*Every heart has
love to give...*

D1290851

AWAKENING PASSIONS

Slowly, hesitantly, Abby reached for him. In a flash of movement Samuel grasped her wrist in his strong fingers before she could touch him.

"Abby . . ." he groaned, "don't do this. You don't know what you're askin'."

"Yes," she breathed and stepped even closer. "Yes, I do know, Samuel."

His breathing staggered, but he didn't move away.

Deliberately then, Abby pushed the first button of his shirt free. When he still made no move, she went on to the next one. She felt his body jerk with her every touch, and his fingers tightened on her wrist. Slowly, inch by inch, his shirt front was opened to her view.

With her one free hand Abby pushed the edges of his shirt further apart, baring his hard, muscled chest. . . .

PRAISE FOR *MOUNTAIN DAWN* BY KATHLEEN KANE:

"Delicious . . . charming . . . an author to watch for!"
—*Romantic Times*

Diamond Books by Kathleen Kane

MOUNTAIN DAWN
SMALL TREASURES

Small Treasures

Kathleen Kane

DIAMOND BOOKS, NEW YORK

This book is a Diamond original edition,
and has never been previously published.

SMALL TREASURES

A Diamond Book / published by arrangement with
the author

PRINTING HISTORY
Diamond edition / March 1993

ISBN: 1-55773-866-1

Diamond Books are published by The Berkley Publishing Group,
200 Madison Avenue, New York, NY 10016.
The name "DIAMOND" and its logo
are trademarks belonging to Charter Communications, Inc.

PRINTED IN THE UNITED STATES OF AMERICA

10 9 8 7 6 5 4 3 2 1

ACKNOWLEDGMENTS

I would like to thank the TV cowboys of the sixties for feeding my western fancies. From Sugarfoot to Cheyenne, Matt Dillon to Palladin, the Maverick brothers to Bat Masterson, they kept the West alive. And most especially, I'd like to thank my favorite TV cowboy, the first big, *gentle* man, Hoss Cartwright/Dan Blocker, for always touching my heart.

Small Treasures

Chapter One

A naked giant stood in the open doorway, a rifle held in one of his huge hands.

Abby Sutton stopped short on the threshold of the tiny cabin and stared unblinkingly up at the man. He was several inches over six feet tall and the breadth of him was just as intimidating. His too-long blond hair hung to his incredibly wide shoulders, and the lower half of his face was covered by a full reddish-blond beard. He had a straight, almost elegant nose, and his pale green eyes sparkled with surprise and what she guessed to be a slowly simmering anger.

Almost before she saw him move, he reached behind him to the rumpled bed, grabbed a threadbare-looking quilt, and tossed it over his shoulders. The material draped across the front of his body, successfully hiding his nudity.

"Who the hell are you?"

His voice was every bit as deep as she'd expected

it to be. She watched as his gaze moved over her and waited until his eyes had lifted to hers again before answering.

"*I* am Abby Sutton," she said simply, "and *you* are trespassing."

"What?"

Really, she told herself. Perhaps that wasn't surprise she'd read in his eyes. Perhaps he was simpleminded. If so, she wanted to reassure him quickly.

"Please don't worry, though," she said, smiling. "There is no need to involve the local sheriff. I really don't mind at all, your 'borrowing' my house for a while." She inclined her head and added gently, "Though, of course, now that I'm here, you'll have to leave."

The giant's mouth dropped open, and he lost his grip on the quilt. He let the rifle fall to the floor and made a desperate grab at his only covering.

"Trespassing? Me? *I'll* have to leave?"

Abby shook her head slowly. Yes. Simpleminded. What a shame. Looking past the giant into the cabin, Abby spied a dented coffeepot. Suddenly the last few hours of travel caught up with her. All she could think of was having a nice hot cup of coffee and getting right to sleep. She glanced back at the man still blocking her way.

"Would you mind terribly if we continued our little talk over a cup of coffee?"

His bushy blond brows drew together in confusion. "Lady," he finally said, "who the hell are you?"

She smiled and gently shook her head again. Poor man. It must be such a trial going through life with the mind of a half-wit. In sympathy, she spoke quietly and carefully. "Oh, dear, you don't remember. I've already told you, you know. I'm Abby Sutton and this is my home."

The giant inhaled slowly. She watched awestruck as, under the quilt, his chest filled out to amazing proportions. Finally, when it seemed that he would explode, he countered, "I'm Samuel Hart. And this is *my* cabin."

Perhaps, she told herself, the giant was too thick-headed to understand even simple English! But she'd keep trying.

"There must be some mistake." She chuckled.

"Uh-huh. That's the first thing you've said that's made sense."

Abby's eyebrows shot up. Deliberately she bent down to pick up her bulging carpetbag, brushed past the big man, and plopped her burden down in the center of the floor. "Mr. . . . Hart, is it?"

He nodded.

"I think we should talk this over."

Samuel looked down at the tiny woman, and his grip tightened on the old quilt. He felt ridiculous, standing there naked as the day he was born, the only thing between him and complete humiliation, a blanket.

"All right," he said quietly. "We'll talk. But first, you go on outside for a bit so's I can get some clothes on."

"It's really very cold outside, you know. Wouldn't it be acceptable if I simply turned my back?"

He felt his jaw drop again. Snapping it shut, he managed to say, "No. I ain't dropping this quilt till you're outside that door and it's closed."

She sighed, and Samuel thought for a moment that she was going to fight him on it. Didn't being in the same room with him . . . *naked* . . . bother her at all?

Frustration and the first stirrings of anger were beginning to boil together in the pit of his stomach. He *had* to get her out of that cabin! Frantically he began murmuring softly to himself.

"Very well." She walked back to the door and grasped the latch. "But please hurry, Mr. Hart. I'm very tired, and I'd like to get to bed."

For a long minute Samuel simply stood, staring at the closed door in open-mouthed astonishment. Get to bed?

Abby took a deep breath of the cool mountain air and seated herself uneasily on the tree stump just a few paces from the cabin. The sun was almost completely gone now, leaving the clearing and the surrounding pines in a soft twilight.

She heard Samuel Hart's hurried movements inside the cabin and frowned uncertainly. Abby had heard his odd muttering just before she stepped outside. Yes, she told herself solemnly. Just like Mr. Hufnagel.

Poor Mr. Hufnagel. Sixty-five years old and not a wit in his head. Abby sighed and let her mind create an image of the little town in Maryland she'd left what seemed years ago. Not big enough to be called a town rightly, it was more like a few dozen souls clustered for company around a winding road that led, eventually, to Baltimore. And every night at suppertime poor Mr. Hufnagel would wander into whichever house he chose for that evening's meal. No one ever knew where he would show up next, and no one had the heart to deny him.

Abby smiled softly. It was a sad thing of course for *anyone* to be so sorely lacking . . . but for Samuel Hart, it just didn't seem fair at all. Not when the good Lord had been so generous with everything else! As long as she lived, Abby would never forget the sight of him brazenly blocking the doorway with his massive frame.

He was really a magnificent man! Blood rushed to her cheeks, and she fanned herself frantically with her hand, trying to cool the rush of excitement the memory had stirred.

No stranger to the sight of naked flesh, Abby had been helping the local doctor since she was a child. Why, she'd probably seen more folks in the altogether than most big-city doctors.

But she'd never seen anyone like Samuel Hart before. He was just as she'd always imagined Thor, the god of thunder, would look.

A loud bang from inside the cabin caught her attention, and Abby shook her head to dislodge the silly notions her tired brain was creating.

Instead, she looked around her at her land. True, she couldn't see much of it in the fading light, but she'd seen enough on the climb up the mountain road to know that she'd finally come home. She glanced up at the deep blue sky and sent a prayer of thanks to her uncle Silas. If not for him she'd still be moving from house to house in Maryland, living mostly on the charity of others.

A frown crossed her features for a moment as she remembered the long years since her parents' death in a carriage accident. With no family to care for her, Abby had been deemed the responsibility of the entire town. And so she'd lived first with one family, then another. Moving every couple of months to avoid being too much a burden on any one family, Abby had belonged nowhere.

Until now.

She looked over her shoulder at the cabin. And *no one* was going to make her leave.

Samuel snatched at his pants and pulled them on, hopping from foot to foot. He set the coffeepot on the stove and fed some kindling into the banked fire, then buttoned up his pants. Grumbling, he then reached for a shirt and drew it over his head.

What in the hell did he ever do to anybody that he deserved this? All he'd asked for was privacy. Solitude. That was the reason he'd bought the little cabin in the first place. High on the mountain, it was far enough away from the town of Rock Creek to discourage visitors and close enough to get supplies easily.

He pushed at the stove door to close it and burned his fingers. Shoving them into his mouth, he shot a murderous glare at the closed door, thinking of the woman beyond. What did she mean, this was *her* home? And what did she say her name was? Abby Sutton. That was it. *Sutton?* As in Silas Sutton? The old drunk who'd sold him the cabin?

That curl of anger was coming back, and immediately Samuel began the familiar pattern to regain control. Slowly, calmly, he forced himself to say the alphabet. He could still hear his mother's warnings. "*Samuel,*" she'd say, "*you're just too big to allow yourself to get angry like any other man. Why, one hit from a hand the size of yours would kill a man! You just got to keep a tight rein on that temper of yours.*" And so she'd taught him to say his ABCs whenever his temper started to rise.

Usually, by the time he reached *K* or *L*, he was feeling better. Tonight he'd had to go all the way through to Z. Twice. And it wasn't *just* temper riding him tonight. It was something else as well. Something he couldn't put a name to, but it scared the hell out of him.

Samuel shook his bushy head. He had to admit, though, that this little woman was really something. She hadn't been afraid of him at all.

What was wrong with her, anyway? Didn't she have the sense God gave a beaver? Didn't she know that *everyone* was afraid of him?

Why, the last time a woman was left alone with him, she'd swooned dead away. Frightened just by his size. And he'd been *dressed* then.

He shoved the coffeepot closer to the heat, then glanced down at the bulging carpetbag the woman had left behind. Curious, he bent down and lifted the bag, balancing the weight of it on his hand. It had to weigh twenty or thirty pounds, at least.

Samuel felt a grudging admiration for the woman. She had to have carried the damn thing all the way up the mountain. He knew damn well none of the townsfolk would have brought her to the cabin. They were too afraid.

Of him.

The door opened and Abby turned. Samuel Hart stood in the doorway, silhouetted against the lamplight within. Even dressed, he was an imposing figure. Abby frowned slightly and gave herself a silent but strong lecture. It simply wasn't proper to continue thinking about how he'd looked the first time she'd seen him.

"Coffee's ready," he said gruffly.

"Wonderful." Abby pushed herself off the stump. "Now, if you'll just help me for one minute . . ."

"Help you what?"

She pointed off toward the road that led from the isolated cabin to the small town at the foot of the mountain. "My trunk."

He took a step into the yard and looked where she pointed. A trunk?

"I'm afraid I had to leave it behind." She smiled, then started walking, clearly expecting him to follow. "I had planned on fetching it in the morning . . . but, since you're here to help . . ."

Grudgingly Samuel fell in behind her, letting her chatter fall around him like autumn leaves.

"I simply couldn't drag it one more step," she admitted reluctantly.

Samuel saw it then. A trunk, just like she'd said. A big one, with securing ropes tied around its sides. She stopped beside it and looked up at him, smiling. He shook his head, reached down, and grabbed the leather handle. As he lifted the trunk clear of the ground and hoisted it over his shoulders, Samuel couldn't help giving the little woman beside him an unbelieving stare.

She'd actually dragged this thing up the mountain? he asked himself. Why, between that damned carpetbag of hers and the clumsy trunk, she must've been dealing with well over sixty pounds. Or more.

"Isn't that wonderful?" Abby said with appreciation. "It must be so handy to be strong. You've simply no idea what I went through, trying to move that trunk."

He grunted and started walking toward the cabin. She kept pace with him, though her continuous prattling ran far ahead.

"I couldn't drag it more than a few feet at a time, then I'd have to drop it and rest. Honestly, I didn't think I'd ever reach the top of this mountain."

"You still haven't."

She went on as if he hadn't spoken.

"But I couldn't leave my trunk in town. Everything I own in the world is in there." She slowed down for a minute as if thinking seriously about that last statement. "Besides," she continued determinedly, "I wanted to have my things with me when I reached my home."

"*My* home," Samuel corrected.

"Hmmm . . ."

It didn't matter what she thought, Samuel told himself. The cabin belonged to him, and that was how it was going to be. He shoved the trunk up farther on his back and realized that at least he knew now what had made the unusual noises he'd been hearing just before her arrival.

Only an hour ago he'd been lying in bed, enjoying his hard-won seclusion and trying to identify the strange sounds that kept coming closer to the cabin. After six months of solitude Samuel knew the fading-day sounds of the mountains surrounding his small cabin. He could recognize in an instant the scrabbling of a raccoon or the soft footfalls of a stalking wolf. The sighing of the wind through the pine trees was familiar, comfortable. Even the eerie creaking of the cabin walls was, in its own way, soothing.

But the occasional scraping, followed by a heavy thud, didn't belong. He'd been about ready to go investigate when the cabin door flew open and Abby Sutton arrived to destroy his peace.

Small consolation indeed to find out that the noise he'd been listening to had been Abby trying to drag the damn trunk up the mountain!

He walked into the cabin and dropped the trunk to the floor beside her carpetbag.

She sighed happily. "Thank you, Mr. Hart."

He nodded and moved for the stove and the now hot coffee. After grabbing down two tin cups from a nearby shelf, he filled them and set them down on a small, hastily built table that sat close to the fire. Straddling a chair that looked far too flimsy to support him, Samuel watched her.

She made no move toward the coffee he knew she wanted. She only stared at him. He stared back, allowing himself to look her over carefully for the first time.

Abby Sutton was the tiniest, most beautiful woman he'd ever seen. She couldn't stand any higher than five feet. The top of her head barely reached the middle of his chest. In seconds his gaze swept over her small, well-shaped form, noticing every detail, from the neatly mended tear in her dress to her unusual golden eyes. Most of her deep chestnut-brown hair was hidden by a particularly ugly bonnet, tied with a violently purple bow . . . but a few stray curls had escaped confinement to lay against the smooth ivory skin of her cheeks. Her full lips were parted, and finely arched honey-colored eyebrows lifted slightly above the remarkable eyes that held him.

"Have you finished?" she asked quietly.

"What?"

"I *asked* have you finished your inspection?"

He shook his head and pushed his shaggy blond hair away from his eyes. Then he heard a faint tapping noise. Her little foot was moving quickly against the floorboards. Deliberately he looked back up at her and forced his lips into a halfhearted smile.

"Yeah, I'm finished."

"Good." She held her skirt aside and seated herself gingerly on the chair opposite him. After taking a sip of the strong black coffee, Abby set her cup down and said, "Now, Mr. Hart. We should talk about what we're going to do."

He crossed his arms over the back of the chair and rested his chin on them. "*We* ain't gonna do anything. *You* are gonna be leaving. First thing in the morning."

Abby smiled and toyed with the cup handle. "That is no way to begin our little discussion, Mr. Hart. Now. Perhaps you would tell me how you came to be living on my property?"

Samuel's eyes narrowed slightly, but he stayed calm. "Well, Miss Sutton, I bought this property from Silas Sutton six months ago."

"Well—" she smiled— "that explains it." Abby took another sip of the coffee, ignoring Samuel's sputtering.

"Why don't you tell me what it explains?"

"Certainly." She reached up for the bow at her chin, untied the ribbon, and pulled her bonnet off. Setting it on the table beside her, Abby said, "Uncle Silas must have changed his mind."

"Changed his mind?" Samuel's only recollection of Silas Sutton was that of an old man, beaten by life, trying to find a way to pay for the whiskey he craved so desperately.

"Of course." Abby picked up the coffee cup and leaned her elbows on the table. It rocked precariously. Leaning over, she inspected the lopsided legs. "We'll have to fix this, I see."

"I like my table just the way it is," Samuel said.

"Really?" She sat up straight again. "I can't imagine why."

"What about Silas?" His voice was much louder

now, and he made a valiant effort to control himself.

"Oh, yes. As I was saying, Uncle Silas sold you the property six months ago."

"That's right."

"But," Abby added with a secretive smile, "he left it to me in his will just *two* months ago!"

Samuel's brow wrinkled, and he ran one of his big hands over his face. What she'd just said proved his case. The property belonged to him. He glanced at her. Why, then, did she look so pleased with herself? Quickly, silently, he recited the alphabet, feeling the old familiar calm flood through him once more. He'd simply have to try to get through to her again.

"Miss Sutton—" he began.

"Please call me Abby," she said with a smile.

"All right." He swallowed heavily. "Abby."

"And your name is Samuel, is that right?"

"Yeah."

"That's a lovely name. It's from the Bible, you know."

"Yeah, I know." His fingers curled over his arms, and he pressed down tightly. "Now, Abby, about that will . . ."

"Wasn't it lovely of Uncle Silas to remember me like that?"

"Hmmm?"

"Uncle Silas. Leaving me this cabin." She was watching him with that sympathetic look again. Speaking slowly, she went on. "It's been so long since I've had a home of my own, I mean a *real* home . . ."

He watched her eyes as she looked around the shabby little place. A gleam of pride and excitement shone in those golden depths, and Samuel had to force himself to look away. It wasn't his fault. He hadn't sent for her. He hadn't told her to come. He hadn't promised something he had no right to give.

Damn Silas Sutton for doing this to him!

It wasn't going to get any easier, he knew. So Samuel finally decided to just spit out exactly what Silas had done.

"Abby, this isn't your home. It's mine."

She shook her head gently and smiled. This was her home now, and she intended to stay no matter what it took.

"And will you stop lookin' at me like I'm some dumb dog beggin' a meal?"

Abby straightened and her smile vanished. He seemed so sure. She couldn't bear the thought he was right. But he wasn't overly bright, and perhaps, she told herself, she could muddy the waters a bit. At least until she could figure out what to do! "But, Samuel, I've just told you that Uncle Silas named me in his will only two months ago."

"Exactly!" The flat of his hand slammed down on the tabletop, and she grabbed for her coffee cup. "Since I bought this property *six* months ago . . . Silas *couldn't* have left it to you!"

"But that's what I meant when I said he'd obviously changed his mind."

"Huh?"

"He may have sold you the cabin first . . . but he changed his mind later and left it to me!"

"Don't you understand?" Samuel said, his frustration mounting with every breath. "The property wasn't his to leave you."

"Well, of course it was his." Abby smiled. "If it wasn't his, how could he have sold it to you?"

"It *was* his. *Now* it's mine!" Samuel felt as though his

mind were covered in cobwebs. He knew he was right! So why was it even he was beginning to doubt it?

"No, it was his, then you thought it was yours, but now it's mine!" She looked around her again and sighed. "And I can't tell you how exciting it all is. Only a few weeks ago I was in Maryland, and now I'm in my own home!"

Samuel groaned.

"Of course, I had no idea the trip would be so expensive." She leaned toward him slightly and confided, "I had to sell Mother's ring and locket . . . and of course, the horses."

"Horses?"

"Oh, yes." She leaned over and reached for her carpetbag. Pulling it onto her lap, she went on. "Papa's matched set of grays. My, they were lovely." She shrugged. "But I'm sure Papa would have wanted them to provide the means to reach my new home. And Mr. Pentwhistle was certainly eager to get them."

After digging into her bag, Abby finally pulled out a sheaf of papers. She gripped them tightly for a moment. Then, handing them to Samuel, she said, "Here is my copy of the will, Samuel. You can see for yourself."

Abby was thinking fast. She couldn't lose her home! Not now . . . not after she'd come so far. Her eyes narrowed thoughtfully. How did she know her uncle had sold this giant his property? Did *he* have a paper to prove what he said? *She* did.

As he read over the papers, Abby restlessly began moving around the cabin. From the corner of his eye he saw her run one finger over the long shelf that held his cooking supplies. Grimly she shook her head at the layer of grime she'd picked up.

Samuel grunted and let his eyes go back to the papers he held. She was right. The old bastard really had left her his property. Why the hell would he do something like that when he knew he had no right?

Abby was down on her hands and knees, poking into a low cabinet. Lord alone knew what she'd find down there. Samuel shook his head again and told himself it was none of her business what his place looked like. After all, he had no reason to keep the place clean . . . no one ever saw it but him. At least, not until now.

Fingers tightening around the useless will, Samuel forced his gaze away from Abby and tried to think. Reluctantly he allowed himself to remember that Abby had said she'd spent every last cent of her money to reach the mountain cabin.

His full lips thinned into a grim line. What would she do if he made her leave? Where would she go? How would she live if he forced her out?

He sat up straight. *If?* Of course she had to leave. There were no *ifs* about it. And it wasn't any concern of his what happened to her, either.

Chapter Two

"Abby?"

She didn't answer.

"Abby?" Samuel looked down. All he could see was her back side. The upper half of her was completely hidden in the cabinet she was inspecting. He rubbed a hand across his bearded jaw and ground his teeth together. "Abby, about this will . . ."

She backed out slowly. When her head was clear, she sat back on her heels and looked up. Samuel sighed. With that streak of dirt across her forehead and the splotch of grime on the tip of her nose, she looked far too vulnerable. He forced his gaze back to the papers he held, then calmly he said what he must, knowing that it would no doubt bring tears to her golden eyes.

"Abby," he began, "this will don't prove anything. All it says is that Silas left you property that didn't belong to him."

Samuel waited uneasily for the tears to start. He didn't enjoy doing this. But dammit, this cabin belonged to him. And he had to make her understand that.

Abby reached up and patted at her cobweb-covered hair, then brushed at the front of her dress. For several minutes she didn't say a thing. Samuel finally realized that she didn't look the least bit upset, and somehow, that didn't really surprise him.

"The will says this place is mine," she said quietly. "Do *you* have a paper proving that Uncle Silas sold it to you?"

Samuel squirmed a little under her steady gaze. He should have known this wouldn't be easy. "No, I don't have a bill of sale. . . ."

Her eyes lit up and she clapped her hands together.

"But," he continued, "the sale is recorded at the county seat."

"Oh."

"Yeah."

"Well, then," Abby said determinedly, "we'll simply have to let the court decide who the cabin belongs to."

"The court?"

"Of course." Abby pushed herself to her feet and dragged one of the rickety chairs over to the wall. She glanced over her shoulder at Samuel before stepping up onto the chair seat. "You say the land is yours, and I *know* it's mine. So, we'll tell our stories to a judge and let *him* decide."

Dammit, he thought indignantly. The court! Hell, there was no court in Rock Creek. The closest thing they had to law around there was a fat sheriff everyone called Sunshine, 'cause he never did any sheriffing after dark.

Mentally Samuel once again went through the alphabet. Now he would have to ask questions about how

to find a judge. And that meant he would have to talk
to those folks in town. He swallowed heavily. In six
months he'd managed to avoid the damn town except
for his few trips down the mountain for supplies. Now
he would be forced to talk with those people who
stared at him with fear-filled eyes.

He looked over at Abby in disgust. This was all
her fault.

No. It was Silas Sutton's fault. Damn his sneaky
hide.

Samuel shook his head. Now she was sticking her
nose into his gun cabinet. Nosiest damn woman he'd
ever seen! Samuel looked back down at the will in his
hand and then tossed it onto the table. Why had this
happened to him? Hadn't he already been given more
than his share of troubles in life?

Abby's squeal of surprise came at the same instant as
the crash. Samuel spun around and saw her stretched
out on the cabin floor, the remains of the splintered
chair beneath her.

Wills, courts, and judges forgotten, Samuel jumped
up and reached her side in two long strides. Immediately he knelt beside her and ran his hands over her
body, checking for breaks.

Abby lay perfectly still. Her eyes closed, she felt
the giant's huge hands on her body. Feather-soft and
gentle, his touch moved over her like a breath, and she
knew she'd been right about the big man. For all his
mumblings and his wild appearance, she had nothing
to fear from Samuel Hart.

"Are you all right?"

She opened her eyes and stared at him. His shaggy
blond hair hung down on either side of his face, and
that beard of his completely hid his mouth. But Abby

saw the concern in his gentle green eyes, and it was to that she answered.

"I think so." Gingerly she sat up, grateful for Samuel's easy strength. She moved her arms and legs, then tilted her head to look up at him. "Nothing seems to be broken." She shifted, then pulled a rung of the chair out from under her behind. "Except the chair."

He frowned and stood up, leaving her to stand under her own power. "You're lucky you didn't break your fool neck. You got no call to be climbin' up on things lookin' into other folks' business."

Abby stood and wobbled only slightly before meeting his glare with one of her own. "Well, if everything in this cabin wasn't built for a giant, I wouldn't have needed to climb up on anything."

He inhaled again, deeply. Once more Abby watched fascinated as his chest grew.

"I built everything in this cabin to suit me. I like things to be where I can reach them."

"And where no one else can," she added under her breath.

"What?"

"Nothing."

A scratching at the door broke the uneasy silence between them. Samuel brushed past her, yanked on the latch, and stepped out of the way. Two dogs leapt into the tiny cabin and rushed straight at Abby.

Instinctively she took a step back. Then she stopped. The dogs, despite their looks, obviously had no intention of tearing into her flesh. The bigger of the two looked to be a cross between a wolf and a pony. His gray fur was covered in dirt, and his bark was as deep as he was big. He also had a wooden splint on his left hind leg. It didn't seem to bother him much, though.

He simply dragged that limb behind him, crashing and banging into furniture and walls. His companion was so small it was laughable. His white and black mottled fur was missing in places, leaving huge bald patches over his tiny body, and one ear was completely gone. His upper lip was curled up over two jutting teeth, giving him a permanent cocky smile. He was the ugliest dog she'd ever seen.

Delighted with the homely but friendly animals, Abby dropped to her knees and was rewarded with several sloppy kisses on her face. She ran her hands over the dogs' backs and laughed when the little one moved to stand under his friend's body.

"They're wonderful!" she cried to Samuel, who was watching the dogs with a disgusted look on his face. "What are their names?"

Samuel shoved the door closed and jammed his hands into his pockets. Damn fool dogs. Didn't even bother to look at him. So much for loyalty. He fed them and took care of them, but give them one look at a pretty face and they forgot all about him.

A whine from the little dog snapped him out of his thoughts. Moving toward the stove and another cup of coffee, Samuel said, "The little one is Harry. The other is Maverick."

At the sound of their names, both dogs turned to the big man as one. Tongues hanging out, they watched him hopefully as he stood next to the shelf that they knew held food.

Samuel ignored them.

"Harry?" Abby laughed and scratched the tiny dog's chin when he responded to his name. "You named a bald dog Harry?" She looked up at him but turned away at his careless shrug. "And Maverick?" The big dog's tongue took a swipe at her cheek. "What sort of name is that?"

Samuel finished the dregs of his coffee in one long gulp, then tossed the empty cup into the basin. "Just a name. Cattlemen call unbranded or unwanted cows mavericks. Well, nobody wanted him, either."

Abby's face softened as she ran her hand down Maverick's back. "*You* wanted him," she said softly.

"I didn't *want* him. I just got him." Samuel's voice sounded harsh even to his own ears, but it was too late to soften it now. "Look, Miss Sutton—"

"Abby."

He sighed. "Look, Abby. It's late. I'm tired."

"Yes, I am, too." She pushed herself to her feet and smiled down at the dogs. "If it's all right with you, I'd like to go to bed now."

Samuel pushed his hair back from his face. "That's what I was sayin'."

"Well, fine then." Eyes solemn, she stared up at him. "Where will you be sleeping?"

"Right here."

"Here?" She glanced uneasily at the only bed.

He followed her gaze and grumbled quietly. Quickly he crossed the small cabin, grabbed a blanket from the bed, and threw it onto the floor. "It's too da . . . dang cold to sleep outside, Abby. I'll take the floor. You take the bed."

"Well," she said, "I suppose that would be all right." Her face brightened as she added, "After all, until the courts decide who really belongs here . . . the cabin *does* belong to both of us."

He gave her a look that had been known to frighten grown men. Abby only smiled and reached for her carpetbag. Samuel blew out the lamp and stretched out on the floor. He heard her moving around for a while longer, then finally the familiar squeak of the bed as she lay down.

His eyes screwed tightly shut, Samuel tried to banish the image of the little woman lying in his bed. It had been so long since he'd even spoken to a woman, it wasn't easy for him to ignore her presence. Every time she shifted position or sighed gently into the darkness, he flinched. The quick scrabble of nails on the wood floor followed by a soft *whump* told Samuel that Harry had joined her on the big bed. He listened to her whispers, straining to make out what she was saying to the little dog, but couldn't quite get it.

Maverick dropped to the floor, curling as closely next to him as his splint would allow. Though Samuel was grateful for the dog's company, he knew, even as his hand moved over the dirty fur, that if not for his broken leg, Maverick, too, would have been in the big bed with Abby.

Coffee. And bacon. Samuel's nose twitched at the delightful odors filling the cabin. A soft, lilting song reached his ears then, and he recognized Abby's voice even though she sang in a whisper. Slowly he opened his eyes, surprised to find it was still dark. He turned his head toward the stove where a lamp, wick turned low, was burning.

Abby moved quietly. There was no wasted motion as she went about morning chores that were obviously familiar to her. He watched in silence as she broke eggs into a frying pan with one hand and with the other turned strips of bacon. In the soft glow of the lamp, Samuel saw her smile and he let his gaze move over her appreciatively. He'd never before awakened to such a lovely image.

Maverick's tail brushed across his nose, and he sneezed in response.

Abby turned to him and grinned. "Good. You're awake. Breakfast is almost ready. Why don't you wash up while I pour you some coffee?"

Gently he pushed the big dog away and propped himself up on his elbows. He stifled the groan that sprang to his lips with the movement. Every bone in his body ached. His neck was stiff, and he rolled his head around, trying to ease the kinks out of it. He must be getting soft. He could remember when he'd had nothing to sleep on *except* the floor. It hadn't bothered him then.

Slowly he turned to his side and pushed himself to his feet. Hands at the small of his back, Samuel stretched and moved for the door. Outside, the darkness was just beginning to dissipate, dawn only minutes away.

He couldn't remember the last time someone had actually risen before him. Even as a child, he'd always been up and moving before his mother. On cattle drives and even through a short stint in the army, Samuel had always been the first to be up and busy. It galled him to admit that Abby had beaten him.

He poured icy water into the basin beside the door and splashed it over his face and neck. The sting of the cold liquid washed away the last traces of sleep, and as he reached for the dirty towel, Samuel told himself that today he would find a way to be rid of Abby. Though something inside him warned that he would miss her, he had to find a way back to his solitude. Back to the lonely life that assured him safety.

Resolutely he went back inside and sat down at the table. He flicked a quick glance at Abby as she poured two cups of coffee. "You didn't have to do all this," he chided her.

"Oh, it's no bother." Abby grinned. "Morning is my favorite time of day."

"It ain't even light out yet."

"I know." She set a plate in front of him, then reached behind her for a bowl that she then placed in the middle of the table. "But I was so excited . . . I just couldn't help myself from getting up and starting the day."

Samuel's eyes widened with appreciation as he stared down at his laden plate. Six strips of bacon, four eggs, some fried potatoes, and right in front of him, a bowl filled with baking-powder biscuits. His stomach growled and his mouth watered just looking at it all.

Maybe it wasn't so bad a thing after all, her helpin' herself to his cabin and supplies.

He wasn't much of a cook. Generally, he'd just throw some meat in a pot of water and boil it until it was soft enough to chew. Most mornings he made do with a stick of jerky. He hadn't had a feast like this in years. As he dug into the food, he asked halfheartedly, "Excited? About what?"

She took a sip of coffee and reached for a biscuit. "Why, it's my first morning in my new home! There's so much to do, Samuel!"

His jaws stopped moving, and he tilted his head to look at her through suspicious eyes. "Do? What is there to do?"

Abby set her cup down and leaned her elbows on the table. Clasping her fingers together tightly, she looked him dead in the eye and said, "First thing to do is clean this place. Honestly, Samuel, I don't know how you can live like this."

He reached for his third biscuit, dipped it into an egg yolk, and popped it into his mouth. "I like it just like it is," he said softly.

"Well, no matter. I'll take care of it," Abby enthused.

He opened his mouth as if to argue, then thought better of it and reached for another biscuit instead.

"Oh, and Samuel," Abby continued, "I think we'd better fix up that chicken coop. Doesn't it snow up here?"

Samuel's eyes widened again, this time at her assuming manner. "Yeah, it snows up here. And don't worry about *my* chickens."

She pushed the biscuit bowl closer to him and smiled when he took another. "Oh, I'm not worried at all, Samuel. I'm sure our chickens will be well cared for this winter. It's only that the roof of the coop looks as though it's ready to cave in any time."

He grabbed the last piece of bacon off his plate and asked, "Why were you out wanderin' around anyway?"

"That's silly." She smiled and shook her head. "I heard the rooster crow and followed the sound to the coop. I had to gather the eggs, after all."

"*You* didn't have to do a damn thing," he ground out. "The chickens are mine. I take care of them."

Abby reached for the coffeepot and poured him another cup of the steaming brew. "For heaven's sake, Samuel. They're only chickens. I've gathered eggs before, you know."

"No," he said, much too evenly. "I don't know. I don't know a damn thing about you except you showed up out of nowhere, claiming to own my house!"

Her pale eyebrows shot up. "There's no need for you to curse at me, Samuel. I hear very well."

"Sorry." He looked down regretfully at his empty plate, then reached for the last biscuit. "But I don't want you stumblin' around outside by yourself. Hell—sorry—you'll probably fall off the da . . . dang mountain."

"Nonsense." Abby grinned at him, not the least put off by his gruff manner. "I can take care of myself." She fed a slice of bacon to each of the dogs and chuckled at their obvious gratitude.

Samuel shook his head slowly, and she heard him mumbling something.

"What was that?"

"Nothin'."

She looked at him speculatively for a moment before shrugging and going on. "I wanted to ask you something, Samuel."

He sighed heavily before saying, "What?"

"I noticed some cages earlier, while I was at the chicken coop. I didn't get a chance yet to go over and look, but I was wondering—"

"You stay away from those cages, you hear?"

"Why?"

Samuel scooted his chair back from the table and stood up. Abby had to tilt her head back on her neck to look at him.

"Those are wild critters out there, Abby. Hurt, sick, and scared." His usually shuttered green eyes glared at her meaningfully. "There's no tellin' what they might do to a stranger. You stay clear of them."

"What happened to them?" she asked softly, clearly unbothered by his anger."

Samuel rubbed his hand across his bearded jaw. "Some was shot. Some caught in traps." He shrugged his massive shoulders. "Some're just sick."

"Ah, poor things," she murmured. As her gaze locked with his, she asked, "If they're wild, Samuel . . . why are you safe with them?"

"They know me." He looked away from her and stared out the dirty window. His voice soft, he added, "They know I ain't gonna hurt 'em. They trust me." Suddenly he turned back to her and said on a harsher note, "But they don't know you. There's no tellin' what they might do."

"Well, then," Abby said, standing up, "perhaps it would be best if the animals got used to me right away. You could take me there now, Samuel."

Samuel stood his ground, staring at her. Abby held her breath, waiting for his decision. She noticed the tiny droplets of water still clinging to his beard and straggly hair. She saw the hesitation in his eyes and could sense the difficulty he was having with her request. Then Abby noticed that his lips, almost completely hidden by his beard, were moving. He was mumbling again.

"Samuel?" she said softly.

His green eyes focused on her, but she saw that he'd once again dropped an invisible barrier between them.

He turned from her and crossed to the far wall. After lifting a rifle from the gun rack near the bed, he bent and picked up a small leather sack. Only then did he look back at her. "I'm goin' huntin'. Low on meat."

"All right. But, Samuel . . ."

He reached the door and swung around to face her. "Abby, you stay the hell away from those animals. You hear me?" Without waiting for an answer, he whistled for the dogs.

Abby watched as Harry and a limping Maverick hurried out the door after the big man already striding away from the cabin. It took only minutes for him to disappear from sight.

In the sudden stillness Abby slumped down onto the nearest chair. The wood quivered but held. Shaking her head, she looked around her at the cabin. Everything about it, from the walls to the shelves to the furniture, had been built hastily by someone more interested in getting it done than in doing it well. Somehow, Abby felt sure Samuel had built most of the furniture in the cabin. Perhaps he hadn't taken much care with it because he was all alone here.

But, she smiled. *She* was here now. And she'd soon have the cabin in order. She looked out the still-open door and stared in the direction the big man had gone. Though she couldn't see him anymore, her thoughts continued to center on him.

Sighing, she poured another cup of coffee. Glancing down at the empty dishes, she smiled to realize that whether he wanted her there or not, it was obvious that he approved of her cooking. She'd never *seen* a man eat so much. But then, she'd never seen a man as big as Samuel Hart, either.

Abby sipped at her coffee and tried to straighten out her thoughts. So far, nothing had gone as she'd planned. All the way from Maryland, she'd nurtured the dream of having her own little home high on a mountain where she could look out any window and see forever. She gave a quick glance at the three windows and sighed again. All you could see there was dirt.

She'd imagined that she would finally have room to be herself. Plenty of space that she could fill any way she wanted to. After years of living in other people's homes and taking up as little room as possible, she'd been looking forward to spreading her wings a little. She turned her gaze on the floors and shelves of the cabin and shuddered. Every square inch of space was covered by guns, furs, supplies, dirty clothes and old, half-eaten food. It seemed that there was no room for her here, either.

She flicked a quick glance at the huge bed in the corner. Even there she hadn't found any peace. She'd hardly slept a wink all night. Knowing that Samuel lay only a few short feet from her had kept her from resting. Though she'd been fairly sure that he wouldn't bother her, there was still the fact that she didn't even know the man to consider.

She smiled to herself then as she realized that she'd been right to trust the big man. True to his word, he'd slept on the floor. She remembered clearly the soft murmurings he'd made in his sleep. He didn't snore, and for that, she was grateful, but he also didn't rest easy. Perhaps, though, her presence had made him as restless as she'd been.

Outside, the tall pines dropped long shadows in the softly growing sunlight. Birds called out in the stillness, and once again, the rooster crowed.

Abby stood up suddenly and walked to the door. Inhaling deeply, she drew in the clean scent of the pines and exhaled on a smile. She loved this place. She loved the quiet, the beauty, the miles of emptiness around the tiny cabin.

She'd finally come home. And no matter what, she wasn't leaving. There was no place left to go.

Oh, she wasn't foolish enough to believe that her claim to the land could stand up against Samuel's. After all, he wasn't *really* simpleminded. He knew this place was legally his. But surely, the judge would see fit to give her *some* claim to the property. After all, she'd come such a long way in good faith.

Abby let her gaze wander around the cluttered yard of the cabin for a moment. Her eyes gleamed with determination. Maybe if she made herself indispensable, Samuel would at least be willing to *share* his mountain.

Spinning around, she looked at the cabin with a wicked light in her eyes. Pushing up the sleeves of her simple blue dress, Abby stepped into the middle of the mess, determined to put her own stamp on the place before Samuel returned.

She would just have to show him how much he needed her.

Chapter Three

Samuel stopped at the edge of the clearing. With one shrug of his broad shoulders, the dead deer dropped to the ground behind him. Maverick and Harry moved anxiously around his legs, urging him forward, wondering why he'd stopped. So was he.

His eyes narrowed and he squinted at the familiar but now different cabin. Walking alone through the woods all day, he'd almost managed to convince himself that Abby really didn't exist. That she was nothing more than a dream created by a man who'd been too long alone. He'd told himself over and over that by the time he got home, the cabin would be empty. As it was supposed to be.

Now that he'd returned, he realized that it wouldn't be that easy.

In the forest, surrounded by the pine and spruce trees, Samuel had clung to the silence. He'd wrapped it around him like an old, comfortable blanket. He hadn't even spoken to the dogs. He'd wanted nothing to disturb the untroubled comfort of the quiet.

How many times in his life had he retreated to the high mountains to find peace? To escape from the people who stared at him as if he were a monster ready to destroy them? To wander freely without worrying about losing his temper or frightening someone else simply because of his size? And no matter how often he went, the woods and the animals that lived there welcomed him.

Harry jumped against his legs, and Samuel bent down, smiling, to pat the homely creature gently. Maverick added a loving lick and a hungry whine, hoping to get his master moving again.

Samuel sighed and squinted again at the cabin. No sense putting it off, he knew. Abby would be inside, probably ready to talk his head off. He couldn't imagine the woman keeping quiet for longer than two minutes at a stretch. Just then a lamp appeared in the front window. He stared at the soft light, spilling freely through the now cleaned and shining pane of glass.

"Dammit to hell and back again," he muttered fiercely. Who the hell did she think she was, cleaning and working over his house? By God, if he wanted his place covered in dirt—that was his business!

Samuel squatted, grabbed the deer's antlers, and swung the dead weight over his shoulders. The two dogs ran ahead of him toward the cabin and the circle of light.

As he drew nearer to the house, he heard her singing. It didn't sound like anything he'd ever heard before. More like she was making it up as she went along. Reluctantly Samuel admitted to himself that her voice was pleasant. Almost soothing in its softness. He glanced at the shining window again and frowned.

Nice voice or not . . . she didn't belong there.

He dropped his burden to the ground with a heavy thump. The singing inside stopped. Samuel looked with disgust at the two dogs, their tails wagging and their tongues hanging out, staring at the closed door. No sense of loyalty at all.

Immediately he flung the door wide, and the animals raced in. Right behind them, Samuel stopped dead on the threshold.

He hardly recognized the place. Quickly he stared around the once familiar cabin. Brightly checked red-and-white curtains were now hanging over spotless windows, and there was a matching cloth on the lopsided table. The distinct odor of lye soap hung in the air, and Samuel noted that the walls had been scrubbed, removing months of smoke stains. The stocks of his guns had been polished, his food supplies were now neatly stacked on a lower shelf, and the cooking pans were hanging on nails pounded into the wall. Even his bed had been covered by a wild-looking flowered quilt.

He couldn't believe it! He'd only been gone *one* day!

And where the hell had she got all the damn stuff?

Maverick and Harry were wandering around the cabin as though they were afraid to lie down. Samuel knew just how they felt.

Finally his gaze fell to Abby. She looked so damned pleased with herself, there was only one thing he could say.

"GODDAMMIT!"

Abby's eyes widened and she had the urge to plug her ears. Good heavens, the man's voice was as big as the rest of him. She saw the dogs duck for cover under the table, and though she'd have liked nothing better than to join them, she forced herself to stay put.

Dropping her gaze to the pile of dirty clothes on her lap, she calmly went back to what she was doing before he'd walked in. She couldn't help but hear his heavy footsteps as he walked toward her. Abby had already noticed, more than once, just how quietly he moved, despite his size. So she knew instinctively that he was stomping across the floor in an effort to intimidate her. Well. It wouldn't work.

"Abby?"

He hadn't lowered his voice any, either, she told herself.

"Yes, Samuel?" Her eyes never left the material she was examining.

"What the hell did you do in here?"

Honestly. That voice kept getting louder. Did he think she was deaf?

"As I told you last night, Samuel. I hear very well. There is no need to shout. *Or* to curse."

He took a deep breath. Abby heard the air rushing into his lungs and knew without looking that his chest was growing to an incredible size.

"Sorry," he said gruffly.

He didn't sound the least bit sorry to Abby.

"*Why* did you—?"

"*Clean,* Samuel?" She finally raised her gaze to meet his. "Because my cabin was a disgrace!"

"*My* cabin!"

She shook her head, unmoved by his shout or by his fists, tightly clenched at his sides. "That hasn't been decided yet. And until it is, I don't have the slightest intention of living in a pigsty."

"Living *here?*"

"Of course." Abby dropped her hands to her lap, tilted her head to one side, and looked at him.

"You can't live here, Abby. With me."

"Why not?"

"*Why?*" He looked around the room desperately, as if looking for help. "Because you can't is all. It ain't done."

She smiled. "Why, Samuel, are you concerned for my reputation?"

"Somebody should be!" He shoved his big hands through his hair.

Abby faltered for a moment. Of course, she'd considered what her living arrangements might look like to an outsider. But there really was no help for it. She simply didn't have the money to stay anywhere else. And besides, the cabin was as much hers as his. At least for now. Why should *she* have to leave? Her mind raced with that thought, and before she could think better of it, she blurted out, "If you really think it isn't proper, Samuel, *you* could go stay in town until we settle this matter."

"No."

One word. No explanation. No argument. Just one word. Abby watched as his hands dropped lifelessly to his sides, and if she hadn't known better, she would have said that he was the very image of a man defeated.

"But, Samuel—"

"I said no, Abby."

She didn't understand any of this. Why, she'd worked like a demon all day, bringing order to his months of chaos. Scrubbing the soot off the walls alone had taken hours. She'd cleaned and dusted and polished. She'd opened her trunk and used the few things she'd been able to bring with her to try to brighten up the tiny cabin. All of that work, to be treated like this.

He might at least have said thank you.

Her fingers clenched tightly around the fabric she held in her lap.

"Fine, Samuel. We'll do it my way, then." She dropped her gaze and went on with her work.

After a long moment's silence, broken only by the now familiar sound of Samuel's muttering, he spoke to her.

"What are you doin'? Are those my clothes?"

She didn't look up. "Yes. I'm checking them to see what can be mended and what cannot."

"Leave my things alone, Abby."

"What?" Her fingers stopped. "Why, Samuel?"

He bent down and pulled his torn shirt from her. "Just leave 'em be, Abby. I take care of myself. Been doin' it for years."

"I didn't mean to—"

"Don't matter." Samuel tossed the shirt onto a nearby pile. "Just leave 'em be. Leave *me* be."

Abby saw his features tighten and watched silently as his eyes shuttered against her. She wanted to say something. *Anything* to make him see that she was only trying to help. That she was trying to earn her keep.

But before she could, he turned on his heel and slammed out the door.

Samuel's razor-sharp knife sliced into the shank of venison, carving off strips of meat to be hung and dried for winter. Occasionally he tossed scraps of meat at the dogs but didn't stop to watch them wrestle for them, as he usually did.

Instead, he saw over and over again the look on her face when he'd told her to leave him alone. Couldn't she see that what she was doing was destroying the life he'd made for himself? Dammit, he didn't want to hurt her . . . he just wanted her to go away.

No.

He wanted for her to never have come.

Samuel had spent years getting used to being alone. At first he'd hungered for the sound of another voice besides his own. He'd yearned to have even one friend. But finally, on his thirtieth birthday five years ago, he'd come to accept that it would never be. That he was slated to go through life alone.

He'd stopped craving the things other men took for granted. Long ago he'd given up any dream of having a woman of his own. A wife. Children. And with that acceptance, he'd found peace.

Until now.

Until her.

Stopping his work momentarily, Samuel let his head drop back on his neck. He stared unblinkingly up at the sky through the slatted roof over his workbench. He couldn't let this happen. Abby was bringing long-dead dreams to life. She made him want the impossible. In the short time she'd been on the mountain, she'd awakened hungers he'd spent years learning how to ignore.

He shook his head and bent back to his task. In less than twenty-four hours one tiny woman had turned everything he'd ever known around. She didn't look at him with fear. She didn't slink away when he was angry. Instead, she smiled at him. Talked to him. And stood up to him with anger enough to match his own.

He found that he liked the sound of her voice. Her singing, her smile, even her addlepated logic.

His mind wandering from his task, the knife he held slid across his middle finger, slicing deep. Samuel dropped the knife, grabbed at a nearby rag, and wound it tightly around his finger. The throbbing pain seemed to underscore what he already knew. He had to make her leave quickly. Before he became too used to having her near. Otherwise, when she finally left, as he knew she would, it would kill him.

He stepped inside and looked expectantly at Abby. After how he'd treated her, he wouldn't blame her if she threw something at him. Though he'd lived alone for years, his mother hadn't raised him without teaching him manners. And she'd be right ashamed of him today. He'd not said one kind word to Abby about all the work she'd done. Hell, he hadn't even thanked her for breakfast that morning. And he hadn't eaten that good in years.

"Supper's ready," she said softly.

He wanted to kick himself good and proper. All the joy had left her face. Samuel felt like he'd stomped a puppy.

"Smells good," he finally answered.

Hesitantly he walked to the table and sat down. As she took her place opposite him, she stopped abruptly.

"What happened to your hand?"

"Huh?" His gaze followed hers, and he remembered slicing his finger. "Nothin' much. Just a scratch."

"Let me see it." She stepped around the table and held out her hand.

He looked at her and recognized the steely look of determination on her features. Sighing, he laid his palm across hers.

Gingerly Abby unwound the dirty rag he'd tied on. Samuel tried to ignore the touch of her fingers and concentrate instead on the pain shooting up from his hand.

"Great heavens, Samuel!"

He looked up.

Her eyes wide, mouth opened in shock, she went on. "This looks very deep."

"It'll be fine."

"Perhaps."

He tried to tug his hand away, but she held firm.

"Come over here." She moved toward her trunk, now sitting on the floor against the far wall.

"Abby," he began.

She turned on him. Hands on hips, she said, "No nonsense about this, Samuel. That hand needs sewing up."

"Sewin'? It's just a scratch."

She ignored him and opened her trunk. Leaning into the half-empty trunk, she reached for a small box. As she threw back the lid, Samuel saw rows of needles, all different sizes, and spool after spool of various colors of thread. He took a step back when she selected a needle and pulled off a long length of black thread.

"Abby, you ain't gonna sew up my hand like you would a new dress!"

She frowned up at him and moved to the stove. She grabbed up a pan of still-boiling water and poured off some of it into a bowl. Carefully Abby then dipped first the needle then the thread into the water.

"What're you doin'?" Samuel asked cautiously.

"Something Dr. Talbot back home taught me." She threw him a quick glance and noticed that he'd backed up another pace or two. Shaking her head, she threaded the needle. "He believed that everything that touched a wound should be clean. Said it cut down on infections and fevers and the like." She looked up at him and smiled. "It always seemed to work."

He nodded but didn't look convinced.

Abby pointed to the bed. "Sit down, Samuel."

He shook his head.

"For heaven's sake." She held up her hands. "It's just a needle and thread, Samuel."

"I can see that."

Maverick and Harry lay on the floor, their heads turning first one way then the other, as though following the conversation closely.

"Then come sit down and let me take care of your wound."

"You ever done this before, Abby?"

She met his gaze squarely. Her face calm, mouth curved in a gentle smile, she looked up into his worried eyes and lied like a drunk politician. "Many times, Samuel."

He relaxed and moved reluctantly toward the bed. As he dropped slowly to the edge of the mattress, Abby reached for a chair and told herself that it was for his own good that she lied. After all, she'd seen Doc Talbot do the same thing to any number of people. And she *was* the best seamstress in Maryland. How much more difficult could it be stitching together jagged flesh rather than torn fabric?

Before she began, she took more of the hot water, and with a fresh cloth she cleaned the area carefully. It really was quite a gash, she thought worriedly. Her mouth suddenly dry, she swallowed convulsively and inhaled deeply.

Samuel held his hand rock steady, and she gave him one more smile before starting. "This will probably hurt, Samuel. I'm afraid there's nothing to be done about that."

"I been hurt before." He nodded. "Like you said. It's just a needle."

She nodded back, then bent her head to her task. When the needle pierced his flesh for the first time, Abby sensed his discomfort. He hadn't moved an inch. He'd said nothing. But just the same, she knew. And she shared his feelings. Constantly her mind reminded her that she'd seen blood before. She'd seen other wounds, some far more severe. That what she was doing was necessary. But just as often she remembered that this was Samuel she was working on. And she found it hard to ignore that. Quickly, neatly, she aligned small black stitches along the length of his finger. Every time she made a knot though, she couldn't help wishing it were the last.

His hand lay in her lap, and as she worked, she couldn't help noticing the other scars and the old calluses that marked his skin. She wondered briefly who had tended to him before her.

It seemed to take forever. She heard his regular breathing, felt the strength in the hand she held. His nearness brought an uneasy warmth that she tried to push aside. Time and again Abby pulled air deeply into her lungs as she fought the faint-headedness creeping up on her.

The room was so quiet, she could hear the snapping of the fire and the dogs' rapid breathing. As she made the last knot, she even heard her own heartbeat pounding in her ears. She sighed with relief when her task was finished at last. But when she moved to look up at Samuel, Abby saw instead columns of blackness closing in on her from each side.

Samuel's face seemed to move farther away. She thought she saw his lips moving, but whatever he said was lost in the rushing sound that suddenly filled the cabin. Instinctively she reached out for him, hoping to reach him before the blackness swallowed her up. But it was too late, and she fell forward into the dark.

"Abby? Abby? . . . Dammit, Abby! Wake up!"

She turned toward the voice calling her and tried to open her eyes. Someone kissed her cheek, and Abby smiled.

"Cut that out, now! You get on out of here."

The voice again. Samuel.

"C'mon, Abby. You're commencin' to worry me some, Abby. Wake up, now."

She stirred and for the first time felt a rhythmic patting on her right hand. She pulled away, but the patting continued. Her eyes opened then, and the first thing she saw was Samuel's worried face.

"What happened?" she asked quietly.

"What happened? You fainted clean away . . . that's what happened." Relief crashed over Samuel with the force of a hurricane. She was making sense, anyway.

"I never faint," she countered as she pushed herself up to a sitting position.

"Then how come you're on the floor?" His bushy blond brows quirked up.

She looked around quickly, her surprise evident.

"I tried to catch you," he went on, "but you went over too damn fast."

"For heaven's sake," she mumbled as she struggled to her feet.

"Now, hold on, Abby." She wobbled and he reached out to steady her. "No need to rush about, now. Go slow, will ya?"

"I'm perfectly well, Samuel."

"Yeah, well . . ." He studied her carefully. She was still a little too pale to suit him. But stubborn as she was, she wouldn't be staying on the floor, he knew. So he scooped her up in his arms. One part of his mind marveled at how light she was . . . how tiny . . . while another part was fully aware of the soft curves of her woman's body pressed so close to him. Reluctantly he placed her gently on the nearest chair.

Samuel immediately poured her a cup of coffee and threw in plenty of white sugar. He set it in front of her and ordered her to drink every drop.

One sip and her face screwed up. "Too sweet."

"Drink it," he said again, "or I'll let Maverick get back to washin' your face to bring you around."

The dog sat on his haunches at her feet, his head tilted curiously.

"Maverick?" She looked back at Samuel. "Oh. I thought . . ."

"Thought what?"

"Nothing. Nothing." She lowered her head and took another sip.

Samuel watched her for a moment, then, satisfied that she wasn't going to keel over again, allowed his gaze to wander over what used to be his home.

Curtains. A rag rug. Flowers in an old pot. Everything so damn clean it hurt to look at it. He shook his head. She'd stuck more damned froo-froo around the place than he'd seen in most bawdy houses. It amazed him to realize that in less than a day, she'd managed to make his house look like he'd never lived there at all.

"Do you like it?" she asked.

"Huh? What? Oh . . . the cabin. What you've . . . done to it."

"Yes. Isn't it lovely?"

He wanted to tell her what he really thought of it, but looking into those gold-colored eyes of hers . . . eyes so full of hope . . . he couldn't. No matter how badly he wanted to have his home to himself again. She'd worked so hard. "Yeah, Abby," he said finally, "it looks real nice."

She rewarded him with a smile that was lit from within. Her color was better, too. That pleased him. Samuel wasn't quite sure what he would do if she fainted again. Without another word he got up, filled two plates with the beef stew she'd made, and sat back down. He waited for her to begin, then he, too, started eating.

After the first bite it was all he could do not to wolf the food down. He had no idea what she'd done to it, but that stew was the best he'd ever eaten. In minutes he'd finished his plate and had gone back for a second helping. In between bites Samuel asked, "Why'd you tell me you'd done that stitchin' up before, Abby? That was the first time, wasn't it?"

She chewed thoughtfully for a moment before answering. "You seemed so nervous, I didn't want you to be scared."

"Scared? Me?" He dropped his spoon onto the plate with a clatter. "You thought I was scared of the pain?"

"Well . . ."

He chuckled deep in his throat. He couldn't even remember the last time someone had been concerned about him. Hell, if she only knew how many times he'd set his own bones or stitched up a tear in his skin by himself. If he hadn't, he'd have died. There was never anyone around him *to* help. Until now. But he didn't say any of that. Instead, he only asked quietly, "Why did you want to do it, if the sight of blood makes you faint?"

"Oh," she said lightly, "blood doesn't bother me at all. Why, I've probably seen oceans of it."

His eyebrows shot up.

"It was the stitching, Samuel. Knowing it was your flesh that I was sewing up like a quilt . . ." She shook her head as if to clear the vision away.

"Well . . ." Samuel's voice was thick, and he cleared his throat nervously. "It's done now." He tried to change the subject then. To get them both thinking of something else. He couldn't allow himself even to think her concern might have been for his pain. That was far too dangerous. "With all the work you've done around here, Abby," he said, forcing a smile, "you still didn't solve one problem."

Her brow furrowed as she tried to think what she'd missed.

"We still only got one bed. . . ."

"Oh!" Abby grinned and jumped up. She grabbed the edge of the table as dizziness struck again. In moments her vision cleared, and she smiled at his worried frown. "I'm all right. But you have to close your eyes, Samuel."

"Close my . . . what for?"

"It's a surprise. Now, close them."

He did as he was told, though he hated surprises. Generally they weren't good ones. Besides, he couldn't imagine what there was left to surprise him with, anyway. She'd taken over his house, claimed his land, refused to leave . . . what else was there?

"All right. You can look now."

He opened his eyes and knew that he would never doubt her ability to "surprise" him again.

She was standing beside the big bed, a proud smile on her face as she looked at her latest addition to the cabin. A plank of wood two feet high was set length-wise down the middle of the mattress. Somehow, she'd found a way to attach it over the head and footboards with hooks at either end of the board.

His mouth open, his eyes wide, Samuel managed to croak out, "What the hell is that?"

"A bundling board."

"A what?"

"A bundling board. They were used quite a bit in New England years ago."

"Used for what?"

"Why, to separate an unmarried couple when they were forced to share the same bed, of course." She pat-ted the plank. "It was actually used by courting cou-ples, mainly. And naturally, the couple didn't remove their clothing."

"Uh-huh."

Abby kept going. "Well, Samuel, I know you can't sleep on the floor every night. And I don't want to, either. *And* since neither one of us is willing to move out . . ." She glanced at him hopefully.

Samuel shook his head.

She sighed and nodded. "This seemed like the per-fect solution. After all . . . it's such a *big* bed."

Samuel clamped his jaw shut, rubbed his hand over his eyes, and looked again at the bundling board. No. It hadn't disappeared. It was real. She meant what she said. He couldn't believe this was happening.

"Of course it's a big bed," he said, managing through sheer will to keep his voice down. "I'm a big man! And it's *my* bed!"

"Well, I know it's your bed. And because you're such a big man, I divided the bed accordingly." She grinned and pointed. "See? Your side is much bigger."

"Abby," Samuel said, pausing to mutter his ABCs under his breath, "it's bad enough, you stayin' here with me . . . alone. But dammit, we *can't* share a bed!"

"Whyever not? I trust you." She smoothed her skirt down and clasped her hands firmly in front of her. "And I assure you, Samuel, the proprieties will be observed."

He was all the way up to M before she stopped talking. The proprieties. There seemed to be no arguing with her. And he'd be damned if he was gonna sleep on the floor in his own house while *she* took over his bed.

She *trusted* him. How long had it been since anyone had said that?

See, he told himself firmly. This is what happens when you get soft. When you start worryin' over folks' feelin's. You should have just told her flat out that she couldn't stay. You should have made her leave.

But somewhere deep inside him, he knew he hadn't *wanted* her to leave. At least not yet. And now he'd have to answer for that.

Racing through the rest of the alphabet, Samuel reached Z, looked at the bed and her beside it, and knew that it would take far more than the alphabet to keep his mind off of what lay on the other side of that damn board!

Chapter Four

The dark cabin seemed to close in around her. Abby lay on her side of the bundling board, stiff as a poker. She couldn't hear Samuel, so she guessed that he was still caring for the caged animals she'd seen earlier that day.

He'd hardly said a word since supper. No. Actually, it was since he'd seen the bundling board. Abby bit down on her bottom lip and folded her hands together over her bosom. She was cold. So cold that her long white nightgown and the heavy quilt that covered her did nothing to remove the chill that shook her body.

And she was certain that the weather had nothing to do with it. She was scared. Scared that no matter what she did, she'd have to leave the cabin she'd already come to love. Despite all her efforts, Abby knew that Samuel wasn't pleased with what she'd done to his home.

She stared up at the ceiling and watched the flickering firelight shadows. Her fingers clenched together as another fear entered her head. One she hadn't even considered until she'd seen that strange look on Samuel's face. Abby's mind raced with the possible consequences of what she'd thought was a brilliant idea.

Suppose Samuel tried to force himself on her? No. She shook her head, ashamed of herself for even thinking it. For heaven's sake . . . if that was the kind of man he was, he'd already had ample opportunities to ravish her.

But if Samuel did insist on her favors as payment for staying in the cabin, she'd have to refuse. And then where would she be? No place to stay, thousands of miles from a friendly face, and no doubt the townspeople would have nothing to do with what they would consider a fallen woman. Of course, she conceded, simply staying at the cabin unchaperoned would successfully ruin her reputation. Her lips thinned into a determined line. And she'd already made that decision.

Oh, she told herself, this was doing no good at all. There was simply no help for it. This was how things had to be until a decision was made about the ownership of the cabin. And torturing herself over the questionable respectability of the situation wasn't going to help.

The dogs. She heard the dogs coming close to the cabin. That meant Samuel wasn't far behind. What should she do? Pretend to be asleep? Sit up and greet him? Or play dead? She chose the latter.

The front door opened and both dogs raced inside. Already, she knew Harry's quick steps from Maverick's limping gait. As the dogs plopped onto the floor, Abby listened with breath held to Samuel's movements.

He set the lamp he'd taken with him on the kitchen table, then turned to shut and latch the door. Slowly, quietly, he walked confidently to his side of the big bed and stopped. In the stillness Abby was sure she actually *heard* him undoing the buttons of his shirt. She tried to close her mind to the mental images that continued to rise up. It was no good.

Behind her closed eyelids, she saw him shrug down his suspenders and pull the gray shirt off. She imagined the breadth of his chest covered only with the faded material of his winter underwear. Even in her mind, she refused to remove these.

She heard one of his heavy boots drop to the floor and managed not to flinch again when the second one joined its mate. A soft brushing of fabric against fabric told her that he'd removed his pants. She swallowed nervously. Deliberately and completely, then, Abby wiped away her imaginings.

The mattress dipped when Samuel lay down on his side of the board, and Abby bit down on her bottom lip. Hard.

Samuel knew she was awake. He felt her agitation as surely as though she'd shouted out her distress. In fact, he shared it. Even as he lay down on his half of the bed, he told himself that if he had the sense God gave a gnat, he'd jump back off that bed like it was on fire!

He'd put off returning to the cabin as long as he could. But his own exhaustion had finally forced his hand. Samuel threw one arm behind his head and glanced furiously at the damn board in his bed. He still didn't believe that so much had happened in so short a time. The life he'd built for himself so carefully over the last ten years was falling apart. All because of one tiny woman. And his own reaction to her.

He snorted quietly in the darkness and cursed his stupidity. He should never have let her get a foothold in the cabin. In his life. He should have *made* her leave the first night. He should have taken her to town by force if he'd had to. His lips twisted in a bitter smirk. Oh, yes. And if he'd done that, the folks down in Rock Creek would probably have shot him for the monster they thought he was.

None of this was right, he thought angrily. He'd spent most of his life learning how to be alone. Teaching himself not to *need* anyone. Protecting himself from hurt by shutting out the world that wanted no part of him. And now he was in danger of losing the peace that had come so hard to him. Abby Sutton was worming her way into his feelings. Feelings he'd thought were long dead.

He couldn't let that happen.

Straightening out, he decided suddenly to try the idea that had come to him while he was caring for the animals. He already knew just how nervous she was. If he could build on that, perhaps he could scare her into leaving. A quick flash of shame shot through him, but he ignored it. This was the only way.

Deliberately Samuel stretched, moaning softly as though relaxing his too tense body. His elbow struck the board and he felt the mattress shift as Abby jumped in reaction. He smiled sadly. It was working. Leaning into the board, Samuel pressed his weight against it until it creaked a loud protest.

"Samuel?"

He stopped. Had he succeeded so quickly? "Yes, Abby?" he whispered.

"Pleasant dreams, Samuel."

Shocked, Samuel moved away from the board slightly and lay still. What was it about this woman that was so damned confounding? He'd been trying to *frighten* her. And she wishes him pleasant dreams. A wave of self-disgust washed over him, and he was grateful for the darkness, that she couldn't see his face.

A quick scrabble of nails on wood caught his attention just before ten pounds of bald dog landed on Samuel's stomach. Harry's forward motion kept him going until he banged his head on the plank he hadn't expected. But when Samuel reached to pet the little animal, Harry nimbly leapt over the bundling board to join Abby.

Abby's whispered words and the dog's happy slurping sounds faded away after a few minutes.

He lay perfectly still on his side of the bed, staring at the ceiling. Disgusted, he imagined the disloyal Harry cuddling up to Abby's warmth. And for one long, torturous moment, he was insanely jealous of a mangy dog.

It was much easier traveling the mountain road in a buggy, Abby told herself with a smile. She hugged her cloak around her tightly against the chill air, but kept looking around with delight at the passing landscape. It really was so beautiful, she thought happily. She would have said so, except that Samuel didn't appear to be in the mood for conversation.

In fact, he'd hardly said a word all morning. All through breakfast and the entire trip down the mountain, he'd been remarkably silent. She shook her head slightly and rearranged the purple bow under her chin. Her hands then deftly checked to see that her bonnet was tilted at just the right angle before coming to rest in her lap again.

Abby had thought that after a good night's sleep, Samuel would be easier to get along with. But it seemed that plenty of rest had just the opposite effect on him. Perhaps she should have suggested that he remain on the floor. At least then he'd spoken to her.

Actually, she was rather surprised that he'd invited her along on this trip to Rock Creek. But when he offered to go with her to town to find the nearest court so that they could clear up their problem as quickly as possible . . . she wasn't about to say no.

Abby threw a quick glance at Samuel from the corner of her eye. What if the court decided that the cabin belonged to him? And it probably would. What then? She couldn't go back to Maryland. Even if she had the money to make the trip, she wouldn't want to go back. Not to living on the charity of others. No matter how kind or well meant.

She shook her head and shoved all those worries aside for the time being. There really was no point in trying to come to a decision now, when it might not even be necessary.

If the worst happened and she did lose the cabin, well, then, she would still be able to make her living as a seamstress, just as she'd planned. She'd simply have to make enough money to pay for a room in town.

If only Uncle Silas had never met Samuel Hart.

If only Silas Sutton hadn't been a drunk, Samuel thought angrily. None of this would have happened. He'd be living in his cabin *alone*, and, if not happy, at least content.

Samuel spared a quick look for Abby. She looked

worried. Even her excitement over visiting the town couldn't mask that. And she *was* excited. She'd checked that ugly hat and retied the damn ribbon at least three times already. Why in hell she even wore the thing was beyond him. Her hair, hanging free to her waist, was much prettier.

He frowned ferociously. For godsake. You got no call to go thinkin' about what's pretty and what ain't, he told himself. He needed sleep, that was all. Samuel scrunched up his eyes, then widened them again. He'd be willing to bet that he hadn't slept more than twenty minutes at a stretch all night. And he knew he couldn't take much more of that.

"Samuel?"

"Yeah?" he answered.

"Is there a judge in town? I mean, will we be able to have the matter settled right away?"

"No." He saw her shoulders slump with relief. "But there's a circuit court judge that comes through regular. We should be able to find out when he'll be back next."

She turned toward him and smiled. Well, he told himself, that sure as hell brightened her up. And he was curious as to why.

"Why's that such good news?" He winced at the harshness of his voice, but she didn't seem to notice.

"Because, if there's no judge in town, we'll have to wait a while for a decision."

"Yeah . . . so?"

"So," she said, grinning, "that means that for now, at least, the cabin belongs to both of us."

"Abby . . ."

"And neither one of us has to worry just yet about finding some other place to live." She took a deep breath of the pine-scented air and exhaled happily. "We can go on as we are."

"I don't think so."

"Whyever not?" She turned to face him, her brows drawn together.

"Because we just can't is all." He slapped the reins against the horses' backs needlessly.

A long moment of silence dropped between them as each of them wrestled with their own thoughts. Then Samuel spoke again.

"I been thinkin', Abby."

"Yes?" She turned to face him and saw that his face mirrored the hesitation in his voice.

He glanced at her, then looked back at the winding mountain road. "I got plenty of money put by. . . ."

"Yes?" Abby had a feeling that she knew where he was headed.

"I figure I could give you enough so's you could stay in town until we can get this mess settled and behind us. Hell," he added in a much louder tone. "I'll even give you enough to get back home on."

Her mouth hung open momentarily, then she snapped it shut. She couldn't believe it! Did he really think that she would leave so easily as that? Without even trying to fight for her cabin? She stiffened her spine and threw her shoulders back. Eyes straight ahead, she told him, "No, Samuel. It wouldn't be right."

"What wouldn't be right?"

"Taking money from you, that's what." Abby lifted her chin and grabbed the side of the buckboard as the wheels hit a huge hole in the road. "For heaven's sake, Samuel. You're practically a stranger! It certainly wouldn't be proper for me to accept money from you,

even if I *did* want to leave." She smoothed her skirt.
"Which I don't."

Grumbling, Samuel bent down, picked up a weatherbeaten brown hat, and jammed it down on his
head.

"If you have something to say, I wish you'd just say
it," Abby said softly.

"Oh, no . . ." Samuel shook his shaggy head in disbelief. "What could I say? I'm just a stranger!" He turned
halfway toward her and glared in her direction. "But
can you explain to me why it's all right to *sleep* with a
stranger but not take money from him?"

Really, Abby thought helplessly. Perhaps he wasn't
a total half-wit as she'd feared at first, but neither was
he as bright as she'd hoped. "Taking money from a
stranger would be . . . improper. I can't explain it better
than that, I'm sorry."

"But you *can* sleep with one?"

"Samuel, you know as well as I that the circum-
stances we find ourselves in are rather . . . special."

He snorted.

"And so," she went on, ignoring his rude comment,
"as long as the proprieties are maintained, of course
it's all right." Abby reached over then and patted his
hand gently. "Besides, as I've already told you . . . I
trust you."

Samuel gave her a look that told her he still didn't
understand. But no matter, she thought happily. He
will. Then she heard him mumbling again. She wasn't
sure, but it sounded like the alphabet.

Abby stared back at the little man standing beside
the livery stable corral. For heaven's sake, she thought,
you'd think people here had never seen a stranger

before. Ever since their wagon had begun rolling down the one narrow street, she'd felt the eyes of the townspeople on her. She glanced up at Samuel and almost smiled her relief. Either he hadn't noticed his friends' odd behavior or he'd chosen to ignore it.

Still, she couldn't help feeling disappointed. She'd so wanted the people here to like her. In her mind's eye Abby envisioned her hometown. The smiling faces, the greetings called out when she passed, the children following her, hoping to talk her out of some candy from the store.

It was all even further away than she'd thought.

As Samuel drove the wagon past the blacksmith's Abby pointedly ignored the rude, barrel-chested man who stared at her with his jaws agape. But she couldn't help sneaking peeks at the buildings as they passed. It was really too bad that the people weren't very friendly. The town itself was everything she'd hoped.

Neat, clean homes lined the well-tended street. A scattering of stores with freshly swept boardwalks and brightly painted signs took up the last half of the street, and the tiny town ended in a grove of pines.

Samuel pulled the wagon to a stop outside the only general store, pushed the brake on, and tied the reins securely. She noticed that he kept his eyes down, looking neither right nor left as he came around to her side to help her down.

Poor man. He was probably embarrassed. Her presence had caused all of his friends to look at him so oddly.

Abby lifted her chin defiantly. Well, she told herself, if they want to stare, then give them something to stare at. No matter how rude the people were, she'd simply have to win them over. This little town was going to be her home now, and she just had to make them like her. She had to show Samuel that she *could* belong.

There were so many interesting things to look at! Abby turned in a slow circle, her gaze moving over the merchandise stacked on irregularly placed shelves. From horse collars to hair ribbons, Mullins's Mercantile had anything you could possibly want or need. Sacks of grain were stacked beside a table holding a varied assortment of fabrics and sewing notions. Just above that display was a shelf holding three well-read books, two rifles, and a towering pile of ammunition boxes.

"May I help you?"

Abby turned and smiled at the older woman who'd stepped out from behind the counter. The woman's prominent nose jutted out from a too-narrow face, and her gray-streaked black hair was pulled back into a severe bun at the back of her neck. But her eyes reflected the smile that stretched across her homely face, and Abby immediately warmed to her.

"Hello. My name is Abby Sutton." She held out her hand, and after only a moment's hesitation, the older woman gripped it tightly, belying her almost scrawny figure.

"Minerva Mullins," she offered. "My husband and me . . . we own the place."

"Oh, it's a wonderful store!" Abby's hands swept out enthusiastically. "Why, you have just *everything* here!"

Minerva preened under what she considered a well-deserved compliment. After all, she went to great pains to see that the store's shelves were fully stocked.

"All I really *need* is some white sugar and some

flour." Abby grinned and added, "But if you don't mind, I'd love to look around a bit."

"Surely, honey," Minerva said as she moved off to collect the order. "You just help yourself to a look-see."

While Abby moved slowly around the room, she managed to keep up a steady stream of conversation. Pleased that the woman appeared so friendly, Abby was determined to make as good an impression on Minerva Mullins as possible.

Minerva staggered under the rush of words from the tiny stranger. She'd never heard anyone talk so fast. Yet, for all that, Abby Sutton seemed a nice woman. Sutton.

The older woman's lined forehead creased in thought. Sutton. Abby Sutton. Minerva cocked her head and watched the tiny stranger as she fingered through the row of hair ribbons. Any relation to old Silas? she wondered silently. There certainly wasn't much of a family look about her. Of course, she reminded herself, Silas was a worn-out drunk, his features marked by years of hard living.

While she was studying Abby, Minerva took notice for the first time of her bonnet. The older woman's eyes narrowed, and she shook her head slowly in disbelief. It was without a doubt the ugliest hat she'd ever seen.

Abby turned then and caught the solemn stare directed at her. "Is something wrong?" she asked.

"Oh. Oh, no. Nothing. Nothing at all," Minerva stammered. "I was, uh . . . admirin' your hat is all."

"You like it?" A delighted smile lit Abby's face. "I made it myself."

"Did you, now?" Minerva asked, managing to avoid the other question.

"Oh, yes," Abby offered, stepping up close to the counter. "You see, I'm really a seamstress. And a very good one, too."

Minerva nodded, unconvinced.

"I'm not nearly as good at making hats, but this one turned out beautifully, don't you think?"

Minerva's jaw worked, but she made no sound. She had no idea what she could say to that statement without telling an out-and-out lie. Briefly her eyes moved up to the hat in question again. It was all she could do not to turn away.

The plain straw base was attractive enough; it was the decorations that created the startling effect. Minerva had never before seen a hat that combined a yellow veil, blue fabric flowers, a pink feather that shot straight up from the brim, and, tilted at a precarious angle, a stuffed white dove with one eye missing. Add to that the wide purple ribbon tied in a flirtatious bow at the side of Abby's neck, and it was truly a hat to be noticed.

Though she could see clearly that the workmanship on the preposterous bonnet was expert, Minerva was sure that a compliment on her needlework was *not* what Abby was expecting!

Thankfully, the bell over the front door rang out, saving Minerva from having to lie to the pretty little woman before her.

"Morning, Minerva!"

Another woman entered the store and walked up to the counter, her eyes never leaving Abby's hat.

"H'lo, Charity," Minerva answered loudly, commanding the other woman's attention. "This here is Abby Sutton. She's new in town. Abby, Charity Whitehall. She's married to the blacksmith."

Abby smiled and refused to remember the big blacksmith staring so rudely when she'd entered town. Instead, she held out her hand to the man's wife, determined to make another friend.

Charity took the proffered hand, and Abby noticed that her own hand practically disappeared in the woman's grip. As tall as Minerva, Charity Whitehall outweighed her by at least a hundred pounds. Her round, placid face was creased in lines that spoke of frequent smiles, and her soft brown hair was braided and wrapped like a coronet around her head.

"Sutton, did you say?" Charity asked. "You ain't kin to *Silas* Sutton, are you?"

"Why, yes!" Abby smiled. "Did you know my uncle?"

The two other women exchanged knowing glances before turning back to Abby.

"Well, now," Charity answered slowly, "I reckon it'd be fair to say ever'body in town knew ol' Silas."

Minerva nodded. "Yes, you could say that. . . . "

Neither of the women wanted to mention the fact that it would have been hard indeed *not* to know Silas Sutton. When you had to step over a man, sleeping off a drunk in the middle of the street every morning, you *did* get to know him. But surely they didn't have to tell this poor little thing all of that!

"I'm so glad he had friends," Abby went on, completely unmindful of the piteous stares directed at her. "He was such a lonely man before he left Maryland."

Again the women looked at each other. Lonely? Silas? Not likely. He'd never had much trouble findin' a drinkin' partner.

"I can't *tell* you how excited I am to finally be in Rock Creek! Why, Uncle Silas wrote to me about this place often—many years ago."

Minerva guessed silently that it had been quite a while since Abby'd received a letter from her uncle. In the last few years the old coot had never been sober enough to hold a pencil. Then something else occurred to her. "You didn't come all the way out here to . . . visit your uncle, now, did ya?"

Abby's smile faded. "No. No, it's all right. I know that he passed over."

Minerva sighed her relief.

"In fact," Abby continued, "*that's* why I'm here!"

"What d'ya mean?" Charity asked.

"Well," Abby said, stepping closer to the other women, "my uncle left me his cabin. So I've come here to live in it!"

Charity and Minerva looked at each other in desperation. The poor child didn't know, then. She had no idea that her cabin was already occupied by that great monster of a man. And how would they tell her that her trip had been for nothing? That Silas Sutton had sold his cabin months before his death to the big man who still remained a stranger to them all.

"You're plannin' on livin' there?" Charity asked.

"Oh, yes." Abby nodded excitedly, sending the one-eyed dove on her hat to flopping back and forth.

"Abby dear," Minerva began, trying to ignore the bobbing dove, "there's something you should know about that cabin." Charity gave her friend an encouraging nod, and Minerva added, "Y'see, there's already somebody—"

The bell on the shop door rang out, and all three women looked up.

While Charity and Minerva stared, speechless, Abby rushed over to the big man standing uncertainly in the doorway and drew him into the store.

"There you are, Samuel!" she cried happily. "I've just been talking with some of your friends!"

Chapter Five

Friends?

Samuel stumbled forward, propelled by Abby's firm grip and eagerness. His gaze never left the two women who stood staring at him as if he were a ghost. Vaguely, his mind registered the fact that Abby was talking again in a steady stream of words, but he couldn't make any of them out. His mind was much too pre-occupied with hoping against hope that neither of the two women would say anything to destroy Abby's belief that he was a normal man. For some reason, still unclear to him, Samuel was desperate to keep Abby from knowing that the people of Rock Creek were terrified of him.

All at once his brain cleared, and he heard Abby say, "You see, Samuel, I was just this minute telling Charity and Minerva about how we're sharing the cabin. . . ."

He looked quickly from her shining face to the two shocked ones across from him. He couldn't believe that she'd said that! Didn't the woman realize that she was about to destroy her own reputation and any standing she might have hoped for in this town?

"Sharing?" Minerva breathed, her hand at her throat.

Samuel shifted uneasily and avoided both ladies' eyes.

"The both of you?" Charity asked. "Together?"

"Oh, yes," Abby revealed. "Of course," she added with a serious nod of her head, "the proprieties are observed at all times."

"Proprieties . . . ?" Minerva echoed with a quick glance at Samuel's blushing cheeks.

"Oh, my, yes," Abby went on, heedless of the ladies' shock. "I've set up a bundling board in the bed so that everything is quite proper."

"Abby . . ." Samuel heard himself moaning softly.

"Oh, Samuel." Abby shushed him with a wave of her hand. "These ladies understand that you can't be expected to sleep on the floor night after night. And there *is* only the one bed after all."

"For godsake . . ." he mumbled.

"Samuel! Really. Your language." She smiled at the two ladies conspiratorially and shook her head at the impossibility of getting a man to clean up his speech.

"A bundling *what?*" Charity asked in a hushed tone as she leaned closer to Abby. Clearly the woman's curiosity far outweighed any fear she held of Samuel. "In the bed?"

Minerva stretched out her hand and laid it atop Charity's. Shaking her head, she said, "I know what it is, Charity. I'll explain it all later."

"Oh, good!" Abby exclaimed. "Because I'm sure Samuel's ready to go now. You know, there's so much to do back at the cabin. Work, work, work!"

The women stared at her in stunned silence.

Unmindful, Abby pulled Samuel over to the table piled high with fabrics. Biting at her lip, she dug through the mountain of material until she'd found the two she was looking for. Holding the goods up for his inspection, Abby asked, "Now, Samuel, I'm going to make you a new shirt. The ones you have will most certainly fall apart the next time I do the wash. So. Which would you prefer?"

Samuel glanced over his shoulder at Minerva and Charity. They were still watching. God, how had he gotten into this mess? Wasn't it enough that everywhere he went, people backed away from him, whispering outlandish rumors? Was it really necessary to now have the two talkingest women in Rock Creek know all about his arrangement with Abby? And did Abby *really* have to act so . . . familiar in front of folks?

He looked back at the material she was still holding out toward him. Suppressing a shudder, he pulled his gaze away from the gaudy red-and-yellow-striped and almost sighed with relief to see she also held a plain, dark blue fabric. He knew very well it was no use telling her that he didn't need a shirt. That he didn't want her to make him one or that he didn't appreciate her fussin' over him in front of the whole blessed world. Samuel had learned in a very short space of time that Abby Sutton was going to do as she damn well pleased, and that was that.

Grudgingly then, he jabbed a finger at the dark blue. "That one," he grumbled.

Abby's face fell. Her thumb and forefinger moved lovingly over the red and yellow stripes as she asked, "Are you certain, Samuel? I really think this one would look lovely with your eyes. . . ."

He heard a collective gasp from behind him and

ignored it. God almighty! What color did she think his eyes were, anyway? He glanced at her hat and silently acknowledged that no matter her enthusiasm, Abby's taste was no better than a hog's.

"I'm sure," was all he said.

She sighed heavily, her disappointment evident. "Oh, all right, then. Minerva, would you mind cutting off a shirt length of the dark blue, please?"

Minerva didn't stir.

Abby went right on. "You'd better make it a little bigger than usual, though. Samuel is a fairly large man, after all."

Minerva's jaw dropped, and with a slight nudge from Charity, she walked toward the fabric, keeping an eye on the "fairly" large man and making a wide circle around him.

Samuel felt the blood rushing to his cheeks again. It was all he could do to keep from shouting. But that would only serve to frighten the women and convince them all—maybe even *Abby*—that he really *was* a wild man. Instead, he said simply, "I'll wait for you in the wagon."

Before he'd taken more than a few steps, he'd begun to recite the ABCs under his breath.

Abby sighed heavily as she watched him leave the store. Behind her, she heard Minerva's scissors slicing into the fabric. Picking up the edge of the lovely yellow-and-red-striped material, Abby couldn't quite contain a sigh. It really was such a shame to pass up such a nice piece of goods when she was absolutely positive that it would look wonderful on Samuel.

She tilted her head and tossed a mischievous grin at the closed shop door. Hadn't he told her to get whatever she needed? Well, then, she would do just that. And what a surprise it would be for him when she presented him with two new shirts. *Then* he'd see that she'd been right about the fabric.

"Minerva," she said thoughtfully, "would you cut off a shirt length of the yellow and red, too?"

The other woman looked up. "But he said he wanted the blue."

"Oh, I know. And he'll get it." Abby patted her favorite fabric again. "But he'll also get a shirt made from this."

Minerva shook her head slowly but reached for the bolt of material. Silently she told herself she could hardly wait to see the big man in a shirt made from the loud stuff. Hell, the size he was, he'd probably look like a walkin' circus tent!

"You know how men are!" Abby laughed gently. "No sense of fashion at all!"

Minerva did indeed know about men's taste. Hadn't it been her own husband, Alonzo, who'd ordered the gawdawful material in the first place? Why, the damn thing had been sitting in the store collectin' dust for almost two years! There wasn't a woman for miles around who'd have anything to do with it!

Until now.

After only a few more minutes Abby was clutching her purchases to her chest and smiling at the two women opposite her. "It was so nice to meet you both," she said sincerely. "Perhaps you could come to the cabin for lunch one day soon?"

Minerva and Charity glanced at each other and knew that neither of them had the heart to disappoint the eager young thing.

When her two new friends nodded, Abby smiled. "Wonderful! Would the day after tomorrow be too

soon? We could do it tomorrow, but there are a few
things around the cabin I'd like Samuel to fix up before
we receive callers. He's such a dear man." She smiled
again. "But, of course, you already know that."

Hurrying out the door, Abby called over her shoulder, "See you both the day after tomorrow!"

Minerva and Charity stood together on the store's
porch and watched the oddly matched couple ride off
toward their mountain cabin.

"If I hadn't seen it with my own two eyes," Minerva
muttered, "I wouldn't have believed it."

"Know just what you mean." Charity nodded em-
phatically, her gaze still locked on the rapidly moving
wagon. "Who'd a thought a big ol' man like him would
blush like a schoolboy!" She snorted inelegantly. "And
just think . . . we was all thinkin' that fella was some
kinda monster or somethin'. What with him never
talkin' to nobody and all the time stayin' up on that
danged mountain! And then to see a tiny woman
like that just grab ahold of him and pull him around
the store was really somethin' to see!" Charity gave
Minerva's shoulder a playful punch. "Wait'll I tell Buck
about this. That man of mine's gonna be plumb speechless when he hears about the 'monster *blushin'*!"

"Oh, heavens, Charity! I ain't talkin' about that. . . .
Minerva turned to her friend. "Didn't you see that
little thing's eyes when she looked up at him? All
sparkly and shiny like a brand-new penny! I'm tellin'
you, there's some sparkin' goin' on up at that cabin!"

"Nah . . ." Charity shook her head violently. "Why,
she ain't big enough to hold her own with a man that
size! 'Sides, he wasn't actin' like he was sparkin' her.
Looked more like he wanted to hog-tie her!"

"Well, if not yet . . . then soon." Minerva laughed quietly. "Whether the big fella knows it or not!"

"Hmmmm . . ." Charity stared thoughtfully at the now empty road. "You could be right, Minerva." Suddenly she turned and locked a steady gaze on her friend. "Now, are you gonna tell me just what in the blue blazes a bundling board is?"

Minerva chuckled and took the other woman's arm to pull her back inside the store. "I surely will. Over a cup of coffee. This is gonna take a spell."

Samuel's big hands gripped the reins as if it meant his life. His knuckles white, his jaw tight, eyes grim, Abby knew without a doubt that *something* was bothering him. She just couldn't understand what it might be.

Surely he wasn't upset because she'd made some new friends. She threw a quick glance at him. No. That wouldn't bother him. If so, he'd never have taken her to town with him. Quickly her mind ran back over everything she'd done and said that morning, looking for the reason behind his anger. After a few minutes she frowned. For the life of her, she couldn't think of a thing.

Then she remembered. Of course. The judge. He must have found out something about the court that had upset him. She fought down a smile. Maybe that meant it was a *good* news for her!

"Samuel," she said.

"Yeah?"

"Did you talk to anyone about the circuit judge?"

His fingers tightened again around the reins, and she watched as his jaw muscles worked.

"Yeah," he finally answered. "The sheriff says it'll be at least five or six weeks till the judge gets back to Rock Creek."

"Five or six *weeks?*"

"We just missed him. He was through here only a week ago."

"What a shame," she offered, then turned her head away. Her lips curved into a satisfied grin. Five or six weeks. *Anything* could happen in that length of time! Abby felt as though a crushing weight had been lifted off her shoulders.

"Yeah," Samuel agreed under his breath. "A shame."

He didn't have to sound so disappointed, she told herself. After all, he'd already made it quite clear that he didn't want her at the cabin. There was simply no need to be rude about it. Unconsciously she straightened the hang of her skirt over her knees, then ran her hand over the brown paper package containing the shirt material she'd gotten for him.

Well, she would show him how useful she could be. Now that she knew for certain that she would have at least five or six weeks before facing a judge, Abby could relax a little. Take the time to plan a campaign that would win Samuel over. She flicked a quick glance at him from the corner of her eye.

His expression hadn't changed. He still looked as if he'd bitten into a rotten apple. Abby smiled softly and looked away. If he had to sulk for a while, that was all right with her. Because no matter what he did or said, the next six weeks still stretched out ahead of them. And they would be spending it together.

Abby crooned meaningless words in a soft, singsong tone as she crept ever closer to the wounded wolf. From behind the wood slats of his cage, the animal watched her through attentive, cold gray eyes. The huge gray wolf's body hardly moved. If not for the slight rise and fall of its rib cage and the steady gaze it directed at her, Abby would have sworn it was dead.

As by all rights it should be. Even at a distance Abby could see that the wound it had suffered must have been a nasty one. The strips of cloth wrapped around its middle covered a large part of the animal's body, and Abby could only guess at the damage that had been done.

Only a few steps away now. She kept up the non-sensical murmurings, hoping to reassure the animal that she meant it no harm. Steadfastly keeping her gaze away from the other animals in different-size cages, Abby concentrated solely on the wolf. There was something about him that seemed to call to her. Perhaps it was his beautiful coloring . . . perhaps it was the fact that he was isolated from his fellow creatures. In a cage far back from the others, the wolf appeared to be so . . . alone.

Somewhere in her mind Abby told herself that he was much like Samuel. Living near those who would be companions, but separated by the bars of a cage. She took another step and thought that a cage didn't have to be a physical one.

Hadn't Samuel distanced himself from her ever since their trip to Rock Creek the day before? He'd said hardly a word to her and had made himself so scarce around the cabin that she was beginning to wonder if he'd left the mountain altogether. In fact, she hadn't seen him at all since the night before.

He was gone before she got up that morning, and now, at late afternoon, there was still no sign of him.

She was almost within reach of the cage. Smiling softly, she stretched out one hand, moving as slowly as possible.

Strong hands clamped around her waist and lifted. Her feet left the rocky ground, and Abby felt herself swinging effortlessly through the air. Before she had the time to screech her surprise, though, she was set back to her feet with a thud that jarred her teeth. Somehow, she wasn't surprised to look up and find Samuel glowering down at her.

"What the hell do you think you're doin', Abby?"

She winced at the booming thunder of his voice.

"I told you to stay away from the animals! Didn't I?"

"Yes, Samuel"—she smoothed her pale green skirt—"you did." Raising her gaze to meet his, she added, "But you weren't here, and they *have* to be fed."

"*Fed?*" He pushed his bushy hair out of his eyes and hollered, "What were you plannin' on feedin' that wolf there? Biscuits? Or maybe your arm?"

She frowned at him. "I hardly think a caged animal would chew off my arm, Samuel."

He shook his head, clearly frustrated. "Abby," he said, taking a deep breath, "that wolf could tear a little thing like you clean in two. Cage or no cage."

Abby threw a measuring glance at the still-unmoving animal, then looked back at the huge man in front of her. "He doesn't hurt you, Samuel."

"Yeah, well, he knows me. He knows I ain't gonna hurt him."

Abby smiled. "Good. Soon the wolf will know me, too, and I'll be able to help you."

"He ain't gonna get to know you, Abby, 'cause you're gonna stay the hell away from him like I said."

Abby leaned back as Samuel's huge body loomed over her. He seemed to think that if his words wouldn't convince her, his size would intimidate her. He was wrong.

"I've told you more than once, Samuel, that I am not deaf and that I don't approve of swearing." As her words picked up speed, she leaned toward him now and was justly satisfied to see the big man shift backward a little. "I'm living here, too, and I don't understand why you should resent my offers to help. I only want to make myself useful. There is simply no reason for you to carry on as though you were still alone."

His lips were moving. Abby squinted up at him. She knew he was saying something, but she couldn't hear it. "Will you at least have the courtesy to speak so that I can hear you?"

Samuel's chest expanded with the long breath he drew in. He pushed his straggly hair out of his eyes and managed to grind out, "I wasn't talkin' to you."

"Hmmph!" Abby brushed past him and began to move along the line of cages. He was right behind her, and she could feel his annoyance. He made no attempt to soften his footsteps, and the ground trembled with every step he took.

Abby tried to ignore him and concentrate on the animals. It wasn't easy. Still she managed to speak a few, soft words to each of the animals that surrounded them, from the cougar to the rabbits, to the doe and her fawn. Before he could stop her, Abby even made a point of stopping beside the wolf's cage one last time. She held her ground stubbornly, even when the animal curled his lip back, exposing several deadly-looking teeth. A low, thunderlike growl rumbled through the animal's chest, and Abby instinctively took a step back.

Samuel's big hands came down on her gently, cupping her shoulders and arms in his palms. A flash of heat rushed through her body at his touch. Warmth flooded her, and Abby relished the feel of his protective strength.

"It's all right, boy." Samuel spoke softly to the wolf, and the big animal cocked his head and looked at the man. The growling stopped. Closing his eyes, the wolf laid his head down on his front paws and went to sleep.

"How did you do that?" Abby whispered. Her gaze was fixed on the wolf. "He listened to you as though he understood."

"In a way, I guess he did." Samuel squeezed her shoulders gently, liking the feel of her beneath his hands. He fought down a sudden, wild desire to caress her and desperately tried to concentrate on her question instead. "Like I told you. He trusts me."

"But . . ." Abby turned under his hands and stared up at him. His eyes were softer, warmer than she'd ever seen them before. Unwilling to break the spell that held them together, she asked her next question quietly, aware that at any moment he might move away. "A wolf. He behaved like Maverick. Or Harry. Samuel, how on earth did you . . . ?"

He shrugged and moved his hands away from her. "I don't know." He jammed his hands into his pockets and went on. "Animals like me is all. Always have. I guess I got a way with 'em."

Abby shivered slightly and wished suddenly that he hadn't removed his hands. Those few moments of closeness had passed far too quickly for her.

She watched as he turned away, unlocked a cage, and reached inside. Her gaze softened as she saw him move his hands carefully over the tiny, injured rabbit. The animal cuddled against Samuel's palm and rubbed its head against the finger Samuel was scratching it with.

Abby wrapped her arms tightly around her and inhaled sharply. She wanted to look away, but she couldn't. Instead, she found herself wondering what it would be like to have Samuel's big, work-hardened hands move gently over her body. To see his eyes soften and know that that look was for her alone. To feel his strength wrapped around her. Her mouth suddenly dry and her breath coming in shallow gulps, Abby made a last deliberate attempt at wiping away the image of Samuel touching her. Holding her. Kissing her.

"Abby? Abby? You all right?"

She shook her head and looked up. Samuel was right in front of her, staring down, concern spreading across his face.

"Of course I'm all right, Samuel." Abby cleared her throat uneasily. "Why?"

"Oh, no reason," he began sarcastically.

Those big hands of his settled over his hips, and Abby wrenched her gaze away.

"I don't understand," she whispered.

"Abby, you been starin' off at nothin' for almost five whole minutes. Like you was asleep with your eyes open!" Samuel shook his head at her. "You dreamin' or somethin'?"

She licked her lips and swallowed heavily before saying, "Yes. I guess I was."

Chapter Six

Her tongue darted out and licked her full, pink lower lip. Samuel's gaze locked on that tiny movement, and a curl of raw desire snaked through his huge body. Good God, the woman had no idea at all what she was doing to him. Being with her the last few days, hearing her voice, watching her guileless face mirror every emotion that touched her, had almost cost him his sanity.

Samuel found himself looking for her. Waiting for her to start in singing one of the little songs that were becoming so familiar to him. Listening for her footstep. He swallowed past the ache of want in his throat and forced himself to turn away from her. God in Heaven, he'd never last the six weeks until the judge came through town. How could *any* man be expected to live with her and not *want* her? And it was far worse for him. He'd been alone so long that he'd reacted to her stubborn presence like a rain-starved field of corn.

It wasn't right. None of this was right. She shouldn't be here, he told himself. She should never have come. Didn't she know that when she left, the loneliness would come again? And that this time it would kill him?

Silently he set the wounded rabbit back into its cage, closed the door, and walked away. He couldn't stay. Not another minute. If he did, he just might give in to his body's demands and kiss her until she couldn't breathe anymore. Instantly his traitorous mind conjured up the vision of Abby in his arms, her perfect mouth puffy from his kisses. The dream Abby reached up and smoothed the palms of her tiny hands over his broad chest while her golden eyes looked at him with hunger.

A sharp, physical pain stabbed him when he realized suddenly that the dream would never happen. He jammed his powerful fists into his pockets helplessly and called himself all kinds of a fool for even thinking about it. Why would a woman like Abby want him? He snorted sullenly. She wouldn't. And he'd best get used to it.

"Samuel!"

He groaned but stopped short. Her quick, light footsteps came up behind him.

"Samuel," she said softly.

"Abby, I got work to do. You best get on to the cabin now." His voice gruff, he looked straight ahead, not trusting himself to look down into her eyes.

"I will, Samuel." She laid one hand on his forearm, and he jerked at her touch. "But first," she continued, "I want to thank you for sharing your animals with me."

Slowly, against his will, Samuel's head swiveled to

look at her. Her face was tilted up, a soft smile on her lips. He knew he'd never seen anything quite so lovely before.

"They ain't *my* animals, Abby," he said, his voice straining. "They don't belong to nobody. When they're well, I'll let 'em go back where they belong."

"I know you will." Her smile didn't waver, and she squeezed his arm slightly. "That's what makes you so special, Samuel. You help those creatures, expecting nothing in return."

Her eyes moved over his face, and Samuel held perfectly still. He was stunned to realize that the quiet admiration shining on her features was for him. Suddenly she reached up, placed her palms on either side of his face and drew him down to her. She smoothed his long blond hair back and kissed him.

It was a quick kiss. Their lips had hardly touched before it was over. And yet . . . Samuel knew nothing would be the same for him again. Like an apple handed to a starving man, Abby's spontaneous kiss had only served to whet his appetite for more.

She released him and drew back. She didn't look the least bit embarrassed. Indeed, she looked quite pleased with herself. Samuel stood, like a great hulking statue, unsure of what to say and not certain he could get his voice to work even if something occurred to him.

"I'll let you get back to work now," Abby said finally. She turned and took a few steps, then stopped. Glancing over her shoulder, she offered, "You know, Samuel, I'd be happy to cut that hair for you."

He opened his mouth, but no words came out. It didn't matter, though. She was already walking toward the cabin, a song on the lips that had just kissed him.

Samuel pushed his hair out of his eyes, then rubbed his hand over his mouth. Abby kissed him.

He'd been gone all morning.

Abby dipped her hands into her bathwater, then let the hot water she'd captured roll down the length of her upraised arms. It felt delicious.

Sighing, she laid her head back against the end of the big metal tub and stared at the ceiling. The lavender-scented water lapped at her breasts with her movement, and some of it splashed over the side, making Harry skitter away uneasily.

Abby chuckled. She didn't even have to see the little dog to know exactly what he was doing. Both he and Maverick had watched her suspiciously while she filled the tub, ready to bolt at a moment's notice. But when they discovered that she was getting the water for herself, they'd both settled down on either side of the big tub.

She was glad of their company, though she couldn't help wondering why Samuel hadn't taken them with him when he'd left that morning. Usually, the three of them would spend the entire day traipsing around the surrounding woods. But today Samuel had slipped off quietly. He hadn't even stayed for breakfast.

Abby reached for the bar of soap on a nearby chair and began to build a lather between her hands. She probably shouldn't have kissed him, she knew. That was undoubtedly the reason behind Samuel's disappearance. It had to be. Why, all last night, she reminded herself, he'd hardly said a word. And she was getting exceptionally tired of his long silences. Even his shouting and carrying on was better than that.

She smoothed the lather over her legs and remembered the feel of his lips beneath hers. Soft and warm, his mouth had moved against hers in welcome, even if it was only briefly. She'd been sorely tempted to linger. To draw out the kiss, to know what it felt like to be held close in Samuel's arms.

Quick, sudden heat flushed her cheeks at the memory of the surprised look on his face when she'd pulled away. No, she admitted silently, it was more than surprise. She'd shocked him.

Dunking her legs beneath the water's surface, Abby also acknowledged that she'd shocked herself as well. Oh, not with wanting to kiss him. That idea, she supposed, had been curling through her brain since the first time she'd seen him. What had so shocked her was her body's response to that brief joining of mouths. Even now her blood boiled far hotter than her bathwater, just at the memory.

She drew a shaky breath, then slapped her hand against the water. This had to stop. For heaven's sake. She had *company* coming to call in just a couple of hours! She couldn't very well spend the entire day lollygagging in the tub dreaming of a man who obviously wasn't the slightest bit interested in her!

Deliberately she stood up and reached for the towel. Bathwater rocked back and forth against her knees, and a chill swept over her wet flesh. Hurriedly Abby stepped out of the tub and crossed to the fire, turning her naked backside to the roaring blaze in the hearth while she toweled herself dry.

Samuel's breath caught in his throat. His fingers tightened over the windowsill, and he wouldn't have been surprised to hear the wood snap under the pressure.

He knew he shouldn't have returned to the cabin so early. He had planned on staying away all day. Just to give himself a chance to bring his desires under control again. And then, just when he thought he might be winning the war, he finds himself in a battle twice as nerve-wracking as the one before.

He wasn't sure how long he'd been standing in the cold staring through the window at Abby. But his feet were numb, and his chest felt as though it might explode for lack of air. He'd hardly been able to draw a breath.

Samuel never would have believed that he would come to this. A peeping Tom of all things! But if it had meant his life, he couldn't have looked away.

When she'd stuck those small shapely legs of hers in the air and then slowly rubbed the soapy lather over the length of them, he'd almost died. He'd watched the water lap and curl around her high, rounded breasts. He'd seen her erect nipples poke above the water's surface, and his mouth had ached to close around them. When Abby's lathered hands moved to her arms, then over her own breasts, Samuel's heart stopped. Her head thrown back, Abby's hands moved over the line of her neck, the soap lather leaving a trail of white foam everywhere she touched. Her lips curved into a smile, and he would have given his soul to know what she was thinking. She sat straighter in the tub and lifted handfuls of water to rinse the soap from her breasts. His jaw locked tightly as he watched the droplets of water cling to her small pink nipples for a moment before dropping into the water below.

The rigid pain of his loins pounded at him, but he couldn't look away. Instead, he watched in dry-mouthed fascination as her hands moved languidly over her wet flesh, touching all the intimate places he longed to know. Slowly she stroked her own flesh as a lover might. His mouth was so dry, it was strangling him.

Then, all at once, she stood up in the knee-high tub, and Samuel knew he was near death. A man could only take so much. In one lithe motion she jumped from her bath and moved to the fireplace. He groaned and tightened his grip on the windowsill when she turned her softly curved bottom to the heat of the fire, leaving him with a vision of her face, wreathed by damp curls, and her lush, pink, bath-heated nudity.

Painfully he shifted position slightly, never moving his gaze from the rise and fall of her breasts. He shuddered at the force of the need that shot through him like a lance. It was all he could do not to crash through the door and sweep her into his arms. His palms itched to hold her, caress her. His tongue moved out to lick dry lips, and he almost tasted her.

Gritting his teeth together, Samuel watched her slowly move the towel over her skin and ached to do it for her. She gracefully propped one foot on the hearth, then bent over to dry her leg. His gaze followed the towel's path. First, her small, dainty foot and ankle, then up her calf, around her knee, then sliding up and over her inner thigh.

His heart hammered in his chest, and the blood racing through his body roared in his ears. As her towel touched the honey-blond triangle of curls, the pain in Samuel's loins became too sharp to bear.

Groaning helplessly, he pushed away from the window and staggered back toward the woods. Behind him he heard the damn dogs barking from inside the cabin.

* * *

"What is it?" Abby wrapped the towel around her nudity and looked at the two dogs, now standing before the door. "Is someone out there?" She whispered the question, then stifled a soft laugh. Honestly, she told herself, it's not as if they're going to answer you!

Quietly she moved to the window. Edging around the glass, she stared out at the empty yard of the cabin. Nothing. No one.

She glanced down at the two dogs and frowned. "What's wrong with you two? There's no one there."

Harry and Maverick looked at her, then at each other. As one, then, they moved to the hearth and laid down, side by side.

"Bad dogs, you startled me." Abby threw another glance out the window. "For a moment I thought Samuel had come home early!" She laughed and added, "Wouldn't *that* have been embarrassing!"

Samuel stopped and stared at the cabin. Even at a distance of two hundred yards, he felt the unmistakable pull of Abby's presence. Dammit! he shouted inwardly. Don't start up again!

In the four hours since he'd torn himself from the sight of Abby's bath, he'd worked like a madman. His meaty hands still tingled from the sting of the wood-handled ax he'd swung for more than three of those hours.

He grimaced and acknowledged that at least one good thing had come from his frustration. He'd finally managed to chop down the damn lightning-struck pine at the edge of his land. Samuel'd been meaning to get to that chore for two months. But he'd put it off. And today he'd been glad he had. The hours he'd spent chopping down the tree, then cutting it up in lengths for the fireplace, had finally cooled the raging fires in his blood. Of course, the bath he took in the icy-cold river water after working probably helped.

And now, as soon as he got within shouting distance of the cabin, he felt the rush of desire again. Well, goddammit, he'd just have to get over it. He wasn't about to leave his home for the next six weeks. Not with winter comin' on. There was too much to do. So, somehow, he was going to have to find a way to live with Abby without lookin' at her.

He snorted derisively. Not likely.

But hell, he was a strong man. He'd been through Indian battles, been stranded in a mountain cave during a blizzard, been in a hand to hand fight with a bear that didn't take kindly to company . . . surely he was strong enough to overcome his own body!

So then, he asked himself . . . how come you're standin' in the cold instead of sittin' in that cabin? He knew the answer, and though it took some doing, he once again started walking toward his home.

As he drew nearer, he distinctly heard the sounds of three or more voices. Immediately he dropped to a crouch and came up on the cabin from the side to prevent anyone from spotting him through a window. His brow wrinkled in thought, he went on. Stealthily, Samuel moved across the open yard. It wouldn't be the first time some drifter had come upon the cabin and made himself to home. The last time was only a month ago. Of course, one look at Samuel had convinced the man to take off for the high country.

But now, Samuel told himself, there was Abby to consider. Suppose some men were even now holed up in that cabin doing God knows what to her? A powerful fear-induced rage swept over him. The kind of raw anger he'd spent his entire life trying to avoid. His hands tightened into fists, and he fervently wished he'd taken his rifle with him when he'd left that morning.

But all he had with him was the razor-sharp axe. It would have to do.

Only a few steps away from the cabin, Samuel squared his broad shoulders and charged the door. Shouting at the top of his lungs, he went crashing through the wood. The ax raised, feet planted wide apart in a combat stance, he stared helplessly at the stunned faces turned toward him.

Minerva Mullins's hand was at her throat, her eyes wide. Charity Whitehall's big body was half out of her chair as though she had every intention of doing battle. And there were two other women, besides Abby, that Samuel didn't know. One of the strangers took a long look at him and swooned gracefully to the floor. The other's lips were moving frantically, though no sound could be heard.

Samuel lowered the ax and let his gaze focus on Abby. His broad chest heaving, he ignored the other women. Gratefully he saw that Abby was already rushing to his side.

"Samuel!" she said with a forced gaiety. "I'm so glad you've returned in time to visit with our guests!" She took the ax from his suddenly limp hand and leaned it against the wall. Then, her fingers tight around his wrist, she led him to the table. Pushing him into a chair, Abby said, "You remember Minerva Mullins."

He nodded and Minerva returned it, slowly lowering her hand from her throat to her lap.

"And Charity Whitehall," Abby went on.

He glanced up at the formidable woman, who kept one eye on him while she dropped back into her chair.

"Of course you must know Esther Knight," Abby prodded, indicating the still mumbling woman on his right. "The preacher's wife?"

Samuel shook his head. The woman gave him a tremulous smile and her lips finally stopped moving. She must have been praying, Samuel told himself in disgust. And who could blame her? She probably thought they were being attacked!

"And this is Mary Smith, the schoolteacher," Abby finished lamely. Then she looked down and cried, "Oh, my heavens!"

Samuel followed her gaze and noticed that the schoolteacher was still on the floor, her eyes closed.

Abby rushed over to the fallen woman and began to pat her wrists with more impatience than gentleness. "She's fainted. Minerva, what should we do?"

Minerva sighed. Glancing down at the prostrate woman, she said, "Just leave her be, Abby. She'll come around directly. Looks comfortable right where she is."

"Do you really think—?"

"Minerva's right," Charity said, throwing in her two cents' worth. "That woman's keeled over more times than a drunk on Saturday night. She wears her stays too damn tight is all."

"Oooh!" Esther fanned a lace handkerchief in front of her flushed face. "Charity, you mustn't mention a lady's uh, uh . . ." She looked at Samuel meaningfully.

Charity's lips twisted. "For corn's sake, Esther! Everybody knows that females wear corsets! And some of 'em tie 'em too tight!"

"Yes, but—"

"Let her be, Charity." Minerva shot her friend a warning look. "If she don't want to talk about them things, then don't worry her any."

Samuel's breath was much more even now. But he agreed with the preacher's wife. He wished to hell everyone would stop talkin' about ladies' underwear!

While the three women waited for the schoolmarm to come around, Samuel took a few quick seconds to study his cabin. There was even more gewgaws around the place than there was yesterday. Abby clearly seemed to be diggin' in for a long stay. He watched her from the corner of his eye as she helped the teacher back into her chair. Concerned gentleness flowed from her as she urged a cup of coffee on the tall, plain woman. The schoolmarm kept directing worried glances at Samuel, but she managed to sip at her drink, and Samuel was pleased to see spots of color return to the woman's cheeks.

He snapped out of his daydreaming when Abby set a cup of steaming coffee in front of him. With the interested gazes of the ladies locked on him, Samuel gingerly lifted the small china cup. His fingers were far too large to fit through the impossibly tiny handle, so he was left to grip it tightly and hope for the best.

Before he could wonder where the damn thing had come from, Abby was telling him, "I was so pleased to find that my mother's china teacups had survived my journey. You know, I had to wrap them up in my clothes to protect them!"

"Still," Minerva added as she reached for another cookie, "with the way those stagecoaches ride, it's a wonder that they weren't all broken!"

Thankfully, the conversation picked up from there.

The women went right on talking as if Samuel weren't there. Occasionally, though, one or the other of them would pass him the cookie plate and ask a question that only required him to nod or shake his head.

Samuel finally felt himself relaxing. In fact, he was almost pleased to find the women there in the cabin. He'd been so worried about being alone with Abby after he'd watched her in her bath, that company was nearly a blessing.

"What do you think, Samuel?"

"Huh?" His head snapped up, and he turned quickly toward Minerva.

"We were talkin' about the barn raisin'."

"Barn raisin'?" he echoed, swearing at himself silently for not listening.

But the older woman was clearly used to speaking with men. Shaking her head as if to say that it didn't surprise her any that his attention had wandered, she repeated, "The Coles'? Over in the valley the other side of the mountain?"

Samuel's brow furrowed, then he nodded uneasily.

"Well, we was plannin' a barn raisin'." Minerva looked him dead in the eye. "Theirs burned down two weeks back, and they're gonna need some shelter for the animals before winter."

"Yeah?" Samuel said, his head cocked. He had a feeling he was about to be roped into something.

"Abby here"—Minerva jerked her head at the younger woman—"said that you might be willin' to help out."

Slowly Samuel's head swiveled around, and he stared at Abby. He couldn't believe it. Wasn't it enough that she'd taken over his home? Did she have to run his life, too?

"Is that right?" he asked quietly.

Abby met his gaze squarely. She smiled at him, and despite his intentions, Samuel felt himself weakening.

"Oh, Samuel," she said excitedly, "I knew you'd want to help your friends. Why, you're so clever at fixing things." She turned to the ladies. "Just yesterday he fixed the pump, and he did it so quickly, it was startling!"

He closed his eyes. For godsake, it was just a broken pump handle!

"And Samuel, as strong as you are, I just know that you'll be needed desperately."

His eyes opened again to find her looking at him hopefully.

"Minerva's told me about the Coles' troubles. They've only been married a year, you know."

"That right," he said quietly.

"Yes," she went on, flashing him a pleased smile, "and already they've had more than their share of problems. What with the barn fire and their new bull dying and now Mrs. Cole is with child and . . ."

He nodded.

Minerva picked up where Abby left off, and Samuel turned to the older woman.

"Yes, well. We all have our troubles. But the point is, Samuel . . ." She paused. "You don't mind me callin' you Samuel, do you?"

He shook his head.

"The point is, Samuel, we need your help. Like Abby says, you're a right strong man. My man Alonzo and the others will be there, of course."

Samuel wondered for a moment if the menfolk knew what their women were up to. Minerva answered that question with her next breath.

"And they say they'd be right pleased to have you."

Samuel sat back against his chair and chewed another cookie. Quickly his brain worked. He'd lived on the mountain for six months. He'd been into Rock Creek at least a dozen times, and he couldn't remember one time when anyone even spoke to him. And now they were comin' to his house and askin' him to be part of a barn raisin'.

He reached for another cookie and avoided the eyes of the waiting women. He had to think about this for a minute. In all those trips to town, he asked himself, did he ever once *try* to talk to anybody? No. He hadn't. But even if he had, he knew no one would have answered. It would have been the same as everywhere else.

And now, because of Abby, he was bein' dragged right into the middle of everyone's danged business!

He hid a smile. For some reason, the idea pleased him. Then he remembered his mother's warning. But this time the words sounded weak and far away. Maybe she'd been wrong, he told himself. Maybe he could be around people.

Maybe.

Was it worth finding out? Should he really bother trying again? His gaze swept the women's faces.

They were all watching him. Waiting. And suddenly Samuel knew that he would have to take the chance. If he was wrong . . . if he found out once and for all that his mother had been right about him . . . well, there were other mountains.

"All right," he finally said. "I'll help."

Abby's hands clapped together. Minerva and Charity exchanged knowing looks, and the preacher's wife, Esther, started in to mumbling again. But Samuel only had eyes for Abby. Her pleased smile and glowing face as she looked at him were worth taking a risk or two.

He only hoped that she wouldn't be disappointed. As for himself, he'd given up long ago any hope for folks to treat him like anybody else.

Some female always took one look at him and fainted. . . . Older men were forever skittering sideways to get out of his way. . . . And young men always tried to find a way to pick a fight, desperate to prove themselves men.

It was the same everywhere. Samuel had little faith that things would be different in Rock Creek. But for Abby's sake, he would try.

Chapter Seven

She was singing again. Samuel's aching eyes focused on Abby's back as she moved about the cabin, getting breakfast on the table.

How can the woman sleep so damn good in that bed? he asked himself. He was just one short step away from madness himself. That no good bundling board idea of hers just wasn't doin' the job. Oh, he acknowledged silently, it kept their bodies from touching during the night, but it didn't do anything to his imagination! And after seeing her in the altogether yesterday, things had gotten worse.

Why, he hadn't gotten more than a few minutes sleep at a stretch all night. Samuel scowled ferociously into his coffee cup as Abby started on another song. Their arrangement didn't seem to be bothering her any.

But he couldn't spend one more night lying in the dark with her only an arm's reach away.

There was only one answer. He had to build another

room onto the cabin. Hell, he'd always planned on making the place bigger anyway. Even after the judge heard their case and Abby finally went home, he'd still need the extra room. It wasn't *just* because of Abby.

Crisp bacon and hen-fresh eggs were set in front of him, and despite his weariness, Samuel smiled. She sure as hell could cook!

As she sat down opposite him, Samuel reached for the baking powder biscuits and helped himself to some blueberry preserves.

"I'm so glad you like the preserves," Abby said. "They're Minerva's, you know. But next summer I'll put up plenty of fruits and vegetables myself."

Samuel glanced up, one eyebrow raised.

"Perhaps you could pick out just the right spot for a vegetable garden, Samuel. I'd like to be all set when spring arrives."

He didn't answer, simply reached for another biscuit.

"Oh, I know what you're thinking," Abby said.

"Hmmm?"

"You're thinking that I shouldn't go on making plans for next summer when I might not even be here for the winter."

Samuel shrugged his massive shoulders and kept his face down. He didn't want her to see what the thought of her leaving did to him.

"But I believe in planning ahead. Besides, nothing is gained by expecting the worst." She poured him another cup of coffee and handed each of the dogs a biscuit. "What are you going to do today, Samuel?"

His plate clean, Samuel took a long drink of the coffee and sat back. "I'm takin' the wagon into Wolf River."

Her brow furrowed.

"A town a day's ride from here. They got a lumber mill over there."

"Oh!" She smiled. "Are you going to pick up the lumber for the barn raising?"

"No." He pushed his chair back and stood up. "The Coles'll have to do that. No, I'm goin' to get enough lumber to build another room onto the cabin."

"Samuel!" Abby jumped up and came around the table to his side. Grabbing his arm and moving toward the door, she went on, "What a wonderful idea! And I know just the place for it!"

As she pulled him through the front door, he had just enough time to grab his hat and think that he wasn't surprised in the least.

At the far side of the cabin Abby stopped. "Right here." She held her arms extended toward the side wall of the house. "It would be perfect right there. Close enough to the fireplace and with a window, I would have a lovely view of the valley! Oh, it will be so nice to have a separate kitchen!"

"Kitchen!" Samuel pulled his arm free of her grasp. Just having her hands on his arm set his body to tingling with wants he had best start ignoring. He stepped away from her and said in a low, controlled voice, "I ain't buildin' a kitchen, Abby."

"Well, for heaven's sake. Whyever not?" Hands on her hips, she faced him curiously. "It's the one thing we need."

"It ain't the one thing *I* need."

"What?" Her features a mask of confusion, Abby asked, "I don't understand. If we're going to make our home more comfortable, I would think it would be best to have the cooking place separate from our living area." She smiled. "It would be nice for when we have guests, not to have the cooking things sitting right out in the open."

"I'm not trying to make a comfortable *home!*" Samuel thrust his balled fists in his pockets. "And I don't *want* guests!" Abruptly he turned away. It was too difficult to think when he looked at her. He didn't know what he'd been doing yesterday when he'd allowed himself to get involved with the womenfolk and their plans. He couldn't even figure out why it was so damned important to him that Abby think well of him. But he knew that if he didn't put his foot down soon, there wouldn't be a place for him to do it. At least, not in his own home.

"Well, what exactly *are* you trying to do, Samuel?"

Jesus! Couldn't she see what was happening to him? Didn't she know how he suffered every night, lying alongside her in the dark? He looked at her carefully. No. She didn't know. Didn't she keep telling him how she trusted him? Didn't she keep smiling up at him, her golden eyes shining? Of course Abby didn't know. Why should she? She felt none of those things for him.

What woman would? Hell, he knew better than most that he was just a big, homely man who didn't even know how to talk to folks. He breathed deeply and felt the cold pine-scented air fill him.

Deliberately he took a moment to control his rising temper. He had no right to be angry with her. It wasn't her fault that her damn fool uncle Silas had caused so much trouble. It wasn't her fault that he, Samuel, had feelings for her that he had no right to.

After another deep breath Samuel said quietly, "I'm fixin' to build you a sleepin' room, Abby."

Her breath caught. She bit down on her bottom lip before a tiny smile curved her mouth. "Oh, Samuel. How thoughtful of you!"

"Yeah, well . . ." He mumbled something incoherent and stared off into the surrounding pines. Thoughtful! Huh! Whatever gods had done this to him must be havin' a helluva laugh, he thought with disgust.

The morning air held a chill that warned of the quickly approaching winter, and Samuel knew that snow could arrive that high up mighty early. If he was going to do this, he'd better get at it, he told himself testily.

"I best get goin'," he said under his breath and walked past Abby toward the barn.

Less than an hour later he stood awkwardly beside the wagon and looked down at Abby. "I should be back by day after tomorrow. You, uh, you bolt the door at night, Abby." He rubbed his bearded jaw. Despite the need to be away by himself for a while, he suddenly felt bad about leavin' her alone. "Nothin'll happen most likely," he added, "but why take chances?"

She nodded.

"And stay the hell away from the animals." He tried to glare at her in warning, but those eyes of hers kept on shinin' at him. "I fed 'em good this morning. They'll be fine till I get back."

"All right, Samuel."

She just stood there, lookin' up at him, and Samuel felt his insides go all which ways. God help him, if he didn't find some peace soon, he'd never last out the six weeks until the judge got to Rock Creek. Why in hell did she have to be so beautiful? He shifted slightly, and Abby leaned closer.

"What is it, Abby?" He ground his teeth together

in frustration. She smelled of coffee and bacon and a touch of vanilla. The morning sun danced in her hair, and she was so close he could count the few freckles across her nose.

"Nothing," she said softly, her eyes never leaving his. "I just thought . . ." Her gaze lowered slightly.

"Thought what?" His voice sounded rough even to himself.

She looked up again, and he was lost in the golden splendor of her eyes.

"I thought you were going to . . ."

"What?" he forced out.

"Kiss me." The words came out softly on a sigh as she leaned closer to him.

God! The fire in his blood that he'd worked so hard to tamp down now flared up again and raged through him. She *wanted* him to kiss her? His chest heaved. He was sure his heart had stopped. His palms itched to hold her, his gaze locked on her mouth, he could almost taste her already. But did he dare? Would he be able to stop with one kiss? Then he realized that it didn't matter. Nothing mattered beyond the miracle that Abby wanted his kiss.

Slowly, carefully, he bent lower. His eyes wide open, he saw hers close just before their lips met. Samuel's mouth touched hers gingerly, and he felt an unfamiliar weakness wash over him at the unbelievable softness of her.

Though his body yearned to grab her and hold her close, he kept his arms at his side and began to pull away after that briefest of kisses.

Then Abby's eyes opened, and she looked deeply into his. Incredibly, he saw desire there. Desire for him. A soft smile curved her lips as she raised her arms to encircle his neck. Of their own accord, it seemed, Samuel's strong arms wrapped around her and lifted her slight weight from the ground.

He felt her hands smooth away his too long hair, and then he dipped his head to hers and claimed her mouth with a kiss he'd been dreaming of since the first time he'd seen her.

The soft warmth of her filled him, and he groaned when she parted her lips for him. His tongue swept inside and caressed hers. His body tightened reflexively as Abby's open palms against his back held him closer, tighter. A soft moan came from her throat just before her tongue moved to stroke the inside of his mouth.

Samuel's heart pounded in his ears, and he pulled away slightly to gasp for the breath he was almost willing to do without. He saw her mouth, swollen from his kiss, saw the glaze of passion cover her eyes, and watched with hunger the rapid rise and fall of her breasts. It was all he could do to keep from tearing her blouse open and burying himself in her soft curves.

But years of control gave him the strength to set her down on her own feet. She staggered slightly and gripped his forearms for balance. He had to stop now. Before he reached a point when he would never stop.

"Samuel," she breathed raggedly, "I—"

"I have to go now, Abby." He turned away, then quickly turned back and grabbed her to him. He simply couldn't help himself. One last time he pressed his lips to hers in a searing kiss that left both of them breathless. Then he turned again and quickly climbed up to the wagon seat. "I gotta go."

"Be careful, Samuel."

He waved but didn't look back as the horses leaned

into their traces and the wagon began its roll down the mountain.

Abby took two shaky steps and raised her hand to her mouth. Rubbing her bruised lips, she whispered urgently, "Hurry back."

Abby stepped back and took a long look at her handiwork. Smiling, she put her palms against the small of her back and stretched. Her back hurt like the very devil, but it would be worth it to see Samuel's face when he got home.

He'd be surprised, she knew. But she owed him a surprise. If she lived to be a hundred, she'd never forget the looks on the other ladies' faces when Samuel stormed into the cabin, ax raised. His fierce expression, his wild hair and beard, and his immense size had given him the look of an ancient warrior that she'd read about once as a girl.

Chuckling softly, she remembered, too, how stunned he'd been to discover that his only opponents were five women having coffee and cookies!

Abby sniffed, then sneezed violently. There was something about the smell of fresh paint that had always made her sneeze. But it was worth it. The new coat of paint looked wonderful!

Picking up her paintbrush once more, she crossed the room and carefully filled in a small space that she'd missed somehow. Abby smiled and turned in a slow circle, getting the full effect of the cabin's new look. For the life of her, she couldn't understand why Minerva had been so stunned when Abby'd picked up the paint that morning at the store. Why, the color was even lovelier than she'd imagined!

Abby frowned momentarily as she wondered what

Samuel would think of the cabin walls being such a bright shade of pink. Then she laughed shortly. If he was like most men, he probably wouldn't even notice, she told herself. But then, she thought dreamily as she stared out the side window, Samuel wasn't like most men.

A curl of excitement started in the pit of her stomach and spread quickly to her arms and legs. She could still feel his lips on hers. His arms wrapped around her, snuggling her in a warm, protective circle. Abby had never known that a kiss could be so much more than a touch.

If she'd known what it would be like, she'd have asked him to kiss her days ago!

Maverick whined and butted against the back of her knees, making her grab at a nearby chair. She looked down at the dog and laughed out loud.

"You're right, Maverick. Enough of this standing around. Let's get this job finished, shall we?"

She set her paintbrush down and walked to the table where two more cans of paint stood waiting for her. Wasn't it lucky, she asked herself, that she'd found the paint in the back of Minerva's store practically hidden under some discarded feed sacks?

Pink was such a nice, cheerful color! It made her think of sunsets and sunrises. Thoughtfully she tapped her index finger against her chin, oblivious to the splotch of pink she left there. Perhaps tomorrow she would take the buggy into Rock Creek again and get enough paint to do the trim in a different color. Abby smiled. Maybe Minerva had a bright, sunny yellow tucked away somewhere . . .

A raucous screeching and cackling burst into the stillness. Harry leapt nimbly down from the big bed and raced to the door. His tongue hanging out, one remaining ear pricked, he turned to look at Abby impatiently. Maverick moved more slowly to join his companion.

Abby glanced uneasily at the closed door. "What is it, boys?"

The hens' wild cackling crept up in volume, and now Abby heard a loud crashing sound to accompany it. Oh, heavens, some animal has gotten in with Samuel's chickens, she thought frantically. She had to do something! But what? She turned around, her eyes scanning the cabin quickly. She didn't have the slightest notion of how to shoot a gun. And if she tried, she'd probably shoot herself rather than the predator out there making a meal of the hens! But there had to be something . . . Her gaze fell on the iron skillet. She snatched it up.

Hurrying now, she moved across the room and opened the door slightly. Before she could stop him, Harry had squeezed through and was racing across the yard. Maverick, though, was stopped by Abby's leg. Awkwardly, she managed to get outside and still keep the bigger dog caged in the house.

Harry's frantic barking was now added to the unbelievable racket coming from the chicken coop. Blast it, she thought as she crouched and sprinted toward the low building, if Harry didn't stop, she would lose all chance of surprising whatever was bothering the hens.

She reached the small outbuilding in seconds and flattened herself against the side wall. Shuffling slowly along the rough planed wood, Abby moved along until she could see the front of the coop. The door was standing open.

Abby gulped and leaned back against the wall.

Holding the skillet to her chest, she tried to make her heart stop racing. The open door meant one thing: Whatever was in there wasn't an animal. Animals can't open closed doors.

A handful of feathers shot out the window over her head, and Abby watched as they floated slowly to the ground. She cringed a little as the hens' agitated screeches got even louder. Another crash from inside and Abby squared her shoulders. It was up to her. This was her home now, too. Not just Samuel's. And it was up to her to defend it. She only hoped desperately that she wouldn't be facing a gun with an iron skillet.

Just as she reached the coop's open door, a hen with wings flapping wildly raced out. Abby's feet moved quickly, trying to sidestep the little animal, but no matter where she stepped, the hen was just underfoot, tangling itself in Abby's skirts. The crazy bird shot free as Abby toppled over and landed on her stomach.

Gasping for the wind that had been knocked out of her by the fall, Abby called out from the ground, "Who is it? Who's in there?"

Another hen raced through the door, skittering over Abby's back on its way out the gate.

Abby got her hands under her and pushed herself to her knees. Over the screeching, she called again, "I know you're in there. You may as well come out. Now."

After a long few minutes, through the cloud of flying chicken feathers, a small figure stepped into the light. Abby squinted and staggered to her feet. Still clutching the skillet in her right hand, she pushed her tangled, paint-streaked, feather-bedecked hair out of her eyes and waited.

It was a child.

Relief swept through Abby as she realized that the boy couldn't be more than ten years old. In the length of time it took him to cross the few feet of space separating him from her, Abby studied him carefully.

Unbelievably dirty, the boy also looked as if he hadn't eaten in days. His torn clothes were threadbare, and his bare feet were purple with cold. As he got closer, Abby noticed the clear, mountain-lake blue of his eyes, his stubborn chin, and his night-black hair, which stood on end in dirty little tufts all over his head. His mouth was set in an unrepentant line, and his thin shoulders were stiff as a board. In one grubby little fist the child held two eggs. This, then, was the reason for the hens' indignation.

Abby looked down at him and tried a smile. No response. Finally she asked, "Would you like some bacon and hot biscuits to go with those eggs?"

The boy's eyes shot up to her face, and he stared at her unbelievingly. After a long, silent moment he said, "Yes'm. I shore would."

Samuel stretched out on his bedroll and poked another branch into the fire. Flames licked at the fresh wood, hit a patch of pine tar, and spat and hissed angrily.

Folding one arm beneath his head, Samuel stared up at the night sky. Pine and fir trees reached out with their branches, etching shadowed silhouettes against the flickering stars and the pale glow of a half-moon. Somewhere in the distance a wolf's howl echoed eerily.

Samuel pulled his blanket up and moved his rifle closer. He could have gone on into Wolf River but had decided instead to spend the night in the wide open. Soon it would be winter and there wouldn't be another chance for lying out under the stars for months. He closed his eyes and breathed quietly, listening for the night sounds.

A scrabble of small feet in the bushes, a tree branch shaken, the crackle of the fire, and from the nearby creek a bullfrog croaking out an invitation to love.

This is what he'd needed, Samuel told himself. Time alone again. Away from everyone. Away from Abby. He couldn't think clearly when she was around.

Hell, he couldn't remember having one clear thought since the night she'd strolled into his home and taken over his life.

He had no time to himself anymore. He had no silence anymore . . . even when Abby wasn't talkin', she was singin'. And people! He rubbed at his eyes with his fingertips. Hell, in the last few years, he hadn't talked to more than maybe one or two folks. And in the last two days he'd seen twice that number. In his own house!

Sleepin' with a board in his bed . . . curtains at the windows, flowers on the shelf . . . his belongings moved every which way. He snorted into the darkness. He didn't know where half his things were—she was so busy fixin' and straightenin' his "messes."

And now she'd managed to rope him into goin' to a barn raisin'. Likely the whole damn town would be there. And they'd all be starin' at him. Waitin' for him to do—something. Well, they wouldn't be alone, he told himself.

How much longer could he last? Every time he felt his temper rise, he worried. Seemed like even the alphabet wasn't helpin' like it used to. And what if he got mad at that get-together at the Coles' place? What if he got into a fight and hurt somebody bad? Then what?

Samuel sat up and tossed another branch into the already raging campfire. He knew what would happen. Those *decent* citizens would run him off the mountain and out of the territory. Hell, he'd be lucky if they didn't try to tar and feather him.

Well, he wouldn't let that happen. No. He'd made his choice when he'd bought the cabin from Silas. He liked the mountain. Liked the loneliness. Liked the emptiness. He was used to it. It was familiar.

And what about Abby? a little voice inside him whispered.

He lay back down again. Abby would be leavin' after the judge came to town. Then everything would go back to the way it was before. The way it should be.

Even as he thought it, he felt the touch of her lips again. Felt the eagerness in her small form as she molded herself to him. Deliberately he closed his eyes and started saying the alphabet. Anything to keep from remembering. To keep from wishing that things could be different.

He had to get that other room built quick. And then he'd have to keep his distance from Abby. No matter what it took. He had no idea why she'd wanted him to kiss her, but he *did* know that it couldn't happen again.

There was no reason for him to pretend that anything could come of it. No woman would want a man like him. And besides, even if she *did* want him, he'd never be able to trust himself around her.

Like his mother had always told him . . . a man his size had to get used to livin' alone. Because, even without tryin', he could do a lot of damage with just a flick of his hand. And it would kill him if he ever did anything to hurt Abby.

Chapter Eight

Abby slipped another biscuit onto the boy's plate. It was amazing. She'd never have believed a child could eat that much. But he'd hardly stopped for breath. Silently she wondered how long it had been since he'd had a decent meal. She knew that she'd never forget the sight of the child's scrawny little body when she'd insisted he take off his shirt and wash before eating. Why, she'd been able to count the boy's ribs! And *dirty!* Clearly, a wash at the pump handle wasn't going to be enough.

But, she told herself, there was plenty of time for that. First things first. She noticed then that he'd finally stopped reaching for more food, so she asked quietly, "What's your name, child?"

He glanced up at her and quirked an eyebrow. "I ain't no child, lady. The name is Luke. Luke Daley."

"Where're your parents, Luke?"

"Ain't got none," he said and pushed away from the table.

"But where's your home? Where are you from?" Surely there was someone *somewhere* worried about the boy.

He paced the small cabin restlessly. "I guess I'm from all over. Ain't got no right *home*."

Maverick and Harry followed him closely, Harry entangling himself in the boy's legs, whining for attention.

"Get on, you dumb dog." Luke frowned at the animal and walked back to the table.

"Harry, Maverick," Abby said softly, "come here." The dogs trotted to her side and laid down.

Luke plopped down onto a chair and shook his head at the two animals. "Them two is about the ugliest things I ever seen."

Abby had a silly notion of wanting to cover the dogs' ears so they wouldn't hear the dirty little stranger insult them. Instead, she said, "They're very sweet dogs."

"Yeah?" His eyebrows rose as if to say it was a good thing they had *something* goin' for them.

Abby decided to try for some information again. "Why were you out in the henhouse, Luke?"

He shrugged. "Just lookin' for some eggs to suck." He looked up defiantly. "I was hungry is all."

That Abby could understand. The poor child all alone in a wide open country like this with winter coming on. No home, no parents. Why, if it hadn't been for Uncle Silas, she reminded herself, she would have been no better off than Luke. She, too, would have been forced into stealing . . . or worse.

"Where have you been staying?" she asked softly. "Around here?"

He shrugged his bony shoulders again. "Here and there. I get by all right."

"But," she said, "there's a town just at the foot of the mountain. Why didn't you go there? Ask for help?"

"I don't need no charity, lady. I make my own way." He thrust his chin out. "And now I'll pay you for that meal, too."

"*Pay* me?"

"Yep. I'm right strong for my size. . . ." His gaze moved over the cabin. "And if you don't mind my sayin' so, this here place looks like it could do with some fixin' up."

Abby blinked and looked around her. She'd thought the cabin was coming along nicely.

"And who the hell painted the place *pink*?"

She stiffened and Maverick whined when her feet shifted and dislodged his head from its resting place. "*I* did. And I would prefer it if you didn't curse, thank you."

Luke shook his head. "I ain't never seen nothin' like it before." Squinting at her, he asked, "How come *pink*?"

"I like pink. It's very cheerful. Bright."

"It surely is that." He cocked his head and looked at her out of the corner of his eyes. "Your man like it too?"

"My man?"

"Yeah. Your man. Husband."

"Well, I'm not married, Luke." She looked around the cabin, a little uneasily. "And Samuel, the man who lives here with me . . . well, he hasn't seen it yet."

The boy snorted. "Don't think I wanta be around when he *does*." Then what she'd said dawned on him. "You livin' here with some fella and you two ain't hitched?"

"Yes." She smiled at him. "We share the cabin."

Luke's blue eyes widened considerably, and he stared at her in astonishment.

"What is it? What's wrong?" Abby asked, concerned.

"It ain't decent, that's what." He shook his head slowly. "And you tell me not to cuss!"

Samuel stepped out of the Wolf River Restaurant and sighed. Nothin' was the same anymore. Why, he used to look forward to eatin' at the place, just to get a break from his own cookin'. But not anymore. That blasted cook couldn't hold a candle to Abby. Now she'd gone and spoiled *this* for him, too! Samuel knew that from here on, he'd be comparin' Abby's featherweight biscuits to everybody else's, and that no one would come up to snuff.

He glanced over at the lumber mill and saw that his wagon was almost completely loaded. Good. He'd be glad to get out of town and back to the mountains for some peace.

Samuel stiffened as a short, balding man, keeping his gaze firmly locked on the dirt road, scurried past him. It was always the same, wherever he went. No one looked him in the eye, women walked a wide berth around him, and children ran from him. He jammed his hands in his pants pockets and marched off down the street. He paid no attention to the folks that jumped out of his way. He was used to that.

In fact, ever since he'd outgrown every other boy in his hometown, people had been fightin' shy of him. It did no good to try to be friendly, he remembered. Folks were just too blamed nervous around him.

When he reached the end of the street, Samuel stopped. Ignoring the curious stares of the townspeople, he looked at the shop opposite him. A barber. Hadn't Abby offered just the other day to cut his hair for him? Maybe, he told himself, she'd been hintin' at something. Just then he caught a glimpse of himself in a store window.

His shoulder-length blond hair hung down from beneath his weatherbeaten hat, and his full, bushy beard looked as though mice had been nestin' in it. Slowly he reached up and rubbed his jawline. How long had it been since he'd had a shave? His brow furrowed as he realized he couldn't even remember the last time he'd seen his own face.

Well, hell, he told himself. He had to wait for the lumber anyways, might as well do it in a barber's chair as anywhere else. Quickly, before he could change his mind, he crossed the street and went inside.

"Luke, what do you think of this one?" Abby held out the red checked shirt for the boy's inspection. She managed to hold her tongue at the boy's grimace, but not without effort. Looking to Minerva for assistance, Abby dropped the shirt back onto the pile and turned to stare out the mercantile window.

As Minerva Mullins took Luke in hand, Abby asked herself again why she'd even bothered to bring the boy along with her to town. It certainly wasn't for his company. The boy had hardly said a word . . . and there wouldn't be much room for supplies in the dilapidated old buggy with Luke riding alongside her.

She sighed helplessly and admitted that it had been the expression on his face when she'd announced she was going into town. Almost as if he was being abandoned.

"I tell ya, I ain't takin' no charity!"

Abby glanced over her shoulder and saw Luke's bottom lip jut out stubbornly as he glared at Minerva. But, judging by Minerva Mullins's features, the boy didn't stand a chance.

"All right, boy," Minerva said with strained patience. "You already been told this ain't charity. I ain't in the habit of handin' out clothes to any scruffy-lookin' youngster I see."

"Scruffy-lookin'?"

Abby smiled at the offended tone in Luke's voice.

"That's right. Scruffy." Minerva shook her finger at him. "I seen half-drowned mutts look better'n you do right now."

He turned to leave, but she caught him. They stared at each other, neither one willing to give an inch. Finally Abby broke into the strained silence.

"Luke, we've already discussed this. Remember?" He glanced at her and she went on. "You said that you would stay at the cabin for a while and help out with the fixing up. That will more than pay for these clothes."

"You reckon?" he said softly, almost convinced.

"I reckon." Abby nodded at him, then turned to Minerva. "While you're fitting him out, I'll just go back into the storeroom and look for some more paint, if that's all right."

"More paint?" Minerva asked, her eyes wide. "Abby, I know I don't have any more pink back there."

Abby started moving toward the storeroom door and threw a quick smile over her shoulder. "Oh, that's all right. I just need a little for the trim. I want to surprise Samuel when he gets home."

Minerva stared slack-jawed at the closed door and shook her head. Heaven only knew what the woman would find back there. But whatever it was, Minerva was willing to bet that Samuel would be *plenty* surprised.

"You mean to say it was *you* sold her that gawdawful paint?"

Minerva looked at the boy and shrugged. "Wasn't nothin' I could do about it. Once that girl's mind gets set, ain't nothin' gonna change it."

"Maybe." Luke cocked his head and looked up at the woman. "But what's this Samuel gonna say about it?"

"Ain't no tellin'."

"I call it mighty strange," Luke mumbled.

"Hmm? What?"

"I say, I call it almighty strange." He looked at the door where Abby'd disappeared. "Some fella and this woman livin' in the same place . . . and them not hitched up proper or nothin' . . ."

Minerva's index finger snapped off her thumb and made a thumping sound against the back of Luke's head. The boy jumped and rubbed the spot with one grubby hand. "Hey! What's that for?"

"Just remindin' you to watch your manners, boy!" Minerva bent down low and looked him in the eye. "That there's a decent woman yonder. And you'd best treat her as such, or I'm likely to remind you again . . . a little harder next time."

He stepped just out of reach and said, "It ain't right."

Minerva straightened up and smoothed her hair back. "I'll say this just once, boy. So you listen. Abby Sutton is a fine woman. She come on some hard times now is all. She's waitin' on the circuit judge to come back to town to decide if that cabin belongs to her or Samuel." Hands on hips, she finished, "Now, her with no money and no place to go, where do *you* figure she oughta be stayin', Mr. It Ain't Right?"

Luke scuffed his bare toes along the floor and avoided her eyes.

"Hmmph!" Minerva reached out and grabbed his arm. "That's better. Now, let's get you fixed up quick so's I can get into that storeroom and hide that blasted orange paint my man Alonzo's so proud of!"

He'd never been this anxious to get home before. Of course, there'd never been anyone at the cabin waiting for him before, either. By all rights, he should have stopped on the road for one more night. He was pushing the horses too hard and he knew it. But he'd make it up to them. Give 'em a good rubdown and some extra grain when they got home. That thought brought to mind all the other animals in his care, and he told himself solemnly that it was for *their* sake that he was rushing home. Even though he knew that the caged animals would be fine for another day or so. It was better than having to admit that he wanted to get back to Abby.

He shrugged deeper into his heavy jacket and hoped she hadn't been frightened all by herself. Samuel knew better than most just how lonely a mountaintop cabin could be. And Abby just wasn't the kind to like solitude.

The nights were getting colder. He could see the horses' breath steam out in front of them as they pulled their load up the rutted trail.

Samuel rubbed his naked jawline nervously, then pulled the collar of his coat up over his now bare neck. Maybe he shouldn't have had his hair cut, too. Not at the same time anyway. It'd been so long since he'd gotten a good look at his own face, he'd hardly recognized himself in the barber's mirror. And now that he was almost home, he was feeling a little foolish about his decision to get cleaned up.

Hell! Abby probably wouldn't even know him!

As the wagon rolled into the yard, he hoped suddenly that he wouldn't scare Abby into fits by arriving in the dead of night like this.

From the corner of his eye, Samuel saw someone move in the shadows near the animal cages. His stomach tightened. It wouldn't be Abby, he knew. She wouldn't be outside in the dark and cold messin' with animals he'd already told her twice to stay away from.

In the dark it was impossible to tell who it was. Samuel's fingers gripped the reins. He had no friends, so there was no reason for anyone to be wandering around his cabin yard. It had to be a thief. Either set on plundering the cabin, or maybe just takin' some of the wounded animals for an easy meal.

A terrifying thought struck him suddenly. What if the shadowed visitor had already been inside the cabin? What if, even now, Abby was lying inside, beaten . . . or worse.

For the second time in his life Samuel didn't bother to recite the alphabet. He allowed the fierce anger swamping him to build and overtake his natural tendency to back away from trouble. Whoever it was sneaking around his place was about to find out what a mistake he'd made.

Samuel knew that in seconds the intruder would hear the wagon wheels and the horses' plodding hooves. There would be no chance of coming in unnoticed. The only thing left to do then was to get the upper hand by surprise.

Standing up, Samuel shouted, slapped the reins over the horses' backs, and charged the team right at the shadowy form. As the wagon careened across the yard, the intruder started to run toward the cabin. But he didn't take more than a few steps. As the charging horses drew nearer, Samuel leapt from the driver's seat and grabbed at his fleeing target.

His huge arms wrapped around the shadowy form, and even as they fell together, Samuel recognized his mistake. He'd attacked a child! Shocked out of the protective rage that drove him, Samuel loosened his hold on the squirming captive. Right away he realized he'd made another mistake.

Luke twisted in the big man's suddenly slack arms and took complete advantage of his opponent's momentary distraction. Without hesitation, Luke drew his thin arm back, clenched his fist, and struck the man beneath him full on the nose.

Samuel bellowed like a wounded bear, but Luke paid no attention. Between punches, the boy shouted angry curses, his high-pitched voice in direct contrast to Samuel's deep roars.

Still flat on his back, Samuel tried desperately to get ahold of the boy's arms, but the kid was just too fast for him. Somewhere in the back of his mind, though, Samuel was filled with admiration for the scrawny child who wasn't the least bit intimidated by his opponent's size.

"Dammit, boy!" Samuel grunted when the child's pointy elbow landed in his midsection, "I don't want to hurt you! Now stop it!"

A short, harsh laugh shot from the boy's throat just before he brought his fist down on Samuel's right eye. "I heard that before, mister!" When the big man's hand finally caught one of Luke's flailing fists, the boy didn't hesitate. He leaned over and sunk his teeth into the restraining flesh.

"Goddammit!"

The cabin door flew open, bathing the yard in the yellow glow of lamplight. Harry and Maverick bolted from the cabin and raced across the yard to the two thrashing combatants. Harry reached them first and leapt at Luke, eager to join the game. The boy brushed the little dog aside and resumed the attack. When Maverick limped alongside, he lay down across Samuel's face, muffling the man's colorful curses.

Finally, with Harry jumping at Luke, Samuel had enough time to dislodge the bigger dog gently, grab the boy, and carefully toss him to one side. It was surely the only way to escape the little fiend's fists. In the soft light Samuel pushed himself to all fours, keeping a watchful eye on the child's furious features.

The two dogs stood uncertainly nearby waiting for the game to begin again.

"Luke!" Abby called out as she ran from the cabin. "Stop!"

Samuel took his attention from the boy for a split second. That was all Luke had been waiting for. Living on his own and fending for himself in a world of adults had taught the boy to use whatever he had to in his own defense. Now he didn't hesitate. He drew his leg back and kicked out at the big man, aiming his blow where he knew it would do the most good.

Samuel's outraged howl of pain splintered the night. Abby winced but kept on moving. She ignored the two dogs, who'd tossed their heads back to add their mournful yowling to their master's. She reached Luke just as Samuel toppled over onto his side. She saw him curl up into a ball and heard his tight-lipped groans as Luke continued his assault.

Abby grabbed the frenzied child and pulled him off the fallen man. But the boy didn't even seem to recognize her. He immediately turned his fists on her.

"Luke!" she called as she tried to capture his hands in her own. "Luke! It's me! Abby!" She shouted to be heard over Maverick and Harry. But there was no answer from the boy. Only the harsh sound of the child's ragged breathing. Then one of his small fists connected with her cheekbone, and Abby cried out in surprise and pain.

A low, guttural snarl erupted from close by. Abby's eyes widened as Samuel slowly pushed himself to his feet. The dogs beat a hasty retreat, and Luke staggered back a step or two, surprised that the man was moving again.

"Samuel," Abby said urgently, one hand on her bruised cheek, "Samuel, I'm all right . . ."

Luke's gaze was fixed on the halting giant.

Samuel took another slow, heavy step toward the boy, oblivious to Abby's words. Just as Luke turned to make a run for it, Samuel's big hand came down on his shoulder. Quickly then, he curled his fingers around the loose material of the boy's shirt and lifted. Like a mother cat moving her kittens from place to place, Samuel effortlessly carried the wriggling child to the nearby watering trough and dropped him in.

The boy bobbed up like a cork, sputtering and cursing wildly. Samuel reached out one hand and pushed him back down. "Cool off some, boy . . . *then* you can get out!"

Luke's head popped up out of the dark water, and he shook himself violently, spraying Samuel with drops of the icy water. Maverick leaned over the edge of the trough and licked the boy's face, determined to remain in the game. Harry leapt straight up and down, trying to see what he was missing.

Abby tried to step around Samuel to reach Luke.

"Leave him be, Abby," Samuel warned.

"That water must be freezing, Samuel." She glared at him. "The boy'll catch his death."

From his hunched over position, Samuel glanced up at her in disbelief. Here he stood, hardly able to draw a breath, and she was worried about the damn kid who'd nearly killed him! He scowled at her and wasn't surprised that it didn't bother her in the least. So he turned his temper on the dog, whose yapping was shooting through his head like a railroad spike.

"Dammit, Harry! Enough!"

Immediately the little dog sat down on his haunches, tilted his head, and stared at his master. Samuel took a tentatively deep breath and frowned down at the impossibly homely hound.

"You, too, Maverick!" Luke yelled and pushed the big dog away from him.

"Don't you shove my dog around, you little . . ." Samuel snapped.

"Who the hell *are* you anyway, mister?" Luke's forearms were propped on the sides of the trough. His dirty, wet hair was plastered down over his forehead, completely obliterating his eyes, and his lips were twisted into a nasty frown.

"Who the hell am *I*?" Samuel shouted. "For godsake!"

"You both know very well how I feel about swearing," Abby interrupted.

Both males turned to stare at her.

"Luke, this is Samuel Hart, the man who . . . *shares* this cabin with me." She turned to look up at Samuel. "Samuel, this is Luke Daley. He lives here, too."

"*What!*" Samuel's bellow startled both dogs who quickly ran for the cabin.

"Of all the ding-blasted, double-damned, cock-eyed sons of bitches . . ." Luke stood up in the water trough and shook a small fist at Samuel. "Why the hell didn't you say so?"

Chapter Nine

Stunned into silence, Samuel stared at the skinny boy hauling himself out of the water trough. Sodden, threadbare clothing clung to the child's body, and it was easy to see that he hadn't been eating regular meals for a long time. An unwanted flash of pity stung Samuel, and he forced himself to look away from the now shivering child.

It wasn't any of his business how long it had been since the kid had eaten. Nor was it his business to find out why the foul-mouthed pup wasn't wearing shoes or why his clothes were falling apart.

Samuel rubbed his hand over his clean-shaven jaw and began to mumble the alphabet.

"What's he sayin'?" Luke asked Abby, who was herself straining to hear.

Samuel abruptly stopped and turned his gaze on Abby. He opened his mouth to speak, but she cut him off.

"Why, Samuel!" She smiled and stepped aside, letting the light from the cabin spill over him. Abby couldn't help staring. She'd had no idea that underneath all of his hair, Samuel Hart was a very handsome man. Well, she acknowledged silently, not *storybook-prince* handsome. His features were too strong for that. But his deep-set green eyes, no longer hidden by stray locks of hair, square jaw, and well-defined lips struck a chord with Abby. She remembered suddenly that kiss they'd shared before he'd left for Wolf River. His beard had scratched at her skin, and she'd had to push his blond hair aside just to reach him. Now she'd like to try that kiss again. "You look so handsome!" The words burst out before she could hold them back.

The big man shifted uncomfortably under her watchful gaze. A wellspring of pleasure poured through him, and he could feel himself flushing with embarrassment. He hadn't wanted to admit to himself just how much he'd wanted her approval. Still, his reaction to her compliment flustered him. Samuel reached up to smooth back a short lock of hair from his forehead, then said more gruffly than he'd intended, "Now, what's all this about *him*"—he jerked his head at Luke—"livin' here?"

"Weren't *my* idea, mister." Luke sneered at him. "This here's a right pushy woman!"

"Pushy!" Abby's brows rose dangerously.

"Here, now," Samuel warned, "that's no way to talk to a lady . . ."

"Wasn't talkin' to her. Talkin' to you."

Samuel noticed that Luke didn't back up an inch. His size didn't seem to bother the boy any more than it did Abby. And the kid obviously wasn't goin' to admit to bein' cold, either, he told himself. The skinny little runt stood straight and tall in his soaking wet clothes, shivering so hard Samuel was surprised he couldn't hear the kid's teeth rattle.

Hell! What had happened to his nice, quiet, peaceful life? He'd only been gone a couple days, and Abby'd quickly moved somebody else into the already too crowded cabin! He couldn't leave that woman alone for a damned minute!

Turning suddenly, he stomped across the yard, snatched his hat off the dirt, and walked toward the wagon. The racing horses had continued to run long after he'd jumped off to attack the child. Lord! he thought. He'd almost hurt a kid!

The heavily loaded wagon was sitting under a clump of aspen a hundred yards away. Sullenly he kept walking. Then he heard Abby.

"Luke, you go on in the house and dry off. Take those wet things and put them in front of the fire and put your new clothes on."

New clothes? Samuel thought disgustedly. Wonder where he got 'em?

"Aw, Abby . . ." Luke said.

"Now."

Samuel stifled the smile that threatened. He knew that tone of hers. It meant, you've already lost. Best do what she wants.

"I'm going to help Samuel," she called out to the boy.

Samuel groaned and all thought of smiling fled. Just what he needed. More of her help. She'd already helped herself to his life, his home . . . what was left? His sanity? This wasn't exactly the kind of welcome he'd been imagining. But then, hoping for anything else would have been a waste of time anyway.

When he reached the horses, he grabbed the hanging reins and tugged, turning the team around for the barn. Quietly Abby came alongside him and matched him step for step.

"Now, Samuel, I think that—"

"Abby," he cut her off, "I had a hard ride. I'm hungry. Tired. And just a little sore."

She cringed at that last remark.

"I don't want to talk about it now," he finished. Halting the team in front of the barn, Samuel quickly unhitched the horses and walked them into their stalls. Abby followed, clearly not intending to leave him alone.

"Samuel," she said softly, "he's just a little boy. . . ."

"Hmmph!"

"You scared him. Jumping at him like that from out of nowhere . . ."

"He didn't seem scared to me!" He threw a hostile glance at her, then went on with his work.

"Well, he was." Abby's fingers pulled at a loose splinter of wood. "And Samuel, I just had to let him stay with us. . . . He has nowhere else."

"Abby." Samuel straightened up after draping a worn blanket over the back of one of the horses. He'd already rubbed both animals down in record time. "You had no right."

"Whatever do you mean?" She took a step closer.

"I *mean* this is *my* cabin. *My* land."

"Our cabin, Samuel." Abby shook her head and smiled at him calmly. "At least until the judge hears our case."

"Dammit, Abby!" He stepped around the shying horse and walked to the next stall. There he draped a blanket over the other horse and turned back to face the tiny woman opposite him. "Even if that's so, don't it mean that I at least get a vote on who lives here or not?"

"Certainly." Abby gave him a brilliant smile. "But you weren't here. And I knew you'd feel exactly as I did about Luke. Why, he was practically starving, poor little thing."

"Oh, you knew how I'd feel, did you?" He stepped out of the stall and crossed to stand before her. "Did you know that I don't like kids? That they don't like me? That they're scared of me?" He loomed over her, trying to intimidate her. It didn't work. "They're noisy, bothersome pests! All of 'em!"

Abby laid her hand on his arm and chuckled softly. "Nonsense. Children are not pests! And *this* child hardly says a word unless you ask him a direct question." Then she added, "Luke wasn't frightened of you, Samuel. You just said so yourself. For that matter, why would any child be afraid of you?"

His head fell back on his neck and he stared sightlessly at the barn's rafters.

"And how do you know you don't like children? Have you ever been around them?"

"No." He threw his arms wide and looked back down at her. "That's what I'm sayin'! I don't *want* to be around 'em." He was losing. Samuel felt the tide of the argument swing to her favor, just as it had every other time. Of course he'd never been around children! Why, he'd spent the better part of his life avoiding *all* people. Especially kids! Usually they took one look at his monstrous size and ran home screamin' for mama.

Although he had to admit she was right about Luke. He hadn't been the least bit scared. Or if he had, he hadn't shown it. In fact, with his bitin' and scratchin' and most especially his well-placed kick, Luke had about won that little set-to they'd had.

Samuel fought down a smile. But dammit, he reminded himself, he didn't have any notion of how to talk to young'uns. And why the hell should he have to worry about it in his own home! Nope, no matter what she said, it wasn't right. And by God, Samuel wasn't gonna stand for it! The kid could stay the night, but tomorrow morning he'd be on the road.

"No, Abby," Samuel said as calmly as he could manage. "You stay here. Me and Luke'll go to town to get the paint."

The sun was barely up, but Samuel was in a hurry to get out of that cabin and down to Rock Creek as fast as his horse would carry him. Surely Minerva Mullins had some *white* paint somewhere in that durned store! He didn't think he could stand one more night surrounded by glowing pink walls.

He looked around unbelievingly. The color was bad enough in daylight. But with the orange firelight shining on it, it was damn near terrifyin'. Samuel glanced down at the boy standing beside him. Thankfully, the kid seemed to agree with him. He didn't know if he could bear bein' around *two* people who thought a pink cabin was "lovely."

Luke looked a sight different in dry clothes and the morning light. True, he was still too skinny, but Abby's cooking would soon fix that up. Samuel wasn't quite sure how he'd come to agree to Luke's staying with them. But he *did* know that what he'd heard during the night had done a lot to persuade him.

Maverick had heard it first. Samuel remembered being wakened by the big dog's soft whine and sudden movement. Harry, sound asleep with Abby, didn't stir. Samuel had lain quietly in the darkness, his side pressed against that damned bundling board, and strained to hear what his dog had.

Then the sound came to him. Softly at first, then as time passed, it came a little louder, a little harsher. It took him a few moments to identify it, and when he did, he hadn't known what to do about it.

On a pallet by the fire, Luke Daley was curled into a tight ball beneath his blankets. In the flickering light Samuel watched as the boy's little body jerked and flinched as if trying to escape something. And with the tiny movements was the sound. Crying. Whimpering. The rough little hellion who'd stood up to a man three times his size was crying in his sleep.

Samuel had shushed Maverick and laid back down himself, though he knew he wouldn't be getting any rest that night. He was sure that Luke wouldn't welcome sympathy from him. In fact, the boy would very likely be embarrassed to know what he'd been doing. So Samuel had left him alone. But he'd also realized that he wouldn't be sending the boy on his way anytime soon.

No child should cry in his sleep.

Samuel snapped back to the present when he heard Abby talking again.

"Are you sure?" Abby asked, eyeing the oddly matched pair before her.

The big man glanced down at the boy beside him. There was no indication of night terrors on the child's surly face. If anything, the runt looked as if he was ready to do battle again.

"Yes, Abby. I'm sure." Samuel grabbed his hat off the nearby peg and jammed it on. "I think we can handle goin' to the store by ourselves."

The fight started in the middle of Main Street. No one was quite sure who'd thrown the first punch, but it was easy to see who was liable to throw the last.

Luke straddled the other boy's chest and pounded his fists rhythmically into his target's face. By the time Samuel rushed out of the store, drawn by the noisy crowd, Luke's opponent had a bloody nose and was yellin' like all get-out.

A raw-boned little man with wispy gray hair was dancing back and forth around the tussling youngsters, trying to get a hold on one of them. Samuel pushed his way through the crowd easily, stepped into the fracas, and lifted Luke with one strong hand.

As soon as he was free, the bloody boy lit into a captive Luke like a weathervane in a twister. He got in a couple of solid punches to the stomach before Samuel reacted. Then the big man laid one hand on the boy's head and held him at bay, easily dodging his still swinging fists.

Finally the gray-haired man plucked the other boy from Samuel's grasp and gave him a good shake.

"What'd your ma just tell you about fightin'?" For a small man his voice thundered over the now quiet crowd.

"Weren't my fault!" the bloodied boy shouted, jerking his head at Luke. "He started it!"

"Ain't so!" Luke squirmed fiercely, trying to escape Samuel's grip. "You're a ding-blasted liar!"

"You can't call me no liar!" The other child rushed forward, but the older man grabbed him again.

"I just done it!" Luke crowed loudly, sparing a sneer for Samuel, hoping to make the big man set him free. "You're a no-account liar, like I said!"

The tired-looking man sent a weary glance at Samuel and nodded at the store. Samuel understood at once and completely agreed. Without a word, he turned around and half pushed, half carried Luke to Mullins's Mercantile.

Murmurs of disappointment from the crowd washed over the two men and boys as they stepped inside. Minerva hurried from behind the counter, wiping her clean hands on a stiff-with-starch white apron. She shot a quick look at Luke, then turned her full attentions on the other boy.

Stepping up close, she ignored the older man and grabbed the boy's left arm in a firm grip. "Obadiah Mullins!"

Luke snickered at the name, then stuck his tongue out at the furious boy across from him.

"What am I gonna do with you?" Minerva paused only for breath. She didn't wait for an answer. "How many times have I told you I don't want you fightin' in the street?"

"Blast it, Ma, where else can a body fight?"

"Don't you talk to me like that young man . . ." She kept a grip on her son and glared at the gray-haired man behind him. "And *you!*"

He shifted uncomfortably. "Now, Minerva—"

"Alonzo Mullins," she went on, "what kind of father can't keep a child out of trouble?"

Samuel watched with interest as Alonzo and his son, both wearing matching expressions of befuddlement, groped for answers to the rapid-fire questions. Then it was Samuel's turn.

"And shame on you, too!" Her black eyes snapped as she stared at the huge man. "Got no more sense than God gave a rock!"

"But—" Samuel started to remind her that he'd been in her store when the fight started.

"Don't make no difference that the boy's not yours. When you're in charge of a young'un . . . then by thunder, be in charge!"

The boys shared half-smiles as they watched the adults getting most of the grief. The two men stood silent under Minerva's tirade, though Samuel's jaw was clenched and he thought he saw poor old Alonzo grinding his teeth together.

Finally Minerva reached into her pocket, pulled out a plain white handkerchief, and wiped the blood off her son's face. Then she shot a warning look first at him, then at Luke.

"Now, while we finish up our business, I want you two to go on outside and find a way to talk to each other."

The boys started to move, but her commanding voice stopped them.

"You recall I said *talk!*"

"Yes'm," Obadiah mumbled.

"Yes'm," Luke repeated, walking beside the other boy to the front door. Just as they reached it, the adults heard him ask, "Where in hell did you get a name like Obadiah?"

The other boy laughed. "That ain't nothin'! You should hear what they called my brothers!"

Samuel was fairly certain there wouldn't be another fight, but he was determined to get back to the cabin quick, just in case. Luke had surprised him. Somehow Samuel wouldn't have thought that the boy would be so willing to fight. Especially with a boy so much bigger than himself. Though the two were about the same height, the Mullins boy outweighed Luke by at least twenty pounds. But, he thought, smiling, for a little fella, Luke was a ring-tailed terror.

Samuel still found it hard to believe that the kid had inflicted so much damage on the bigger boy. And all Luke had to show for his tussle was a rip in his new shirt and a small bruise under his right eye.

"That'll be enough of that," Minerva stated flatly.

Samuel jumped and turned to face her. "What?"

"I *said* that'll be enough. I ain't blind, you know." She turned her back on him and walked behind the counter again, where she started boxing his order. "I can see you standin' there, puffin' out that chest o' yours all proud as can be of that little scrapper of yours."

Samuel looked to Alonzo for support, but the man just shook his head and moved off toward the storeroom.

"I wasn't . . ." Samuel said.

"Hmmph!" Minerva slammed a bag of sugar into the box and smirked at him. "You're all alike, you men. Why, the last time Obadiah got in a scrape, *he* won, and you'd a thought Alonzo's buttons would fly off." Smoothing her impeccably neat hair, Minerva stopped suddenly and pointed an accusing finger at him. "Young and old, you're all the same. Just interested in struttin' for the hens is all." She pushed the box toward him and Samuel rushed to pick it up and get outside. Her voice followed him out the door.

"If it ain't screamin' Indians, it's outlaws or each other, and when you ain't got no one else, some of you will turn on your women!"

He closed the door after him but still heard her last comment. "You're all alike, I say!"

Alonzo Mullins was waiting by the storeroom's outside door. As Samuel pulled the wagon alongside, the older man picked up two of the paint cans and shrugged.

"She always like that?" Samuel asked quietly.

"Hell." Alonzo smiled. "When she gets a bee in her bonnet, Minerva can talk till she gets blue in the face. But she finally wears down."

Samuel grabbed the last two paint cans and set them in the wagon beside the others. He looked down at the smaller man and found himself returning Alonzo's conspiratorial grin. Suddenly they were both laughing. And Samuel realized with a start that the other man wasn't scared of him. In fact, Alonzo just might even like him a little.

A few minutes later the wagon was rolling out of town. Samuel somehow wasn't surprised to find Luke and Obadiah smiling and waving goodbye like lifelong friends. And he didn't even mind when Luke started in chattering about "what Obadiah said," though it appeared the other boy had an opinion about everything. Just like his mother.

Alonzo Mullins stood on the freight platform behind his store and thoughtfully watched the big man's wagon until it disappeared from sight. He'd heard all about Samuel Hart from Minerva, but he hadn't put much stock in what she'd said. To Alonzo's way of thinking, womenfolks changed their minds too damn easy. He remembered quite well all the times he'd heard Minerva and her nosy friends speculating about the silent giant who'd hardly opened his mouth to the townsfolk until the last week or so. And now, after spendin' a little time with him over coffee and cookies, they all decide that he's just a *wonderful* man. Just a little shy is all.

Alonzo himself hadn't been so sure. But now, after seein' how he took Minerva's tongue lashing without battin' an eye, well . . . maybe the women were on to something this time. The man sure hadn't acted like no ragin' monster. Not even when the kids were havin' at it.

Minerva called to him from the store, and Alonzo pushed away from the plank wall he'd been leaning on. Turning to go back to work, Alonzo let thoughts of the mysterious Samuel Hart drift away. Only time would tell what kind of man the big loner really was.

But in the meantime, maybe ol' Samuel'd like to do some fishin'.

"I still don't understand why you don't like the pink," Abby said quietly as she watched Samuel stir the open can of white paint.

He tried to keep his eyes down. If he looked at her crestfallen face, Samuel was afraid he'd weaken. And he couldn't afford to this time. "It ain't that I don't like pink, Abby," he said. "It's just that . . ."

"It ain't fittin' for a man!" Luke commented and continued to cover the pink walls with a fresh coat of white.

"I don't see why not," Abby said, frowning at the boy's back. "White will look so . . . plain."

And thank God for that, Samuel told himself silently. But she sounded so disappointed that he added, "When your sleepin' room is finished, you can paint it anything you want, all right, Abby?"

Her lips curved slightly. "I suppose it will have to do," she said quietly. "But, Samuel, could we at least use my bright yellow on the trim in this room?"

He sighed, surrendered, and looked at her. She looked so damn hopeful, he knew he couldn't refuse her. Besides, when she was gone he could paint over the whole mess. Samuel looked away. He didn't want to think about that now. "Sure. You just show Luke. He's doin' a good job there."

The boy glanced over his shoulder, then went back to work.

"Yes, he is," Abby agreed, smiling. Then she frowned suddenly and asked, "How did you say he hurt himself again?"

Luke stiffened slightly, and Samuel cleared his throat uneasily. The two of them had agreed not to mention anything about the fight to Abby. Didn't seem worth the trouble. She'd only get herself in a state fussin' over the boy.

"He . . . uh," Samuel said, "fell off the freight platform at Mullins's."

"Strange," she mused to no one in particular, "that he could simply *fall* off."

"Yeah, well." Samuel grabbed his hat and moved for the door. "Gotta keep your mind on what you're doin'."

"Where are you going, Samuel?" she asked.

"I'm gonna get started on that room," he answered and opened the door.

"Oh, good!"

He turned to look at her and felt his blood race at the brilliant smile she gave him. "Oh, and Samuel—do you think you could make up a bed for Luke today, too? He shouldn't have to sleep on the floor, you know."

He stared at her. She was amazing. The woman could think of more things for a body to do.... Finally he nodded and went outside before she could come up with anything else.

Why did she always have to look at him like that? With complete trust and faith shining from her eyes. Samuel knew that for some reason, Abby Sutton believed in him. He didn't quite understand why, but a part of him liked it very much.

It felt good to please her.

Chapter Ten

Abby filled the coffeepot for the second time that morning, then set it on the stovetop. The breakfast dishes were sparkling clean, the cabin floor neatly swept, even the windowpanes glistened in the sunlight.

Then she sighed and looked around at the plain white walls. Samuel was wrong, she told herself glumly. The cabin didn't look nearly as cheerful as it had when it was pink. Why, even the red and white curtains lacked a certain something when surrounded by plain walls.

She jumped when the pounding started up again. Samuel was certainly working hard at adding that room. Why, he'd worked until long after dark the day before and was at it again right after breakfast today! Now her head pounded in time with Samuel's enthusiastic hammer.

But she couldn't complain. Not since the man was building her a bedroom, for heaven's sake. And she had to admit that since Luke had arrived, she wouldn't mind having a little privacy. Although, a little voice inside her whispered, she would miss having Samuel so close to her every night.

She reached for the bundle of clothes she'd left at the edge of the bed, then carried them to the still lopsided table. Sorting through them, Abby picked out a pair of Samuel's long johns, laid them out across the table, and snatched up her sewing kit. Quickly, she threaded a needle then began the long task of mending the poor man's clothes. There were more rips, tears, and worn spots in Samuel's clothing than she'd ever seen before.

Actually, she told herself, his and Luke's clothes were in the same sad shape. She shook her head slowly as she realized that the two males were probably much more alike than they would admit to.

She'd noticed it right away. They both had the same haunted, lonely shadows in their eyes. They each acted surprised when she did something for them. Even something as simple as baking cookies. Abby chuckled softly. The two of them had eaten an entire batch of sugar cookies just the day before. So, she'd gotten up early today to make more and knew they'd probably be gone by nightfall.

Abby smiled as her needle whipped expertly through the faded - material. This is what she'd yearned for. A place to belong. People who needed her. Her own man. Children.

She stopped. Samuel? Yes, she smiled. Samuel. Maybe she'd known it from that first night, but now she was sure of it. He was the man she'd waited and prayed for. All she had to do was help him realize how much he needed her.

The hammering at the back of the cabin intruded on her thoughts, but now the sound was pleasant. Samuel was here. Softly she began to sing.

Samuel reached for another board from the slowly shrinking pile of lumber, then stood up and stretched his tired muscles. The sooner he got this room built, the better he'd like it. Between Abby's tempting presence and Luke's tossing and turning, he felt as though he hadn't slept in a year.

He looked down at what would soon be Abby's room and ignored the fact that he was building it exactly where she had decided it should go. After all, it was the only place that made sense, he told himself. He certainly wasn't doing it *just* to please her.

Frowning, Samuel picked up his hammer again but stopped in midswing and listened. She was singing. He knew the song. "Greensleeves." Abby's voice moved over the old, familiar words like a kind friend, filling the air with sudden warmth. He leaned his forearm on his bent knee and allowed himself a moment to enjoy her presence.

Her low, soothing voice warmed him every bit as much as the late morning sun. Samuel stared out at the land surrounding him and realized with a start that his customary ache of loneliness was gone. Before Abby came into his life, all he'd seen in the country around him was the emptiness. The unbearable silence of his self-enforced solitude.

Now, with the magic of her voice touching him, he finally knew what other men must know and take for granted. The quiet peace and comfort of knowing that someone else is near. He smiled.

Then his smile froze on his face as he heard the unmistakable sound of wagons rolling into the yard. Voices, a lot of them, talking, laughing, shouting. Samuel dropped his hammer in disgust. Peace and comfort? he told himself silently. Not likely.

Luke came running from the chicken coop and reached the two wagons at the same time Abby stepped out of the cabin. Quickly she looked around the empty yard for signs of Samuel. She caught just a glimpse of him as he poked his head around the corner of the cabin. He ducked out of sight immediately, and Abby knew she couldn't wait to greet her guests before going to fetch him. Otherwise, she knew he'd disappear.

She tossed a smile at Minerva, Charity, and their families, then lifted the hem of her skirt and ran for the back of the cabin. She'd been right. As Abby rounded the corner, she saw that Samuel was already halfway toward the woods and moving quickly.

While she was running toward him, Abby decided to pretend that she hadn't seen his furtive peek at their guests and that she had no idea that he was running away.

"Samuel," she called and grabbed at his arm.

He didn't stop, merely slowed down. "Got some things to do, Abby."

"Well," she went on as she dragged him to a stop. "I'm so glad I caught you before you left, then." She took a few gulps of air and laid her palm on her chest, trying to quiet her breathing. "We have guests, Samuel. Minerva, Charity, and their families just arrived. I know you wouldn't want to miss them."

He cleared his throat uneasily and managed to avoid looking into her golden eyes. "Yeah, well . . ."

"Come along, Samuel." She tugged at his arm but didn't budge him. "We can't let them continue to sit out in their wagons."

Why not? Samuel wondered silently. He hadn't asked 'em to come. He didn't want 'em there. He glanced down at her shining face, so full of excitement over unexpected visitors, and knew that she would never understand his feelings about people. Hell, it was getting so that even *he* didn't understand anymore.

"Please, Samuel," she asked quietly, her eyes watching his features carefully.

"But I got a lot to do, Abby . . ." he started.

"Can't it wait?"

She laid her hand on his, and the warmth of her touch swayed him as no words could have done. He read the hope in her eyes and the anxiousness of her expression and knew that he couldn't disappoint her.

Swallowing back his reluctance, Samuel forced a smile. "All right, Abby."

She grinned happily at him, linked her arm through his, and started for the cabin at a fast walk. "Isn't this nice, Samuel?" she chattered. "A surprise visit. Just like it used to be back home in Maryland. Why, then the neighbors would just decide to go out calling on other folks for no reason at all . . . and it was such fun!"

He nodded grimly.

"Oh, and Samuel," Abby added excitedly, "they've brought their children today, too! Won't Luke be pleased?"

Oh, Lord, Samuel groaned. It ain't enough he's got one woman and a child around the place. No, now there's got to be wagonloads of 'em.

The Whitehall and Mullins families were all standing around in the yard waiting for their hosts when Abby and Samuel walked up.

Luke and the others were making enough noise to account for thirty children, though Samuel could only count nine including Luke. Reluctantly he allowed Abby to draw him closer to the adults standing uncertainly alongside the wagons.

"Minerva! Charity!" Abby sang out. "It's so nice of you to come calling!"

"Well," Minerva said, "we got to talkin' and decided that if we was to come up and see how you was gettin' along, we'd best do it soon. My achy knee tells me snow'll be comin' mighty thick this winter."

"But it's a lovely day," Abby protested.

"Likely will be for a few weeks yet," Minerva agreed, raking her gaze across the deep blue sky. "But then you'd best be ready to stay inside by the fire."

Samuel shifted uncomfortably under the direct stares of Charity and Buck Whitehall. Minerva didn't seem angry anymore over the boy's fight, but from the looks the big blacksmith was throwin', he wasn't any too pleased to be drug along on this visit.

Alonzo Mullins, though, stepped up to Samuel and extended his hand. Over their handshake Alonzo said with a grin, "Minerva wanted to come for a visit. . . . Me, I got to thinkin' about that nice trout stream up here." He rubbed one hand over his stubbly cheeks. "Used to do a little fishin' with Silas now and again." He tossed a wary glance at Abby, and Samuel knew the man meant that they went fishin' whenever Silas was sober. Which wasn't very often.

"Anyways," Alonzo went on, "thought maybe you and me and Buck here could catch us a few fish before the big snows come."

Samuel felt a smile growing inside him. He hadn't been fishing in a mighty long time. And he'd never gone fishing with a friend. He looked at Abby and caught her smile. She was pleased for him, he knew. Maybe she *did* understand how it was with him and other folks. Maybe.

"What a wonderful idea," Abby crowed delightedly. "And I just know that Luke would *love* to go fishing!"

Maybe not, Samuel told himself. "Luke?" he said quietly.

"Yes." Abby nodded.

"That there's a good idea, Abby!" Minerva joined in. "Why, the menfolk can take all the children with 'em. Be good for 'em for a change."

"Sounds good to me," Charity offered, speaking for the first time since they'd arrived.

"Now, Minerva," Alonzo said on a sigh, "if those young'uns come with us, we'll never catch a fish. Their caterwaulin' will scare every fish for miles clean off the mountain!"

"Hmmph!" Minerva shook her finger at her husband, then included Buck and Samuel in her comments. "If you three grown-up men can't make some children be quiet for a while, what good are you?"

"I ain't takin' my three," Buck said and threw a proud smile at the other two men.

"Oh, yes, you are, Buck Whitehall!" Charity glared at him, and the big man's expression changed instantly. "I got them three underfoot all day every day. You can damn well have a day yourself once in a while."

Abby knew how to settle the matter. "Luke!" she shouted and smiled when the boy and his new friends came running from the barn. As Luke skidded to a stop in front of her, she asked, "How would you like to go fishing with Samuel and his friends?"

Samuel's eyebrows shot up. *His friends?*

A grin flashed across the boy's small face, then disappeared. He looked from Samuel to Abby before saying softly, "Don't know how. Ain't never been before."

Abby tilted her head and stared up at Samuel. But there was no need. Samuel had seen the excitement fade from the boy's face to give way to disappointed embarrassment. Briefly he wondered what kind of life Luke had led before he'd shown up on the mountain. Samuel couldn't imagine a boy his age never having been fishing before. Why, even Samuel had spent many a summer afternoon sitting on a riverbank with a pole in his hands. Sometimes you didn't even have to catch anything to enjoy yourself. The pleasure was in the sittin' and waitin'.

Abby opened her mouth, but Samuel said quickly, "Well, then, boy, it's high time you learned how."

Luke's gaze flew up to meet the big man's. Disbelief warred with delight in the child's shadowed brown eyes.

"Get goin'. There's some poles in the barn. You go fetch 'em." Samuel jerked his head at the building across the yard. When the boy didn't move right away, he added, "Well, come on! Them fish ain't gonna wait forever!"

Luke took off like a shot for the barn. Obadiah turned to his father hopefully and asked, "Me, too, Pa? Can I come?"

Alonzo glanced at his wife before nodding. "Yeah. I reckon you can all come along." He pointed off at the chicken coop. "Go and get your brothers."

Buck grumbled something unintelligible, then called to his children. Turning back to his wife, he said, "Hope you're satisfied, woman! We ain't gonna be bringin' back much fish!"

"Just enough for dinner, Buck." The plump woman smiled at her husband and waited. In seconds Buck smirked, kissed Charity's cheek, then swatted her backside playfully.

"Awright. But remember"—he pointed at her—"we catch 'em. You all cook 'em."

"We'll be ready," Abby said and watched enviously as Alonzo stepped up to his wife and gave her a kiss before turning to get his poles from the back of the wagon. She looked at Samuel hopefully, not sure really what she wanted from him. But she *did* know that the sudden feeling of family, of belonging, was fading in the realization that she and Samuel were not like the two other couples. They shared no history together. They didn't smile at secret exchanges. And the only child they had between them was like themselves. He didn't belong anywhere, either.

Still, she couldn't let Samuel leave without trying to express what she was feeling. As Minerva and Charity got their respective children ready for an afternoon with their fathers, Abby followed Samuel to the corral.

He was leaning on the top fence rail, his strong forearms crossed over each other, his expression blank as he stared at the surrounding pines.

She stepped up beside him and laid her hand on his right arm. He didn't turn to look at her but kept his gaze fixed on the woods.

"Samuel," she said, unsure of how to proceed. His arm flexed beneath her hand, and once again she was astonished at the sheer strength of him. Unconsciously her fingers moved lightly over his tanned flesh until his hand clamped down over hers, stilling her actions.

"Don't," he groaned softly.

Stung, she tried to pull away. But he wouldn't release her. Her gaze lifted to his, and she was surprised to see the raw hunger in his eyes. Abby's breath caught, but she couldn't bring herself to look away. She was held fast by her own matching need. The flesh of his jaw, still a shade lighter than the rest of his face for having been hidden by a beard for so long, twitched nervously. His lips were compressed into a tight line, and his eyes begged her not to push him any further.

Abby hadn't intended to kiss him. Only to somehow let him know that she . . . cared for him. But now, faced with the knowledge that he shared her desires, she couldn't turn away. Just as she knew that he would not be the one to initiate a kiss.

Deliberately she held his gaze with her own as she rose up on her toes to reach him. She noted absently that his massive chest expanded with his indrawn breath and that he didn't release it. Their guests, Luke, the animals, everything faded away into nothingness as Abby moved closer to her goal. Hesitantly she touched her lips to his and loved the clean-shaven feel of him. She heard him moan softly as his hand tightened over hers. But he made no other movement. Even his mouth refused to relax. If not for the grip he had on her fingers, Abby would have thought him completely unmoved by her kiss. Instead, she knew that he was using every ounce of his great strength to hold himself in check.

She pulled back and watched him. His eyes were shuttered now, but it didn't matter. Abby was convinced that Samuel cared for her. She was just as sure that it would be up to her to make him admit it. She just had to figure out how.

* * *

Charity stared at the bundling board and shook her head. It was still hard for her to imagine a man and woman sharing a bed and lettin' a little thing like a plank of wood stop 'em from . . .

"Charity!"

She turned, flushing to meet Minerva's impatient gaze.

"Hmm?" Charity said. "What?"

"I was askin'," Minerva repeated, "if you'd got all the food arranged for the Coles' barn raisin' next week."

"Oh!" Charity looked guiltily from Minerva to Abby, then back again. For heaven's sake. She'd missed the whole conversation. "Uh, yes. Yes. It's all settled. Even Sarah . . ."

Minerva's eyebrows rose. "Yes . . . ?"

Charity frowned at her old friend. "Well, Sarah and her girls are part of the town, too. They wanted to do their share."

"Who's Sarah?" Abby asked.

Minerva shook her head at Charity's stubborn expression and answered, "Sarah Dumont runs the saloon and—"

"Now Minerva," Charity broke in, "it ain't kind to carry tales."

"Tales my great aunt Matilda!" Minerva turned to look at Abby. "Everybody knows that Sarah's two girls, well . . ."

Abby blushed. "Oh. I see."

"Anyway," Charity added quickly, "the Coles ain't gonna care if Sarah and the others bring along some food to this here gathering. As long as they get that barn up by winter."

"S'pose you're right," Minerva said. She turned to Abby. "I ain't got nothin' against Sarah, you understand. She's only doin' what she has to get by. And her girls, Stacey and Jennifer, are sweet little things. It's the menfolks' reactions to 'em I don't like."

"What do you mean?" Abby asked quietly.

"Hmmph!" Charity snorted. "What she means is, the men take one little gander at Sarah and her girls and forget all about their wives."

Minerva straightened her hair. "Until we remind them, of course."

Charity grinned. "Yes, indeedy! Why d'ya think there's so many children in Rock Creek, Abby? I'll tell ya! 'Cause we're all the time remindin' our husbands, that's why!"

Minerva choked back her laugh for a moment, then let it go.

Abby smiled at the others and told herself that she could hardly wait for Samuel to get a look at Sarah. Maybe that would give Abby the courage she'd need to convince the big man they belonged together.

"Maccabee Mullins!" Alonzo stood up and hollered at his son again. "You get down outa that goddamned tree this minute! You hear?"

The boy giggled, and Alonzo cursed softly before sitting down once more. "Durn kids! Never listen to a damn thing. Probably fall outa that damn tree and break his fool neck. Minerva'll never let me hear the end of it!"

"Fortune!" Buck shouted at the redheaded boy leaning out over the stream. "You fall in again, and so help me, I'll let you drown!"

"Ah, Pa . . ." the boy whined.

"Don't 'ah, Pa' me," Buck warned. "Get away from there. Go on and look for gold with Jedediah and Ezekial."

Fortune Whitehall kicked at a rock, disgusted. "Gold! There ain't no gold out here. 'Sides, them two is babies!"

"Well, you can gold hunt or you can look out for your sisters!" Buck pointed down at his two daughters, Chance and Treasure. The four- and five-year-old girls wore identical blue and white dresses with white ribbons tied at the ends of their copper-red braids.

"I'll go with Zeke and Jed," Fortune answered quickly. Even three- and four-year-old boys were better than girls—especially at Fortune's advanced age of seven!

"I thought so," Buck mumbled, then shouted, "you two children stop that!" His daughters were scooping up handfuls of mud and rubbing it on each other. "Your mama's gonna skin me alive!" Quickly he brushed the mud out of the girl's hands and tossed a disgusted glance at his unused fishing pole. "Hell, I knew I wouldn't catch no fish today."

"Don't matter," Alonzo said on a laugh. "These three here already caught enough to feed everybody." He pointed to the boys at the stream edge. Luke, Obadiah, and his brother Nimrod did indeed have a long string of fish. "Sam," Alonzo said with a chuckle, "you must be a helluva teacher. That boy's gonna clean out this stream!"

Samuel smiled and caught Luke's excited glance. He would never forget the boy's expression when his first fish had nibbled at the hook. Delight, joy, surprise, and hesitation each took its turn on the boy's features. Poor Luke was so afraid he'd lose that fish, he'd jerked his pole too hard and the fish had come flyin' out of the stream, narrowly missing Buck's head. The man had about choked to death on his chewing tobacco, and Alonzo laughed so hard he'd dropped his own pole into the swiftly moving stream.

Samuel grinned, remembering Luke's shaking hands as he took the still squirming fish from the hook and proudly added it to the stringer. After that first catch, Luke hadn't moved an inch away from the stream. For the last three hours the boy had done nothing but talk to Obadiah and Nimrod and study his pole for the telltale jerking of the bait.

Samuel had never spent such a pleasant day. He'd enjoyed Buck and Alonzo's conversations and for the first time in years got a taste of what friendship must be like. Even the children running up and down the bank, dropping out of trees, and falling into the stream didn't upset him. Because for some reason, none of the children were afraid of him. In fact, Nimrod had even allowed Samuel to tie a hook on his line.

Samuel glanced at the Whitehall girls and caught Treasure's gap-toothed smile. Her little fingers curled over in a wave, and he returned it, only slightly embarrassed. Though Buck whined and complained about those two, Samuel saw the man's pleasure in his daughters and was himself more than a little envious.

"Sam! Sam!" Luke called excitedly. "I got another one!"

Samuel leaned forward and whispered, "Take it slow, Luke. Like I showed you. . . ."

"But thisn's a big one, Sam!" Luke's teeth ground together, and his scrawny arms strained with the weight of the fish.

"Hell, if it's that big, don't throw it around this time, boy." Buck laughed. "This'un might kill me!"

"Sam"—Luke ignored the other man—"you gotta help me. I cain't get it by myself."

"Yeah, you can, boy," Samuel encouraged, moving closer.

"Come on, Luke!" Obadiah cheered.

"Bring 'er in," Nimrod added his voice to the crowd.

"Just take it easy, boy." Alonzo was caught up in the fight.

Luke's scrawny back and shoulders moved with his effort, and the veins on his thin arms stood out. His lips pressed together, he concentrated solely on landing the prize fish at the end of his line.

"That's right, boy," Samuel said softly, "slow and steady. Don't jerk him. He'll come along soon's he's tired."

"Samuel . . ."

"It's all right, boy." Samuel laid his big hand on the boy's shoulder. "I'm right here if you need me."

"I *do!*"

"Nah, you're doin' fine." Samuel wanted the boy to know the victory of winning the battle himself. But rather than see him lose the fish altogether, he was ready to jump in and help.

Luke stood and backed up slowly, keeping the line tight and his face a rigid mask of control. The fish leapt out of the water, and Obadiah gasped. "I swear, Luke, that one's a monster! Must weigh ten pounds!"

Luke's arms ached and he wanted nothing more than to sit down and rest, but he kept going.

"Almost, boy," Samuel crooned as he matched the boy's steps. "You about tired him out now. Just stay with him."

Luke took another two steps back, gave a mighty yank on his pole, and the granddaddy of all trout lay on the bank flopping madly.

"You did it!" Samuel grinned and clapped his hand down on the boy's shoulder. Luke looked up at him, a smile toying with his trembling lips. His narrow chest lifted and fell quickly with his shuddering breath. The boy looked at Obadiah and Nimrod, taking the fish off the hook, and he heard their words of praise. Luke's eyes filled, and he rubbed the back of his hand over them roughly. He took a deep breath, then suddenly dropped his pole and threw his arms around Samuel's waist.

Surprise shot through the big man but was quickly replaced by an overwhelming sense of satisfaction. Pleasure raced through him as he looked down at the small boy plastered against him. Samuel knew exactly what the boy was feeling. He knew that terrible, overwhelming mixture of joy and fear that it all would end somehow.

The others were busying themselves with the fish and gathering up the children to head back to the cabin. No one glanced at the boy and man.

Samuel'd never known the joy of a spontaneous burst of affection from a child, and he realized with a jolt how grateful he was to have been given this chance.

Awkwardly he ruffled the boy's hair with one hand and patted his back gently with the other. He hoped he was doing it right.

Chapter Eleven

The cookfire was dying. An occasional flame shot from the red-hot, crumbling wood and sent a shower of sparks into the dusk. The children, half asleep, lay sprawled around the circle, content to listen to the adults' low-pitched voices.

Abby looked around her with a smile on her face. It had been a lovely day. They'd all eaten outside, since the cabin was far too small to hold so many people. Dirty dishes and blackened pots lay scattered around the quiet group, and for once, Abby was in no hurry to begin cleaning up.

Instead, she wanted to enjoy the last moments of their impromptu party.

"Yeah, Sam," Buck was saying, "you're doin' a fine job on that room you're buildin'. If you need any help when it's time to lay the roof, you just give a holler."

Abby saw the surprise on Samuel's face, but he said nothing, only nodded.

Alonzo pulled a drowsy Ezekial onto his lap and

said, "You're gonna be almighty handy at that barn raisin', Sam."

"I should smile." Buck chuckled. "Why, with Sam on our team, we're bound to win. Hell, we don't hardly need nobody else. . . ."

"Win?" Abby asked quietly. "Win what?"

Minerva snorted and gently slapped Alonzo's thigh. "These men, Abby. They make a durn contest out of everything."

"No doubt there'll be bettin', too." Charity eyed Buck thoughtfully. Her husband gave her an innocent smile.

"What?" Abby asked again.

"Well, see," Alonzo started, "the menfolk split up into teams. Four of 'em. Then each team raises a side of the barn. First team to finish up proper, wins."

"The trick is"—Minerva's brows rose—"to make sure the dang fools don't kill themselves tryin'."

"Is there a prize?" Abby wanted to know.

"Sometimes," Charity answered with a shake of her head. "But most often, not."

"Hell," Buck intoned, "don't need a prize. It's enough to know you won."

"Yes," Minerva shot back, "so's you can throw it in the faces of the losers until the next raisin'."

Alonzo laughed. "Honey, that's half the fun!"

"So you say," his wife answered tartly as she pulled Ezekial from his lap. "We best get goin', 'Lonzo. These children are tuckered."

"Yeah." Alonzo groaned and pushed himself to his feet. "You're right, ol' girl. I'll get the team hitched. Want to get off the mountain before full dark."

"Us, too, Buck," Charity ordered, but her husband was already up and moving.

Abby looked over at Samuel. She saw his eyes follow the movements of the others and read her own disappointment at the end of the visit in his wistful smile. She wanted to go to him. Stand beside him while they said good night to their guests. She wanted to know she belonged with him.

"Abby?"

She looked down and smiled at Luke's half-closed eyelids. The poor child was asleep on his feet. "Yes?"

"All right if I go to bed now?" He stifled a yawn.

Abby looked up and saw that Obadiah and the other children were already bedding down in the backs of their parents' wagons. "Go ahead, Luke." She reached out and tentatively brushed his hair off his forehead. "You've had quite a day."

"Yes'm." The boy turned toward Samuel but kept his gaze on the ground. "I . . . uh . . ." Suddenly his gaze lifted. "Ah, hell. Thanks for takin' me fishin' with ya."

Samuel looked at the boy and saw for himself how hard it had been for Luke to say that. Damn, he wished he knew what to say to children. Right now he'd give just about anything to have the right words come to mind. He glanced at Abby and noticed the way she was watching him. Waiting. She'd prob'ly know just what to say to the kid. Samuel ran one hand over his face and said gruffly, "Had to take you. Hell, if it wasn't for you, we might not've had enough fish for this crowd to eat."

Luke's eyes widened, and a sudden grin lit up his face. Just as quickly then, he turned on his heel and ran for the cabin.

Samuel stared after him for a long moment.

"That pleased him," Abby whispered.

She'd stepped up beside him, and Samuel shifted uncomfortably. "Think so?" he wondered aloud.

"Yes." She laced her fingers through his even as he tried to pull his hand free. "Everyone likes to be needed."

"Yeah. I, uh . . ." Samuel said as he began to move, "best help hitch the wagons." But the men were already finished and climbing to their perches on the high bench seats. Samuel found that he couldn't unloose Abby's fingers without making a big show of it, so together, they walked to say goodbye to their guests.

Everyone was gone. The fire had been reduced to a few glowing embers easily swallowed by the encroaching darkness. Samuel stood just inside the barn and watched Abby make a final trip into the cabin carrying the last of the cookpots. He'd managed to avoid her for the last half hour, busying himself with caring for the caged animals while she cleaned up. But now there was nothing else for him to do.

The lamplight shining through the cabin windows looked warm, homey. It beckoned to him, promising warmth and welcome. But he couldn't go in.

Samuel cursed softly. It was being around the others that had done this to him. Seeing those families, close up—watching the loving, hearing the easy teasing . . . It had made him hunger for things he'd long since become accustomed to doing without. He'd even allowed himself to pretend for a while that he and Abby and Luke were a family. That they were no different from the others.

He snorted and kicked at a rock. He was a fool.

Deliberately Samuel turned his back on his home and moved deeper into the shadows of the barn. The sleepy horses stirred nervously and only quieted at the familiar sound of his voice. His shoulders hunched, his steps heavy, he walked slowly to the empty stall in the far corner of the barn. Samuel had already laid down fresh straw, and now he shook out an old wool blanket and spread it out over his bed for the night.

He couldn't go into the damned cabin and sleep in the too small bed with Abby snuggled up just out of reach. Not tonight. Somehow, he'd been able to control himself when the others were there, but now . . . now his mind gave free rein to the torturous images he'd been fighting all evening.

Samuel flopped down onto the blanket and threw his forearm over his eyes. It didn't help. Nothing did. No matter what, Abby's face haunted him. With little effort he still felt the touch of her hand on his, the warmth of her breath when she stood on her toes to kiss him. Samuel remembered clearly having to summon every ounce of his strength to keep from grabbing her and clutching her to him.

"Dammit," he mumbled and tried again to push the memory of her body pressed to his from his mind.

"Samuel?"

He groaned and squeezed his eyes shut. Just the sound of her voice whispering in the darkness was enough to inflame the desire that never ended. Why the hell didn't she just leave him alone? Couldn't she see what she was doing to him?

"Samuel?" She stepped into the barn. He heard her footsteps scuff on the dirt and straw. "Are you in here?"

It was no use. She wouldn't leave. He knew that.

The horses moved restively in their stalls at Abby's approach. Soon she'd have them all worked up. Samuel surrendered to the inevitable and pushed himself to his feet. "I'm over here, Abby," he said quietly.

She moved closer. He didn't even have to hear her. He could smell her. Even after sitting around an open fire, amid the flying ash and the stink of burning wood, she still smelled like flowers and vanilla.

He jammed his hands in his pockets when she came to a stop directly in front of him. Otherwise, he knew he'd grab her and never let go. And he couldn't do that.

"Samuel"—her voice was soft, confused—"why are you out here? Why haven't you come in the house? There's fresh coffee on."

"I'm, uh . . ." He groped for a reason. Any reason. "Gonna stay in the barn tonight. One of the horses ain't quite right." He couldn't meet her eyes and keep the lie going. "Don't want any coffee, either."

"Oh." She turned quickly to look at the animals behind her. "What is it? Can I help?"

He snorted. "No, Abby. You can't help me any."

Her face fell. Even in the shadows, Samuel could see her disappointed frown. He had to ignore it. Hell, he had to get her out of the barn. "Go on back to the cabin, Abby. Go to bed."

She stepped closer instead. One of her small hands reached for him, and he jerked when her palm touched his chest. "Abby . . ."

"Samuel," she interrupted, "you can't stay out here. It's much too cold. You'd freeze."

He couldn't stand it. Pulling one hand free of his pocket, he grabbed her wrist and pushed it away. Cold? Hah! Right now Samuel's blood was boiling so that he thought he'd never cool off.

"Abby . . ." He took a deep breath and released it

slowly. Mentally, he began the ABCs even as he spoke. "I'll be fine. Just go on to the cabin." *Quick*, he added silently.

"But, Samuel," she said softly, moving even closer, "I don't want to go without you."

He knew what she was about to do. And even though he thought it might kill him, he wouldn't stop her. She reached up and cupped his face with her palms. Her hands were so warm, so soft. Samuel bit back the moan rising in his throat. As she drew his mouth down to hers, Samuel told himself that he was being a fool. That he should push her away. But he knew he wasn't strong enough to do that. Not just yet.

He saw her lips curve slightly just before their mouths met. Her hands moved from his face to snake over his shoulders and lay flat against his back. He felt the warmth clean down to his soul and lost the will to fight.

Tenderly, almost fearfully, his huge hands moved up her spine, his fingers dancing lightly over the fabric of her plain white blouse. Even when she pressed herself tighter to him and opened her lips for his tongue, Samuel held himself in check, terrified that he might hurt her accidentally.

He groaned and his big body shuddered as his tongue moved over the warmth of her mouth. Abby's breath came soft on his cheek, and her fingers moved through his hair.

When the ache in his groin became too much to ignore, Samuel's senses finally snapped back into control. He tore his mouth from hers and gasped for air like a dying man. In the dim light he saw her golden eyes glittering with passion and the rapid rise and fall of her chest as she struggled for breath.

With a muffled curse Samuel spun away, pushing his hands through his hair. This is what he'd hoped to avoid. This was the reason he'd come to the barn in the first place. Because he couldn't trust himself around her anymore. He'd never wanted anything in his life the way he wanted Abby Sutton. And the strength of that desire scared him to death.

It wasn't even the fact that she was so damn little he'd probably crush her if he tried to make love to her . . . it was the fact that she wouldn't be staying with him. And if he allowed himself to love her and she left . . . he would die. Samuel was certain of it.

"Samuel," she said softly.

"Go away, Abby," Samuel groaned, not looking at her.

"But—"

"Goddammit, Abby!" He placed both palms flat against the barn wall and let his head fall forward. Every muscle in his body was tight, strained to the breaking point. "Will you get the hell back to the cabin?"

"Samuel," she tried again stubbornly, "why are you doing this? I wanted—"

A broken laugh burst from his lips, but still he didn't turn to face her. "*You* wanted? You wanted what, Abby? Us makin' love? Shit, you're so goddamn little, I'd prob'ly kill ya!"

She gasped, but he went on.

"You want me to just throw you down on the floor of the barn? In the dirt? Is that what you want?" He groaned again and with a mighty shove pushed away from the wall and turned to look at her. It took every ounce of courage he had to look into her eyes and see the hurt he was causing her. But he *had* to get her to leave. Before it was too late. Though it was like tearing his own heart out, he knew the only way to make her go back to the cabin . . . and safety, was to be brutal. "You want me to treat you like a whore?"

Her breath caught, her mouth fell open, and her eyes filled with unshed tears.

He forced himself to go on. "'Cause, Abby, if it ain't what you want, you'd better clear outa here while I'm still willin' to let you go."

In disbelief Samuel watched as she lifted one hand as if to reach for him. He could see the hurt in her watery eyes, and still she wanted him.

Abby couldn't believe what she was hearing. It was so unlike Samuel to be cruel. And she *knew* that he didn't think of her as a . . . whore. There *had* to be a reason for his callousness. If only she could touch him again. Make him tell her what had gone so wrong . . . but even as she thought it, her courage deserted her.

Deliberately he stepped back and turned away from her. "Go on, Abby. Get outa here."

A few seconds later he listened to her leave. Her steps were slow, and with each one, he had to fight to keep himself from calling her back.

He'd never been more alone.

A strained silence fell over the cabin, bringing a chill as deep as the early morning mists that covered the mountains.

Abby looked out one of the front windows and watched Samuel hitching up the horses to the big wagon. He was wearing the blue shirt she'd made for him. Her interested gaze told her that it fit him far better than any of his store-bought clothes. His massive chest and broad shoulders looked even larger in the plain blue fabric, and she couldn't help staring. His worn, bedraggled hat was pulled low over his eyes, and though she could see his lips moving, she couldn't hear him.

But then, she hadn't heard much from him for the last week. Since that night in the barn when she'd made such a fool of herself, Samuel had avoided Abby as much as possible. Even when she'd forced him to let her take the stitches out of his hand, Samuel hadn't spoken to her. Not a word. He continued to sleep in the barn, even though the nights were getting colder.

And it was no warmer in the cabin. Oh, certainly she had a fire and plenty of blankets and even the dogs and Luke for company . . . but with Samuel's side of the big bed empty, Abby had found it almost impossible to sleep. She missed his sleepy grumbling, the way he banged into the bundling board every time he moved. Abby sighed and dropped the edge of the curtain. She even missed his snoring.

Luke pushed Harry off the nearest chair and looked up. "You want me to take some of these here out to the wagon?"

She forced a smile. Poor Luke. He'd fallen into the midst of a battle he couldn't possibly understand and was doing everything he could to remain neutral. "Yes, go ahead. I'll be along in a moment."

He nodded uncertainly and paused as though he wanted to say something, then picked up the three-layer chocolate cake and moved for the door. The boy had really filled out in the last week or so. Regular meals and the new clothes made him almost unrecognizable as the dirty little urchin he'd been such a short time before. Abby rushed ahead of him, opened the door, and held it for him. Irritated, she noted that

Samuel didn't even turn around when the door hinges squeaked.

It looked as though this barn raising was going to be a *very* long day. Abby walked over to the small mirror she'd nailed up only the day before and checked her appearance one last time. A lavender ribbon held her hair back from her face, and not having the heart to bother with the rest of it, she'd simply let the mass of chestnut curls hang free to her hips. Her faded red dress, though not new, was clean and freshly ironed with enough starch added so that it might stand on its own. Trying to be festive, she'd wrapped a wide, yellow ribbon around her waist and tied it in a big bow. The ends of the ribbon, defying all her efforts to iron them into submission, hung limply down the front of her dress.

Abby sighed, pinched her cheeks, then reached for her bonnet. As she studied herself in the slightly flawed mirror, she realized that not even her precious hat would be enough to cheer her up. The little one-eyed dove seemed to mock her as she tied the purple bow into a saucy knot under her chin on the right.

Even her pink feather looked tired. Instead of standing straight up, it now leaned off to the left, pulling the blue fabric flowers away from the straw base. Her fingers reached for the tiny, yellow net veil and drew it down to the bridge of her nose. It was too late now to try and fix the bonnet. It would just have to do.

"Abby! Samuel says we got to get a move on!"

She stopped and listened to Luke call her from the yard. Straightening her shoulders and narrowing her eyes, Abby mumbled a few well-chosen words to the big man who couldn't even be bothered to shout at her. Disgusted, she turned to the table and picked up the golden brown apple pie. Lifting her chin, she walked out the front door and slammed it behind her.

She was going to have fun at the get-together. Even if it killed her.

Her face hurt from smiling. Abby'd been introduced to so many people, one face blended into the next until she could hardly remember her own name. Of course, there were a *few* people who would be hard to forget. She glanced down the length of the food table.

Sarah Dumont, the woman who ran the Lucky Lady Saloon in Rock Creek, stood with "her girls," surrounded by a swaggering, strutting crowd of men and boys. Each member of their audience jostled the other in a hopeless quest for singled-out attention.

Abby's gaze moved quickly over the three women. Sarah, a tall woman with light brown hair and a blond streak on either side of her face, wore a deep peach gown with a bodice cut so low Abby wondered how she kept it up. Stacey's auburn hair was pulled around to one side of her face and hung down in long curls over the shoulder strap of her bright pink satin dress. Jennifer's pale yellow gown was modest in comparison to the others, yet Abby was glad the woman's almost black hair hung forward, over her full breasts.

It was just as Minerva had said it would be. One look at Sarah and her girls and the menfolk forgot all about their families. All of the men except Samuel.

Abby looked away from the crowd, letting her gaze travel over the Coles' yard. He wasn't hard to find, even among so many people. Samuel was taller by far than any man there, though even if he weren't, Abby was sure that her eyes would go unerringly to him.

Then he stepped out of the almost-completed barn, slipped around the corner, and stood alone in the shadows, watching everyone else. Despite his casual stance, leaning up against the side of the barn, he looked ill at ease. His hands twisted and untwisted the brim of his hat, and even from a distance, Abby could see the scowl on his face.

She couldn't understand it. After his team had won the side-raising contest, Samuel had seemed to be enjoying himself.

Samuel hugged the side of the new barn. From his vantage point he could see everyone at the party. He was well aware of the angry looks all of the wives were firing at the men gathered around Sarah and her girls. And he had to admit that the three women were really something to look at. But even as he thought it, he knew he would never be a part of their admiring throng.

Hell, he'd only been with two or three women in his whole life! And that was because they'd come to *him*. Oh, when he was younger, he'd been like most other young pups, playin' up to the saloon girls . . . but it had only taken a couple of those women to stare at him with dread to cure him of that nonsense!

Luke and Obadiah caught his eye then as they stood at the edge of the crowd, jumping up and down to get a good look. Samuel half-smiled, shook his head, and looked away.

He crushed his hat between his fingers and cursed himself for a coward. Here he was, alone again, when only a while ago he'd been part of a team. Samuel knew he'd never forget those few moments of happy excitement after his team had won the race to put up the barn. His team members clapping him on the back, smiling at him, including him in their victory celebration.

But all too soon it had ended. One by one, the other men had returned to their families, and Samuel was alone again.

You don't have to be alone, his mind chided. All you have to do is go to Abby.

He groaned and clamped down on the thought. How the hell could he go to her after hurting her like he had that night in the barn? Shit, if he was Abby, he'd have shot him by now!

But it had had to be done, he told himself. He'd had to turn her away. He'd had to protect himself from the pain he'd spent so many years avoiding.

And Lordy, how he'd paid for it. He'd just lived through the longest week of his life. Samuel had never really noticed just how small his mountain property was. Until he'd had to try to find places to keep to himself. He grumbled and shifted position slightly. Hell, he'd done more hunting in the last week than he had in the last year.

Well, he told himself, at least there was more than enough meat to see him through the coming winter now. In fact, there was enough for all three of them. *Dammit*, why'd Abby ever come to the mountain?

As if she had spoken, Samuel looked up and found her eyes on him. He wasn't surprised to see that she'd already started walking toward him.

And he had nowhere left to hide.

This is ridiculous, Abby thought stubbornly. If he wouldn't talk to her at home, then by heaven, he could talk to her here. She threaded her way through the crowd, her gaze never leaving Samuel's. At least, she told herself, he was willing to look at her.

Samuel straightened abruptly. Didn't she see the two cowboys closing in on her? Even from where he stood, Samuel could tell that the two men were *very* drunk. Their wobbling steps were determined, though, and taking them directly to Abby.

Someone grabbed her arm, and Abby swung around. A tall handsome cowboy with sandy-blond hair and big brown eyes smiled down at her.

"Hey, pretty lady," he said, breathing the stench of whiskey into her face, "let's you and me dance."

Abby's nose wrinkled and she tried to pull her arm free. "There's no music," she said firmly, "but thank you anyway."

"Don't need no music, little darlin'," said another man, shorter than the first, with black hair, green eyes, and a beautiful smile. "Jas and me, we'll show ya . . ."

Abby jerked back. He was as drunk as his friend. She wasn't frightened, though. They were in the middle of a crowd, and the two men seemed harmless enough. But they both reeked of whiskey, and the smell was making her sick.

"You go on, Chris," the blond one said. "I found her first."

"That ain't so, Jason," Chris countered, "and you know it. Why, just a bit ago, I said to you, I says, looka there at that pretty little thing. . . ."

Jason pulled Abby closer and glared at his friend. "Hell, the day I need you to point out a pretty woman . . ."

Chris pulled at her other arm. "You sayin' I can't pick 'em good as you?"

Abby flew back toward Jason when the man jerked her away from his friend.

"That's what I'm sayin'," Jason countered. "You recall that time in Tularosa?"

Chris spit in the dirt. "Hell, that don't count none. I was drunk!"

Abby simply stared at him. A moment later she was pulled back to Jason again and whirled around in a circle, dancing to music only the drunk could hear. No matter how she tried, she couldn't seem to get away. Vaguely she was aware that the crowd of men had turned away from Sarah's girls and were now staring at her. Desperately she twisted her head from side to side, looking for Samuel. Their eyes met briefly, then she was pulled away again.

"Here now, you two," Alonzo Mullins said, trying to break into the little trio, "that'll be enough of that. You boys go on and have another drink."

Privately Abby thought that they'd had more than enough already, but she said nothing.

Both cowboys laughed. Then Jason said, "After we're through dancin', mister. There's plenty of time. . . ."

"Awright, awright," Chris said, tugging at Abby again. He ignored Alonzo completely. "You had your chance, Jas. My turn now."

"Not hardly," Jason argued. "Still my turn!"

"You're both wrong, boys!" Samuel's voice boomed out. "It's *my* turn!"

Chapter Twelve

Strong hands fell on Abby's shoulders. She felt herself pulled from Jason's eager grasp, then she was lifted through the air and deposited safely a few feet away. Gratefully she smiled up at her rescuer. "Thank you, Samuel," she said with relief. "I'm sure they meant no harm, but thank you."

Samuel wasn't so sure. What he *was* sure of was the minute that cowboy had laid a hand on Abby, all Samuel'd wanted to do was push his fist through that handsome young face. He hadn't even bothered to say the ABCs. Even now his blood was still boiling with rage, but if Abby was really all right, then he was willing to let everything else go. For her sake. He stared down at her and saw her eyes widen with fright.

He was already turning when she screamed, "Look out, Samuel!"

Samuel hadn't even considered not going to Abby's rescue. Even though he knew that most of the people at the gathering would turn from him once he entered a fight. He'd seen it before. A man his size just couldn't act like other men. Folks were just too scared of his strength.

But none of that mattered when he'd seen the shock and humiliation in Abby's eyes. Her trust in him. Her faith. He'd have walked through fire to reach her, and damn to hell anyone who dared step between them.

Then for a moment it had looked as though there wouldn't be a fight after all. He should have known better.

With Abby's shouted warning, though, Samuel ducked into a crouch as he turned and the fist that Chris swung at him missed by a mile. The drunk cowhand turned with the force of his swing and, his balance already gone, spun in a circle again before falling into the dirt.

At that same instant Jason leapt at Samuel's broad back. The young cowhand wrapped his forearm around his opponent's thick neck and hung on, trying to choke the big man.

Samuel hardly noticed. His gaze was centered on Chris, who scrambled to his unsteady feet and charged the giant who had broken in on his fun. As the drunk closed in on him, Samuel shot one beefy arm out, grabbed hold of the younger man and tossed him effortlessly into the clamoring crowd.

Chris landed, spread eagle, on one of the townsmen, and they both crashed to the ground. Other men in the crowd, laughing and shouting, pulled Chris to his feet. Once he was up, Chris threw a frustrated punch at the nearest face.

Buck Whitehall's head snapped back with the force of the blow. Growling menacingly, Buck drew his big fist back. Chris ducked and the blacksmith's hearty bash slammed into another spectator's jaw. In seconds the whole crowd was fighting.

The men of Rock Creek and the surrounding farms took to the fight like kids let loose in a candy store. Amid the shouted insults hovering over the once quiet yard, fists flew and bodies hurtled through the air to land with heavy thuds.

Samuel tried to shake Jason off his back again, but for some reason the damn kid wouldn't come loose. Samuel sidestepped awkwardly as one of the fallen townsmen crashed and landed at his feet. The man gave Samuel a lopsided grin before getting up and rushing back into the fray. How the hell did all this happen? Samuel asked himself.

Then he groaned when he saw Chris slip out from under the brawling crowd. Through slitted eyes Samuel watched the stubborn cowhand brush himself off and prepare to charge.

With a death grip on Samuel's neck, Jason hadn't stopped throwing ineffective swipes at the big man's head and shoulders. Jason was more irritating than anything else, but try as he might, Samuel couldn't seem to get a grip on the man clinging to him. He cursed viciously as Chris ran at him, fists ready.

From the corner of his eye Samuel noticed Abby and Luke watching the goings-on. Abby's gaze was filled with worry while Luke jumped up and down beside her, batting his small fists through the air as if trying to somehow help Samuel.

With one palm against Chris's forehead, Samuel held the young man at arm's length. Then he reached around with his free hand and gave a mighty yank. *Finally* he had Jason off his back. One hand at each man's collar,

Samuel lifted the cowhands, then crashed their heads together as easily as he would clap his hands.

Knocked momentarily senseless, the two drunks fell in a heap to the ground.

Samuel took a long, deep breath and frowned down at the two troublemakers at his feet. Before he could move, though, a shotgun blast echoed over the still-battling crowd.

All sound stopped. Men paused in midswing, their fists poised just inches from their targets. As one, they looked toward the source of the blast.

Minerva Mullins stood, feet wide apart, still clutching the shotgun with both barrels aimed toward heaven. Behind her stood at least a half-dozen angry women.

"I got one barrel left if you fools ain't ready to listen yet," Minerva warned in a steely tone.

A couple of men shifted position, but no one said a word.

"That's better," Minerva stated flatly. "Now, us women say this fight is over right now."

A few mumbled comments floated out into the hush.

"Over," she repeated. She frowned at the men sprawled in the dirt and said, "Some of you pick them up and bring 'em over to the tables. We're gonna have dinner now."

Her eyes narrowed, she moved her gaze slowly and deliberately over the grumbling men. Leisurely then, she lowered the gun and smoothed her skirts. After another long pause she and her cohorts turned their backs on the men.

"Durn women," someone said under his breath. "All the time botherin' a man just when he's havin' a good time. . . . "

"Lonzo," another said, "can't you keep that woman of yours in line any?"

Alonzo snorted as he pushed himself to his feet. "When you can handle yours, Hiram . . . *then* you come talk to me about Minerva."

Samuel just shook his head. He couldn't believe it. It was over. He'd been in a fight and he hadn't *killed* anyone. His strength had done no more damage than anyone else's. In fact, most of the others looked a lot worse off than the two drunks Samuel had dealt with. He'd never seen so many puffy eyes and split lips in one place before.

He stood quietly in the yard as the battered, dirty men filed past him, dragging the unfortunate few who couldn't walk on their own to the tables.

"Some fight, eh, Sam?" one man whispered as he passed.

"Guess you showed them two somethin' about how to treat our females," another said as he clapped the big man on the back.

Samuel twisted his head this way and that, watching the men and returning the smiles they gave him. They weren't afraid of him. Seeing him in a fight hadn't sent a one of them running. Instead, they'd all joined in. Made a party of it. His forehead creased and his brows drew together as he tried to make sense of what had happened.

All those years of fear. Telling himself that people would be frightened by his size. His strength. Hiding away from other folks to keep himself safe. Shying away from talking to people. Was it possible, he wondered, that the reason he'd never had any friends was his own standoffishness? Could it be that simple? If he had tried to make friends . . . talked to people, become a part of a community, would they have accepted him?

Abby's hand on his arm snapped him out of the new, disturbing thoughts. He looked down at his own forearm and noted that her fingers were trembling.

"Are you all right?" she asked quietly.

Against his will, his gaze lifted to meet hers. If her touch hadn't been enough to get his heart thumping wildly, the look in her eyes would have done it. Where he'd expected to find fear and dread, he found instead concern, worry. She wasn't afraid *of* him. She was afraid *for* him.

"Samuel," she said, her voice mounting in his silence, "are you hurt? Did they hurt you?"

He shook his head. "I'm fine. They didn't hurt me any."

She reached up and touched a bruise at the corner of his eye. Already the skin was swelling and turning colors. "I was so worried, Samuel. There were *two* of them picking on you. I didn't know what to do. . . ." She chewed at her lip nervously. "They might have . . ."

Samuel knew very well that those two couldn't have done him any damage. Hell, they were both so drunk they could hardly stand up! But he found he liked her concern so much that he didn't want to argue the point with her.

"Boy, howdy," Luke piped up out of nowhere, "that there was some fight, Sam. I never seen the like! An' the way you tossed them two around like they was no bigger'n me . . ."

"Luke!" Abby turned on him. "That will be enough. Samuel might have been seriously injured, for heaven's sake."

"Nah," the boy countered, waving his hand at the outraged woman. "They couldn't do nothin' to Sam! I'm gonna go see Obadiah. Make sure he seen it all."

Luke made a quick half turn and ran through the crowd in search of his friend.

The last of the staggering warriors passed them before Samuel asked, "Them cowboys didn't scare you any, did they?"

Abby looked up at him, her eyes shining with the trust he'd come to associate with her, and said softly, "Of course not, Samuel. I knew you were close by."

He couldn't think of a thing to say. Her faith in him was something so new, so precious, that he didn't quite know what to make of it. But as she pulled him gently toward the supper tables, Samuel finally admitted to himself how much he needed it. And her.

By the time everyone had eaten their fill, the sun was low on the horizon. Already the afternoon sky was streaked with pale shafts of pink and amber.

It was time to leave.

As Abby was packing up the last of their things, Luke and Obadiah came rushing up to her, pulling Minerva behind them.

"Obadiah says I can stay over to his place tonight, Abby," Luke said, eagerness plain on his face.

"Yes'm," Obadiah added, "Ma says it's fine with her."

Abby looked up at Minerva questioningly.

"Oh, yes," Minerva said with a groan as she tugged her hands free from the boys. "With five of my own, I won't hardly notice one more!"

Abby glanced at the wagon across the yard and watched Samuel move around the horses, hitching them up for the ride back to the cabin. She smiled. It might be just the thing for Luke to stay the night with the Mullinses.

"All right." Abby looked at Luke. "You mind Mrs. Mullins, now."

"Yes'm." Luke took off with Obadiah without a backward glance.

Minerva chuckled and followed after them. "You can come for him tomorrow," she called over her shoulder.

Abby barely heard the other woman. She nodded absently and turned her gaze back to Samuel. His back was to her. She stared openly as the muscles in his back and shoulders flexed and bunched with his movements. A curl of excitement laced with a pang of nerves crept through her body. Her mouth was suddenly dry and breathing was difficult.

She hugged the folded quilt to her chest and told herself that if anything were to happen between the two of them, it would be up to her to start it. Briefly Abby wondered if she would have the courage to go to him again. After that last embarrassing scene in the barn, it wouldn't be easy.

Just then, Samuel paused beside one of the horses. He reached out and ran his hand down the length of the animal's neck. Even from a distance Abby could see the gentleness in his touch.

She shivered and hugged the quilt tighter. Her mind was made up. Samuel wasn't going to ignore her tonight, she told herself firmly. He loved her. And she loved him. Tonight, she would show him how much. Even if she had to go the barn and *drag* him back to the cabin.

*   *   *

Abby lit the lamp, checked the fire for the fifth time, then moved across the room to the bed. She bent over and tugged at the bright flowered quilt, smoothing out imaginary wrinkles. She was dawdling and she knew it. It was only that she wanted everything to be perfect.

Straightening up, Abby looked around the cabin and smiled. The cozy room looked nothing like the worn-out, dirty place it had been when she'd first arrived. But it was more than the curtains and tablecloth and even more than the new paint. The *feel* of the room was different now. Instead of lonely seclusion, the little cabin offered warmth—comfort.

The fire snapped and the flame in the lamp wavered, sending dancing shadows of light moving about the walls. A pot of stew hung from the hook over the fire and bubbled in time with the flames. The door to her unfinished room was closed, and Harry and Maverick were both stretched out, asleep before the hearth.

She glanced down at her best gown. A soft sea green, the bodice molded itself to her body. And above the low-cut neckline, a narrow band of slightly frayed white lace framed the tops of her breasts.

Everything was ready.

Abby clasped her hands together tightly and took a deep, shuddering breath. This might have been much easier. If only Samuel had said something on the ride back to the mountain. But he hadn't. It was as if he was deliberately closing her out of his life. His heart.

She flicked a quick glance at the closed front door. He was in the barn, she knew. Just where he'd been all week. All she had to do was cross that yard and somehow get him to come to the cabin. A nervous laugh shook her. And then what? She had no idea how to go about getting a man to bed her.

Abby shook her head. She wouldn't worry about that now. First she had to get him in the cabin. Later she would worry about the rest of it. She looked over her shoulder at the big bed. Somehow, without the bundling board in the center, it was more . . . disquieting.

She looked away and turned her thoughts to Samuel. His voice, his eyes, the warmth of his touch. She breathed deeply and let the now familiar curl of excitement spread and grow until her limbs almost shook with it.

Before her too rational brain could intrude again, Abby walked to the front door, threw it open, and hurried to the barn.

She stopped just inside the building and listened for a moment to the soothing sounds of the horses' familiar movements as they settled in for the night. Her gaze shifted over the barn, searching for Samuel. Then he rose and moved away from the concealing stall. Her breath caught and she just managed to stifle a gasp.

At the far end of the building Samuel stood in the soft glow of a solitary lamp. He finished pulling off his shirt, and Abby's gaze locked on his muscular chest and brawny arms. She'd never seen him like this before. When they'd shared the cabin, he'd removed his clothing in the dark . . . and she'd always kept her eyes tightly closed anyway.

But now Abby found she couldn't see enough of him. The length of the barn was too great a distance for her, and so she began to walk toward him. Her footsteps were soft on the straw-covered dirt, but still he heard her.

Samuel turned to face her, and as she came even closer, he reached behind him for the shirt he'd just discarded. She wanted to tell him not to put it on. She wanted to see his body in the lamplight. She wanted to run her hands over that broad chest and feel his heart beating.

But his eyes as he watched her were wary, and she didn't want to take a chance on ruining her carefully laid plan.

"What is it, Abby?" he said as she stopped before him.

"Uh," she cleared her throat. "I need more firewood, Samuel. I was wondering if you would . . ."

The watchfulness in his gaze softened. Quickly his fingers moved down the row of buttons, closing his shirt front. "Sure. You go on. I'll be along."

"Thank you, Samuel," she said and forced herself to turn and walk back to the house. But she let a small smile touch her lips. He hadn't seen through her little lie. Thankfully, he didn't seem to recall that he'd just filled the woodbox two days ago.

As she crossed the yard, Abby tossed a quick look up at the night sky. There seemed to be so many more stars here than there were in Maryland. Or maybe it was just that she was so much closer to them, here on the mountain. Her gaze dropped to the lighted windows of her home, and Abby knew that whatever the reason, she belonged there. In that cabin. With Samuel.

She sent a silent prayer to heaven asking for the strength she would need to convince Samuel.

In a few short minutes he entered the cabin, his arms wrapped around a half-dozen good-sized logs. Samuel walked to the woodbox, lifted the lid, looked inside, and stopped.

He turned his head and looked at her from over his shoulder. "What are you doin', Abby? You've got plenty of wood here." His voice was soft, almost regretful.

She closed and bolted the front door before answering him. "I'm sorry, Samuel. It's just that I wanted to . . ."

He dropped the load of wood into the box, slammed the lid, and faced her uneasily. "You wanted what?"

"To . . ." Her face cleared and she smiled brightly. "To have company for a late supper."

His brows drew together. "Supper?"

"Yes," she said quickly, moving to the fireplace and swinging the cooking hook out. "With Luke at the Mullinses' tonight, well, I didn't want to eat alone." She lifted the lid with one towel-wrapped hand and gave the stew a few quick stirs with the other. The damp aroma drifted up into the stillness.

"Thanks," Samuel said gruffly, "but I ain't hungry." He moved for the door.

Abby dropped the lid back onto the pot with a clatter and hurried to head him off. When she stood in front of him, she tossed the towel to the table a few feet away and forced herself to look up at him. For one long, agonizing moment she wished desperately that she had the knowledge that Sarah Dumont and her girls possessed. Then she banished all thoughts of anyone but the man before her.

His pale green eyes were shuttered. She couldn't read his feelings, but knew by his rigid posture that he wasn't going to bend.

Slowly, hesitantly, Abby reached for him. In a flash of movement Samuel grasped her wrist in his strong fingers before she could touch him.

"Abby . . ." he groaned, "don't do this. You don't know what you're askin'."

"Yes," she breathed and stepped even closer. "Yes, I do know, Samuel." She made no effort to pull her hand free of his gentle but firm grip. Instead, she lifted her other hand and skimmed her fingers lightly over his chest.

His breathing staggered, but he didn't move away.

Deliberately then, Abby pushed the first button of his shirt free. When he still made no move, she went on to the next one. She felt his body jerk with her every touch, and his fingers tightened on her wrist. Slowly, inch by inch, his shirt front was opened to her view.

She glanced up at his face and saw that he was staring blankly at the wall behind her. His jaw tight, lips pressed together, he looked as though he was awaiting execution. Abby ignored his pained expression. He loved her. She knew he did.

With her one free hand Abby pushed the edges of his shirt farther apart, baring his hard, muscled chest. His sun-bronzed flesh was dusted with fine, reddish-blond hair that trailed down his chest to disappear beneath the waistband of his pants.

Abby laid the flat of her palm against his skin. Gently her hand glided over Samuel's flesh as she struggled for the air that wouldn't come. His body quivered beneath her hand, and when her fingers toyed with his pale, flat nipple, Samuel jerked convulsively and snatched her hand away.

Now he held both her hands, and though he was gentle, his grip was such that she couldn't break away. Abby's legs were shaking, and she heard her own blood pounding in her ears. A warm, damp heat spiraled through her and centered at the core of her desire.

Looking into his eyes, Abby willed him to see her need for him. Willed him to acknowledge his own need.

"Abby," he whispered as his fingers moved over her wrists, "you gotta stop this. Now."

She leaned toward him. "No, Samuel. I won't stop."

He groaned and let his head fall back.

Abby moved closer until her breasts were within a hair of touching him. "Samuel . . ." Her soft breath blew at his chest. She waited until he looked at her again. "I don't want to stop. And I know you don't really want me to."

"Yes," he ground out tightly. "Yes, I do."

"No." She smiled and shook her head gently. "You're trying to protect me, Samuel. Whether from you or myself, I'm not sure . . . but either way, it's too late."

He snorted. "It's not too late yet, Abby. Not yet."

Abby leaned closer and placed a soft kiss on his chest. She smiled when his muscles contracted. His fingers loosened on her wrists, and she slipped them free. Slowly, teasingly, she moved her palms up over his flesh until she reached his shoulders. Then she pushed his shirt down over his arms until it fell to the floor, unheeded.

Samuel shuddered as her hands moved over him. His lips began to move in a way that she'd noticed whenever he was upset.

Abby moved her hands to cradle his face. Immediately his muttering stopped. When his gaze met hers, she said softly, "Don't protect me, Samuel. Love me."

For a long, agonizing moment Abby waited. Then he groaned in surrender and reached for her.

Chapter Thirteen

Samuel lifted her easily and held her close. Abby's lips parted for his kiss, and when their mouths met, she wrapped her arms around his neck and clung to him.

All hesitation and nervousness fled, and she eagerly opened her mouth to him. His tongue swept inside, and her breath caught in her throat. A warm, heady desire raced through her veins, making her flesh oversensitive to his every touch.

Samuel moved his lips to her throat and lavished kisses down the length of her neck. His strong hands at her waist lifted her higher until his lips found the tops of her breasts.

Hands on his shoulders, Abby arched against him, letting her head fall back on her neck. His mouth hungrily moved over her flesh, and she sensed his frustration when he couldn't reach enough of her.

She straightened in his grasp and lifted her hands to the back of her gown. He held her effortlessly and stared up into her eyes as she slowly unbuttoned her dress. Just as when she'd unbuttoned his shirt, Abby somehow knew instinctively to move without hurry. The waiting, the unfulfilled hunger, brought its own rewards.

One by one, she freed the hooks from their places. As the bodice of her dress dipped lower with each inch of freedom, Abby watched Samuel's gaze darken with a need that matched her own. When the last hook had been undone, she pushed the sleeves of her gown down off her shoulders, letting the material drape over Samuel's arms. A muscle in his cheek twitched, and she knew he was holding himself in check.

Deliberately then, Abby untied the ribbon of her chemise and slid the straps down her arms. It was only then, when she had bared herself to his gaze, that she faltered for a moment. She had to fight down the instinctive urge to cover herself with her hands.

Instead, she cupped his face and smiled tremulously at him. Samuel turned his face and kissed her palm before bringing her bare breasts close. As Abby watched, her heart pounding, Samuel's mouth opened and then closed over one taut nipple.

Her hands moved to his shoulders and squeezed reflexively. She gasped aloud when Samuel's tongue began to draw damp circles over the bud of her breast, and when he suckled her, Abby groaned and once more arched against him. He released her breast despite her sigh of disappointment and slowly lowered her body, her breasts skimming over his own chest.

When their bodies touched, Abby's eyes flew open at the contact. Her hands at his shoulders, she tried to pull herself closer to him. But suddenly he seemed to toss her gently, flipping her into the air and catching her in his arms to hold her cradled against him. Her head nestled against his chest, she listened to the ferocious pounding of his heart. She moved her hand across the breadth of him, smiling when she felt his skin tremble.

Samuel carried her to the bed, leaned down, and with one hand swept the quilt to the footboard. Gently he laid her down on the mattress. Her chestnut hair dark against the white sheet, the bodice of her dress crumpled around her waist, she held out her arms to him.

"Abby"—his voice was hoarse—"God knows, it'd prob'ly kill me to stop now"—he drew in a shaky breath—"but I swear, if you say so . . . I will. If you changed your mind about this . . ."

"Samuel," she whispered softly, "don't stop."

All indecision left his features as he lowered himself to her side. He pulled her close against him, feeling the warmth of their joined bodies. How many nights, he asked himself, had he lain awake wanting nothing more than this? Just to hold her and be held. And now she was offering him so much more.

His hands moved to her waist, and with exquisite care he slid her gown down over her hips, his fingers exploring every exposed inch of her body. The sea-green fabric bunched under his hands, and when it was finally free, Samuel tossed it to the floor. In the golden haze of the lamplight her skin glowed like fine porcelain he'd seen once as a boy. Her breasts were small but full, her waist narrow, and her hips, Samuel noted with relief, were wide and rounded.

He'd been so worried about her size. She still seemed far too fragile to accommodate a man as large as he, and a trace of fear lingered in the back of his mind.

Abby's fingers moved over his chest, and he couldn't deny the sigh that escaped him at the pleasure of her touch. He'd dreamed of this for so long. Then, timidly, her hands moved farther down his body until they reached the wide belt buckle at his waist. He held perfectly still, not wanting to frighten her with any abrupt movements. But he needn't have worried. After only a slight hesitation, Abby's fingers pulled at the leather belt, her desires clear.

Samuel pushed away from her and stood at the side of the bed. As he undressed fully, he watched her. There was no sign of fear in her eyes when she looked at his nude body. Only the desire that fired him on. She was too beautiful for the likes of him, he knew. Her fine, smooth skin, flushed from his attentions, her nipples, erect and waiting for him. Her tongue, darting out to lick her lips, inviting him to taste her sweetness. It had to be a dream, Samuel told himself. And if it was, he prayed silently, please, God, let him never wake up.

"Samuel," Abby called to him, and he dropped his pants on the floor beside her forgotten dress.

He stretched out alongside her, his hands moving over her body with gentle eagerness. Abby moved closer, snuggling as close to him as she could get. Her head just under his chin, she began to plant tiny kisses on his neck and chest. The feel of her lips against his flesh stirred a hunger in Samuel like he'd never known before.

He leaned on one elbow and dipped his head down to claim her breasts, one after the other. Just as Abby would begin to moan and toss her head in pleasure, he would leave the sensitive bud for the other. His tongue swept over her heated skin, marking her as surely as if he'd trailed a red-hot brand over her body. Abby's hands moved up and down his arms, her nails scratching gently as they passed.

He moved one hand down over the curve of her hip and slipped around behind her to cup her bottom. Then, in a smooth motion, Samuel turned quickly and lay beneath her.

Abby stretched out her length atop him. And Samuel held her waist and gently slid her body along his, bringing her breasts to his mouth. Again, he teased her, enjoying her pleasure as much as she did herself. Then slowly he moved her back down along his body until he once more shifted position, laying her gently against the pillows.

Samuel's fingers moved lightly over her abdomen, dancing feather touches to her flesh. His lips moved to claim hers and as his tongue darted inside her mouth, his fingers slipped into the center of her soul.

Abby gasped and her hips began to rock. Her arms wrapped around his neck and pulled him tighter to her. Their tongues met and caressed each other while Samuel's thumb stroked across the most sensitive part of Abby's body. Her moans were louder and fed Samuel's hunger until he, too, felt the overwhelming urge for completion that swamped the woman in his arms.

Finally she tore her mouth free from him and cried out, "Samuel! I need . . ."

"Yes, Abby, I know. . . ." He kissed her and with his free hand smoothed the matted hair back from her brow. Quickly now his fingers moved in and out of her body, creating the rhythm his body would continue when he felt she was ready to accept his entry.

A faint scrabbling sound from behind him startled Samuel, and he turned to find Harry and Maverick trying to hop onto the mattress with them. Samuel growled low in his throat, his desire battling with patience that was already near its end.

Abruptly he pulled away from Abby, stalked across the cabin, and opened the door. The dogs understood and left immediately.

"Samuel," Abby said, "Samuel . . ."

He hurried back to her and lay down once more. "Damn dogs," he mumbled with a kiss. "They must've thought I was hurting you."

Abby smiled and trailed her fingers down his cheek. "The only way you could hurt me is if you leave me like this," she said quietly.

"Never." He kissed her again and moved her thighs apart. Kneeling between them, he looked down at her and hoped to God he *wouldn't* hurt her. She raised her hips in silent invitation.

"Come to me, Samuel."

"Abby"—he swallowed convulsively—"you're so damn little."

She held her arms out to him, a smile on her face. "It will be all right, Samuel," she said softly. "I know it will. Trust me."

Slowly he lifted her hips to ease his entry. Even as his body moved to join with hers, Samuel's fingers stroked the center of her pleasure. Her breathing was fast, ragged. And he knew his own matched it. But still he moved carefully.

As he slipped farther inside Abby, though, Samuel knew she'd been right. Their bodies fit together as if made for each other. After a moment of discomfort, they began to move as one, their souls touching and releasing with each contact of their bodies.

As the first convulsive pleasure shook her, Samuel leaned over and swallowed her broken cries. Finally his own body exploded into hers, and he fell, stunned, into the depths of her eyes.

"The last time I saw somethin' that stupid," Minerva said, glaring down at Alonzo, "it was waggin' a tail and barkin'."

Alonzo cocked his head and looked at her. One of his eyes was swollen shut, and when he tried to narrow the other one angrily, he winced in pain. "Consarn it, Minerva." He groaned and laid his head gently against the chair back. "Ain't I got enough hurtin' already without you startin' in again?"

She shook her head and slapped the piece of raw meat into his extended hand. While he applied it to his eye, she went on. "Well, I don't know what else you'd expect . . . a bunch of grown men rollin' around in the dirt for no good reason a'tall!"

"Hell," he shouted, then moaned and lowered his voice, "I *had* a reason! Look at my eye, for corn's sake! I didn't do that to myself, y'know."

"Hmmph!" Minerva walked to her rocker, picked her knitting up off the cushion, and sat down. As her fingers slipped easily into the familiar pattern, she said, "Might as well have. Don't know why you'd expect to come out of a brawl like that without a scratch."

"Wasn't a brawl," he mumbled defensively.

"Can't call it nothin' else." Her needles clicked furiously.

He glanced at her out of his good eye. "Notice you ain't got nothin' bad to say about Samuel Hart bein' in that fight—and *he* was the first one in it!"

The needles paused in midstitch and Minerva stared at her husband. "Alonzo Mullins! I'm surprised at you!"

Alonzo shifted uneasily.

She shook the half-finished sweater at him. "You know durn well and good that fight wasn't his fault. You figure he should just stand there while those two drunks was hoorahin' Abby?"

Alonzo frowned. "No, but—"

"I should say not." The needles started in again, and her voice picked up speed. "He had just cause to go start smashin' them two up. But did he?" She waited for him to shake his head. "No, he did not!" Minerva nodded abruptly. "It was *them* that started that damn fight. . . ." She stopped and glared at him again. "And I'll tell you somethin' else, Mr. Alonzo Mullins. He didn't do near the punchin' you all was doin'!"

"I know," he muttered, disgusted with himself, the fight, and, mostly, Minerva.

"Why, the way Samuel handled them two was somethin' to see." Her eyebrows shot up. "If you hadn't been so *busy*, you might've seen it, too."

A loud crash from upstairs broke into the one-sided conversation. Heavy footsteps pounded across the parlor ceiling, and Alonzo clapped one hand to his aching forehead. "You children," he started to shout, "aaah . . ." he finished softly.

Minerva's lips quirked. Calmly she got up, walked to a corner of the cluttered room, and snatched up the broom that rested there. Holding it by the straw bristles, she thumped the handle against the ceiling several times. "Obadiah!" she called out. "You and Luke clean up whatever it is you just broke up there!"

"Ah, Ma . . ."

She stared up at the ceiling and thump
"Don't 'ah, Ma' me, either!" After a few s
silence they heard shuffling steps moving a...oss the
room. Minerva, still staring up at the ceiling, remarked
quietly, "'Lonzo, it appears I've knocked another hole
in the blamed ceiling. You best fix it tomorrow."

Her husband groaned.

There were quite a few empty tables in the Lucky
Lady saloon. Sarah Dumont stood at the head of the
stairs and let her gaze drift over her place of business.
She'd built the saloon up from practically nothing, and
she worked hard to see that it stayed the best damn
saloon this side of Denver.

Hardwood floors gleamed in the light thrown from
dozens of sparkling clean oil lamps. The mirror behind
the long mahogany bar had come all the way from
Saint Louis without a scratch, and on either side of the
bar stretched row after row of drinking glasses she'd
shipped in from New Orleans.

Sarah started down the stairs and nodded briefly
at Mac, one of two burly men hired to maintain the
peace at the Lucky Lady. It was Terry's night off, but
as quiet as it was, Sarah didn't think he'd be missed.
She walked up to the bar, flicked a tiny speck of dust
to the floor, and ordered a sherry. When Dave, the
bartender, handed her the drink, she held it up to the
light, admiring the golden lights that shot through the
liquid.

Then, in the mirror, she caught sight of two men
sitting in the far corner, their heads together.

"How long have they been in here, Dave?" she asked
quietly.

The bartender gave the men a cursory glance and shrugged. "Couple of hours. On their second bottle now."

Sarah studied the two in the glass and took a small sip of her drink. Jason and Chris. You'd think they'd have had enough by now. After the mess they'd made of that barn raising, Sarah couldn't help but wonder what they were up to now. She took another sip and decided to find out. As drunk as they were, there was just no tellin' what they might try—and she didn't want any problems in her place.

Carrying her drink, Sarah weaved in and out of the tables scattered over the saloon floor. But even before she reached them, she heard them. Their voices were slurred but understandable.

"'s all *his* fault," Chris pointed out to his friend.

"Yeah," Jason agreed. "What's he care if we dance with the pretty lady?"

"He figure we ain't good enough, you reckon?" Chris's eyebrows rose, offended at the thought.

"Hell, if we ain't don't know who is. . . ." Jason slammed his glass down on the table. "Ain't we the bes' damn cowhands in the state of Texas?"

"Yeah . . ."

"And ain't we got money from the last trail drive we was on?"

Chris frowned. "We still got *some*. . . ."

"And wasn't we all fixed up—shaved and everything—today?" Jason asked indignantly.

"Yeah." Chris sat up straighter and jerked at the string tie that was now over his shoulder.

"Well, then," Jason asked, "why the hell'd he get so damn mad? Who the hell does he think he is, anyway?"

Sarah stopped at the side of their table. "Think you boys have had enough," she said softly and reached for the almost-empty bottle.

Jason snatched it away from her. "This here's ours, lady. We done paid for it already."

She held her hands up. "All right. Then why don't you take it with you? I'm fixin' to close up now."

"What if we ain't ready to go yet?" Chris countered.

Sarah looked at Mac and nodded. The big man started walking toward her immediately.

Jason looked over his shoulder at the approaching man and groaned. "I ain't seen so many grizzly-size men in one place in all my life!"

Chris watched the man in silence as though deciding if he was willing to fight to stay. Then he made up his mind. He stood up, swayed, and grabbed the edge of the table. "C'mon, Jas ... let's git."

Jason pushed himself to his feet and snatched his hat off the table. He jammed it on his head with one hand and clutched his bottle to his chest with the other. "We'll be leavin'. For now ..." He stared at Sarah, and Mac stepped a bit closer.

Chris grabbed his friend's arm and headed for the door. Before they left, though, Jason stopped and said, "This here is a mighty miser'ble way to treat a man, though. We'll be comin' back, y'hear?"

"Yeah," Chris added before following his friend out the batwing doors, "and we still aim to get our dance with that pretty lady, too. And you can tell that tame Griz of hers, too."

The doors swung back and forth noisily after they left. Sarah didn't even hear the whispered conversations from the customers around her. She was thinking about those two and what trouble they could cause.

Oh, she was fairly sure they wouldn't do any *real* harm. She'd seen their kind for years. Cowboys who worked all spring and summer, then holed up in some town for the winter to drink all their money.

Still, she told herself as she thanked Mac and walked back to the bar, it might be a good idea to tell Samuel Hart that he hadn't seen the last of those two.

Abby sighed and snuggled in closer to Samuel. His left arm closed around her and pressed her tightly to his side. Her head on his shoulder, Samuel moved just enough to plant a kiss on her forehead.

"Samuel," she breathed, running her fingertips across his chest, "that was . . ."

He smiled and captured her hand in his. "Yeah, Abby, it was."

She shivered suddenly.

"Cold?" Samuel asked and reached for the quilt at the foot of the bed. He drew it up over both of them, tucking the blanket around her carefully before drawing her back into the circle of his arms.

"Mmm . . . better," Abby whispered.

From outside, one of the dogs barked, and then came the screech of nails being dragged down the length of the door.

Abby buried her face in Samuel's chest to stifle her giggles when he tossed a dirty look toward the intrusive sounds.

"Think it's funny, do ya?" Samuel asked with a wicked grin. He got out of bed and walked nude to the door. His hand on the latch, he turned to watch her as he pulled the door wide.

Harry sped into the room with Maverick only a few steps behind him. The little dog raced across the floor and leapt onto the big bed with Abby. She yelped and tried to burrow under the quilt to escape his attentions. But Harry, cold and dirty, knew just how to deal with that. He slipped his nose under the blanket and by tossing his little head back again and again, he lifted the quilt just enough so that he could move. Maverick, still hampered by his cast, settled for limping back and forth around the bed, barking and whining for attention.

Samuel closed the front door and leaned back against it. Crossing his legs at the ankle, he watched the goings-on delightedly. Every move that Abby made, Harry countered. Finally Samuel knew when the little dog had cornered her by Abby's startled screech.

She sat up abruptly and threw the quilt aside with one hand. In the other she held Harry, squirming excitedly. Abby blew her hair out of her eyes and looked across the room at Samuel.

He grinned and openly studied her. Sitting nude in the middle of his bed, Abby's luscious hair billowed out around her as she juggled Harry and turned to quiet Maverick at the same time. The bigger dog was desperately trying to join his friend on the mattress, and, Samuel told himself, it was only fair. Quickly he moved across the cabin, lifted Maverick's hind end onto the bed, and laughed aloud when the big dog knocked Abby over backward in his enthusiasm.

Laughing and shouting useless warnings at the two animals, Abby rolled from side to side on the pillows trying to avoid their cold bodies and wet tongues. Finally, though, she surrendered and gave herself up to the dogs' adoration. With Maverick licking her hair and cheek and Harry's hind legs balanced on her thighs, his forelegs on her chest, she glanced up at Samuel.

Abby knew that she was seeing the *real* Samuel for the first time. She couldn't remember ever hearing him laugh like that before. And the guarded look in his beautiful green eyes was finally gone. Her gaze snaked over his nude body, and she felt the now welcome curl of desire spread through her limbs.

She knew that he was aware of her thoughts when he bent down and gently lifted Maverick from the bed, then shooed Harry off, too. All trace of laughter gone from his face, Samuel knelt beside her, wrapped her in his arms, and kissed her.

A long moment later Abby asked, "Samuel, can we . . ."

He shook his head regretfully. "Best not, Abby. You're awful new at this." He ran one finger down her jawline. "Don't want to wear you out any. . . ."

Samuel shifted position, leaning his back against the headboard and drawing her up close. A quick glance told him the dogs were settled again in their favorite spot in front of the fire. He ran his hand up and down the length of her back, marveling silently at how soft and smooth she was to the touch.

She was more woman than he'd ever dared dream of. Abby's warm heart welcomed and accepted him just as her body enticed him. He hadn't expected to be blessed with a woman like her. One that would want him as much as he wanted her.

Samuel closed his eyes and listened to Abby's soft, regular breathing. She was sleeping. His hand moved slowly over her back, caressing her, enjoying the feel of her nestled against him.

This was all so new to him. Why, the only women he'd ever been with were paid well for their time. And even then, there had been no real enjoyment or pleasure in the act. Only release.

There had never been any closeness. No softness. No holding each other and listening to the silence together.

He gently scooted down on the bed, drawing Abby in close when she stirred. Samuel was exhausted. She sighed and laid her arm across his broad chest. And, he thought wryly, for the first time since Abby had come into his life, he would be able to get a good night's sleep.

Chapter Fourteen

Early morning light sneaked into the cabin, darting between the folds of the red and white curtains. Abby sighed, stretched, and rolled over. Her eyes flew open as she realized that it was well past dawn and she was still in bed.

She sat upright, and the blankets fell away. For a brief moment she stared at her own nudity with surprise. Then the night before came flooding back into her brain, and she smiled. The memories were so clear it was as if she could still feel Samuel's hands on her flesh.

Samuel.

Quickly her gaze moved over the obviously empty cabin looking for him. She ran one hand over his side of the bed. The sheets were cool. He must have left quite a while ago. But where did he go? She threw the quilts aside and swung her legs over the edge of the bed. Wincing slightly at the unfamiliar aches

assaulting her body, Abby pushed herself to her feet
and snatched her dress from the floor.

While she shoved her arms through the sleeves, a
steady stream of worries and questions picked at her
mind. She remembered very well how she'd had to
practically *force* Samuel into bedding her. He'd fought
her so hard, maybe he was disgusted with her now.
Maybe he thought she was a tramp. *Maybe* he was so
furious with her, he'd up and left the mountain!

Frantically Abby reached around behind her and
tried to do up the buttons of her gown. It was no
use, though. In the state she was in, she told herself, it was lucky she'd been able to get the dress on
at all!

The palm of her hand against her breast to hold the
dress in place, Abby ran across the room and threw
the door open. Heedless of the cold ground beneath
her bare feet, she raced to the barn, ignoring the cackles
and screeches from the chicken coop. The morning chill
seeped through the skin of her exposed back, and her
teeth chattered.

In the barn she saw that the horses were still in their
stalls. But that didn't mean anything, she reminded
herself. Samuel often walked up and down the mountains. He didn't really *need* a horse to leave!

She heard a dog barking then and spun around.
Maverick. The animal barked again, and a few seconds
later there was a loud crash followed by a startled yelp.
Abby started moving and hurried her steps when she
heard Samuel shout, "Goddammit!"

She hurried back across the open yard, around the
corner of the cabin, and came to a dead stop when
she collided with Samuel. Immediately his big hands
reached out to steady her.

"Dammit, Abby," he said as one hand moved over her back, "I'm sorry. I didn't mean to wake you up."

"You didn't." She shuddered and moved closer to him. He hadn't left. His hand felt wonderful on her skin. Her palms crept up his chest, and she tilted her head back to look at him.

Samuel bent toward her, his mouth moving for hers. Both of his hands now caressed her back, sliding up her sides to brush at the edges of her breasts. She released a pent-up breath on a sigh and stood on her toes, eager to reach him.

Suddenly, though, Samuel seemed to notice just what was happening. He released her abruptly and with one hand pulled the edges of her dress together, protecting her from the frigid air.

"Are you out of your mind, woman?" he whispered. "You can't go wanderin' around out here half dressed! You'll be down sick in no time."

"Oh, I never get sick, Samuel," she countered, her fingers toying with the top button of his shirt.

He snatched at her hand, capturing it in his. "Yeah, well, you never lived in the mountains before, did you?"

She grinned. "No, but it *does* get cold in Maryland, too, you know."

"Not like here." He stepped back a pace and shook his head as he looked down at her. "Now, go on in and get dressed, Abby." His eyes widened when he saw her bare toes peeking out from under her hem. "Barefoot?" Samuel swept her up in his arms. "You *are* crazy! Goin' around barefoot and it almost winter! What were you thinkin' of?"

"You."

Her face was almost at a level with his, and Samuel

looked at her steadily. No one, he told himself, should look *that* good first thing in the morning. "What do you mean?" he asked quietly.

"When I woke up," she said, "you were gone." Abby lowered her gaze to the pocket of his shirt. "I thought you were . . . angry."

"Angry?" Samuel held her close against him but was careful to control the urge to squeeze her tightly. A short laugh escaped his lips. "Angry? No, Abby. I don't think you could call it angry."

She looked up. "Then why did you leave? What are you doing out here?"

Samuel leaned over and kissed her. Her mouth opened under his, and for a moment he gave his hunger for her free rein. He'd never experienced anything like this before. His desire for her hadn't been quenched the night before. If anything, it was even stronger now. He'd never known a *need* like this. Finally, gasping, he pulled away.

"Dear God," he whispered, his breath fanning her ear.

"Samuel." Abby's breathing was ragged.

"*That's* why I left the cabin, Abby." He inhaled deeply.

"I don't understand. . . ."

He started walking toward the front of the house, Abby still cradled in his arms. "With what happened between us last night," he said slowly, "I know that— well, we'll probably—"

"Yes?" she prodded.

"Shit, Abby!" He glanced down at her and kept moving. "You're goin' into town today to bring Luke back, ain't you?"

"Well, yes, but—"

"Now, I don't know much about this sort of thing"—
Samuel cleared his throat uneasily—"but seems to me
that havin' a child in the room with us prob'ly wouldn't
be a good idea anymore."

Her brow wrinkled in thought, then as realization
dawned, her eyes widened and she grinned. "Oh."

"Yeah. Oh." Samuel nudged the front door open,
walked inside, and crossed the room to the bed. "So
I got up early to finish up your room. Should be ready
for you by tonight."

"For me?" she asked, running her fingertips over the
back of his neck. "Or for us?"

He groaned quietly. "Reckon that'll be up to you,
Abby."

She smiled. "For us."

Samuel clenched his jaw tight and set her down. He
didn't know what he'd have done if she hadn't said
that. It would kill him if he couldn't touch her again.
"If that's what you want, Abby. If you're sure."

"I'm sure." Abby stood up on the edge of the bed
and wrapped her arms around his neck. Deliberately
she leaned against him, rubbing her breasts over his
chest.

"Abby," he moaned, forcing his hands to stay at his
side, "I got a lot to do out there." She kissed his
throat. "I dropped a whole pile of lumber when Harry
ran in front of me." Her tongue flicked gently against
his earlobe, her breath tickled his flesh. "Mornin's half
gone already." He shuddered. Abby's fingers slipped
the first of his shirt buttons free. "Abby, we best
not. . . . I know you're prob'ly still tender and—"

"No, Samuel," she breathed, moving her lips across
his jawline. "Not tender. Cold." Her mouth teased his,

her tongue tracing the outlines of his rigid lips. "Make me warm, Samuel."

He shouldn't, he knew. But how much could a man take?

Her hand slipped down his chest, over his belt buckle, and rubbed against the hard warmth of him. "Please, Samuel."

With a groan, Samuel surrendered. Catching her to him, he pressed the length of her along his body, then slowly lowered them both to the mattress.

Everyone in Rock Creek was so friendly! Abby smiled at the liveryman and shook her head. It was so different from the first time she and Samuel had come to town together. Then she'd been sure that she'd never be happy . . . that they would never accept her.

"Afternoon, Abby!"

She turned on the wagon seat and waved to Charity Whitehall, busy hanging out her wash. Really, it was such a nice place, Abby told herself and silently sent a prayer of thanks to Uncle Silas.

As she pulled up in front of Mullins's Mercantile, the door burst open and slammed into the wall. Obadiah, with Luke only a step behind, raced from the store and down the steps.

"Luke!" Abby called.

The boy slid to a stop on the wide dirt street, looked over his shoulder, and grinned. "Be back directly, Abby. We're just goin' down to the ice house for Mr. Mullins."

"C'mon, Luke!"

Obadiah stood in the street looking back at his friend.

"All right," Abby said, and when Luke took off, she

shouted, "But be quick about it!"

She reached up for her basket, then slipped it over her arm and climbed the steps to the store. The bell over the front door clanged out a welcome, and Minerva hurried from the back room. When she saw Abby, she smiled.

"Well, now. Been wonderin' when you was gonna get here."

Abby fought down a blush and thanked heaven that Minerva couldn't read her mind. She'd hate to have the woman find out exactly *why* she was late!

"I'm sorry, Minerva. I was . . ." She tried to think of something.

But Minerva brushed her off. "No matter. Like I said yesterday. You got this many kids . . . one more don't much matter!" She took Abby's list of supplies and turned to fill the order. "You folks sure are goin' through the flour and such!"

Abby leaned on the wood counter and idly played with a stray piece of string. "Uh-huh. Samuel and Luke just gobble everything up so quickly. . . . Maybe I should get a fifty-pound sack of flour while I'm here this time."

"Prob'ly a good idea." Minerva made a note on the list, then looked up. "You know, Abby, till you came, I hardly ever saw Samuel. I'll bet he wasn't in this store for supplies but once or twice in six months."

Abby chewed at her lip.

"Yessir, you comin' to town has made him a right good customer!"

Abby watched the woman's back as she moved surely around the store. This wasn't the first time Abby had thought about all the money Samuel had been spending on supplies. And she was beginning to feel very badly about it. But she didn't have any money. She'd spent it all on the trip out from Maryland.

Her mind whirling, Abby turned and let her gaze move over the store. When she spotted the bolts of fabric, her eyes widened. Why not? she asked herself. Wasn't she the best seamstress in Maryland? Hadn't everyone told her that for most of her life? If she could do some dressmaking for the ladies in town, she'd be able to help buy supplies. After all, Samuel's money couldn't last forever. Why, for all she knew, he might very well be almost penniless!

"Minerva," she said suddenly, "are there any dressmakers in town?"

"Hmmph!" The other woman snorted and shook her head. "Not hardly, Abby. When we want something like that done, we either stumble through it our ownselves or go on down to Wolf River. There's a woman there. Charges too damn much for my tastes, though."

"What if there was someone right here in Rock Creek to do dressmaking? Do you think folks would be interested?"

Minerva straightened up and stretched her back. "Reckon so. I know *I* would be. Between the boys, the store, and Alonzo, I purely ain't got the time to be sewin', too."

"Wonderful!" Abby slapped her hand down on the counter top. "You can be my first customer!"

The bag of coffee slipped from Minerva's suddenly nerveless fingers. The woman's eyes widened, and her brows shot straight up. "You, Abby? A dressmaker?"

"Certainly." Abby grinned and walked to the pile of material. "Perhaps I've already told you, Minerva, but back home in Maryland . . . why, folks there thought

I was the finest hand with a needle and thread that they'd ever seen. Of course, I didn't do *just* dressmaking. I also make shirts for men and children. Why, I could do quilts, curtains, tablecloths . . . there's just no end to the business opportunities!"

Minerva sighed heavily when the younger woman lifted the same godawful red-and-yellow-striped material she'd purchased before as shirt material for Samuel. For some unknown reason, Abby Sutton seemed unerringly drawn to the most hideous fabrics. Minerva told herself that she should have known this was coming. She should have been paying more attention. But when Abby got to talkin', sometimes a body just lost count of what she was sayin'. *Now* what was she going to do? Minerva thought frantically. She could hardly tell the poor little thing no. Not after all she'd said about how nice it would be to have a seamstress in town!

But still, visions of *The Hat*, as Minerva had come to think of it, danced before her closed eyes. If Abby could do all that to a plain old bonnet, imagine what she might do to a dress!

"Well, Minerva?" Abby asked excitedly. "What do you think?" The young woman stepped up to the counter, lifted the lid of the closest jar, and took out a piece of rock candy. Then suddenly reached for another one. "For Luke," she said.

Minerva snatched at the boy's name like a drunk after the last bottle of whiskey. "Luke! My, Abby, that's a fine boy. You know, he was so kind to the little ones last night. Obadiah could learn a few things from him, I can tell you."

"Well, I'm glad to hear he was no trouble." Abby smiled. "He *is* a pleasure. I've always loved children, you know. I've missed being around them. It's strange, though, Minerva, he still hasn't said anything about where he came from. About where he belongs." Her smile faltered when she added softly, "He used to cry in his sleep."

Minerva shook her head slowly. "It's a puzzle, all right. Lord knows there's too many orphans runnin' around unchecked in this country. Reckon most of 'em don't have no place to belong. But he surely seems happy up on the mountain with you and Samuel." Her brow furrowed, and she cocked her head. "You give any thought to what's gonna become of the boy after you and Samuel get this land mess all cleared up?"

"What do you mean?" Abby licked at her candy.

"Well"—Minerva picked up the bag of coffee, then moved behind the counter—"just what I say. Once the judge comes in and you two figure out who owns what, where'll Luke be? You figure he'll just head for the hills? Find a new place? New folks?"

Abby moved the candy around in her mouth thoughtfully. Truth to tell, she was ashamed to admit she hadn't given the matter a single thought. Luke had simply become a member of the household. He was *there*. He belonged with them. Abby was almost positive that Samuel felt the same.

Oh, certainly at first, he hadn't been any too pleased with the boy . . . but then, their first meeting hadn't been a perfect one, either. Abby hid a smile when she remembered Luke's well-placed kick. But more and more often, the two of them would go off together. Why, she'd even seen Samuel allowing the boy to help with the animals. Which was more than he'd let *her* do.

The too-sweet candy suddenly turned bitter-tasting.

Heaven help her, she hadn't spent much time thinking about the judge, either. And though she loved Samuel, she couldn't very well depend on his loving her enough to share his home with her. After all, he'd never said anything about love or marriage.

She fished a hankie out of her string bag and took the candy from her mouth. Suddenly worried, Abby told herself that maybe seducing Samuel hadn't been the right thing to do. But she'd needed him so much. Yes, she added silently, but what if you got with child? *Then* what?

Abby swallowed heavily. Good Lord, in all the excitement of that wonderful moment, she'd never even considered that possibility!

"Abby?" Minerva touched her friend's arm. "You all right?"

"Hmmm?" She shook her head and stared at the older woman across from her with new determination. Now it was more important than ever that she begin to make a little money for herself, for Luke, and God help her, possibly a child. "Yes, yes. I'm fine, Minerva. You know, why don't I come back into town tomorrow? Then I could get your measurements, and you could have time to pick out the fabric you'd prefer. There are some *lovely* things over there!"

Minerva groaned helplessly as Abby picked up her packages and headed for the door. There was at least one small thing to be grateful for in all this, Minerva told herself. At least Abby hadn't insisted on picking out the material herself!

Abby cut the fresh bread into generous slices, then stacked them on a small plate before setting it in the center of the table. Here it was, suppertime, and she hadn't seen Luke or Samuel for hours.

As soon as they'd returned from Rock Creek, Luke had raced to Samuel's side, eager to "help." And, Abby told herself with a smile, judging by the incessant pounding of hammers, they'd done quite a bit of work on the new room they were building. Though she hadn't wanted to interrupt their work, Abby *had* enjoyed listening through the cabin walls to the conversations between Luke and Samuel.

No matter how many questions the boy asked, Samuel never lost his patience. She'd overheard him explain the proper way to hammer a nail several times and wasn't sure if she herself could have remained so calm and even-tempered. Abby was positive that Luke's "help" had been much more of a hindrance to the room's progress . . . especially considering how many times the boy had coerced Samuel into playing with Harry and Maverick.

And yet, she was just as sure that the boy would never have reason to suspect it.

She lifted the heavy skillet off the fire grate and carried it to the folded towel in the center of the table. When the poor old lopsided thing didn't even rock, Abby congratulated herself. All it had taken was a small piece of leather folded up and stuffed under the short leg. She hadn't had to bother Samuel with it at all.

"Somethin' smells good, Abby," Samuel called out. Luke was right behind him, nodding his agreement.

"It's only stew again, I'm afraid," Abby said as she ushered the two of them to their chairs. "But what with getting such a late start into town and all . . ." She glanced at Samuel. His pale green eyes caught hers and seemed to glow with the memory of how they'd spent the morning.

"Don't matter to me," Luke said and reached for the serving spoon. "Your stew's almighty good, Abby. Best I ever tasted."

The two adults smiled at each other over his head, then Samuel grabbed a slice of bread and tore off a piece. He popped it into his mouth and after a moment said, "Nothin' better than fresh bread, Abby. Can't remember when I've ate so much of it, either." He tore off another piece. "When I was doin' my own cookin', I only got fresh bread in town. Didn't seem hardly worth the trouble to make it just for me."

Abby served him some of the stew, handed Luke a slice of bread, then filled her own plate. Smiling, she told herself that Samuel had unwittingly given her the perfect opportunity to tell him of her new plan.

"Speaking of bread, Samuel," she said softly, "in town today I was talking to Minerva . . ."

"Yeah?" He grabbed the coffeepot and filled both of their cups.

"Well, she was remarking on how much flour and what not we're going through . . ."

He snorted. "That should please her."

Abby smiled. "Of course it does, but . . ." She waited for him to look at her. "It doesn't seem quite fair to me, Samuel."

"What?"

"The money you've had to spend on supplies in the time I've been here."

His brow furrowed. "What do you mean?"

"Only that since I arrived, we've gone through so much flour and sugar and—so many other things. It must be costing you so much money."

"Don't matter."

"It matters to me."

"Why?"

"Because, since we're sharing this cabin, we should be sharing the expense of running it."

Samuel glanced at Luke and found the boy following the conversation with great interest.

"I told you before, Abby, don't worry about the money. I got plenty enough stashed aside."

"For now." She set her fork down and leaned her elbows on the table. "But how long can it possibly last, Samuel, if you're spending so much of it to keep us all eating?"

From the corner of his eye, Samuel watched Luke set his fork down, too. Eyes downcast, the boy let his hands fall to his lap. Samuel frowned. Why the hell was she sayin' all this now and upsettin' the boy?

"Like I said, Abby, that's for me to worry about."

"No, Samuel."

He dropped his fork and stared at her. "*No,* Samuel?"

"Until the judge comes to town and makes a decision on this property, we are *both* the owners. And I think it's only fair that I contribute my share."

"*Your* share?"

"Well, mine and Luke's of course." Abby smiled at the boy and didn't seem to notice his woebegone expression. "Since it was my idea for Luke to stay here with us, it seems only right that I take on the responsibility for him."

Samuel's mind whirled. Where did all of this come from? She'd been fine that morning. *Better* than fine. One trip into town and she wants to turn everything upside down? He looked at the boy again and ground his teeth together. Couldn't she see what she was doing to the child's pride? For God's sake. Bein' talked about like he wasn't there was bad enough. But the way she was sayin' it, the boy prob'ly felt like a beggar at a weddin'.

"Abby," he finally said as his mind raced through the ABCs, "I don't know what got you all het up like this, but I'm tellin' you one thing right now. Ain't you or me payin' this child's way."

"What?" Confusion etched on her features, Abby stared at him. Samuel noticed that Luke's eyes were studying him, too.

"Luke," Samuel said, turning toward the child slumped in his seat, "do you feed the chickens?"

"Yessir."

"Collect the eggs?"

"Yessir."

"Muck out the barn?"

"Yessir."

"Help me with the sick animals?"

Luke smiled. "Yessir, when you let me."

Samuel nodded briefly and shot a glance at Abby. "That there is what I mean. You got no need to pay for that boy. He pays his own way."

Luke straightened perceptibly and began to eat again. Samuel nodded his approval and turned to Abby. "And you. You do all the cookin', cleanin', sewin', and everything else you can lay a hand to. I ain't never lived this good." He looked at the boy. "Have you?"

"No, sir," Luke answered and reached for another slice of bread.

"See, Abby?" Samuel said, his voice softer now. "We all pay our own way around here." He picked up his fork again and bent to his supper.

Abby's gaze moved from one to the other of them

and finally rested on the big man across from her. He seemed to think everything was settled. She laced her fingers together and rested her chin on them.

Well, she wasn't finished yet.

Chapter Fifteen

"I understand what you're saying, Samuel," she began, "but I don't agree."

Man and boy stared at her.

Well, for heaven's sake, she told herself, she hadn't meant to stir all of this up. And goodness knows, she'd had no intention of insulting Luke, though she admitted silently she could see that she'd managed to do just that. If not for Samuel, she'd have hurt the boy's feelings badly, if unintentionally. So, before they could misunderstand her again, she went on.

"Oh, you're perfectly right about Luke. I should have said that myself." She turned to the child. "Luke, you work just as hard as any of us, and Samuel is quite right. You more than pay your way here."

Luke grinned happily. "Thanks, Abby," he said on a rush. "Samuel and me, we was workin' real hard today tryin' to finish up your room for ya. And Samuel taught me how to hammer a straight nail and how to saw, and he says I can paint the whole room all by myself, seein's how I done such a good job on the rest of the cabin. . . ."

She nodded, took a breath and tried to interrupt, but Luke was too fast for her.

"Course, it was too late to finish up the room tonight, so we strung up a canvas roof over the whole mess so's in case it rains we won't have no mud in there."

She glanced at Samuel. He shrugged his massive shoulders and sighed.

"That's a good idea, Luke," Abby said quickly.

"Oh, the canvas was Samuel's doin'." The boy looked up at his hero with wide eyes. "He can do just about anythin'."

Samuel frowned self-consciously and picked up his coffee cup. "Well, we'll get that roof on for you tomorrow, Abby. Matter of fact, we could maybe use your help."

"I'm sorry, Samuel, but I won't be able to tomorrow."

"Why not?"

"Because I have to go back to town tomorrow." She stood up and carried her plate to the small wooden counter behind her. "I'm going to be a dressmaker, Samuel. And tomorrow I have to meet with my first customer. Minerva."

"What?"

"Yes." She turned around to face him. "That's what I was talking about earlier. I've decided on a way to help out more around here. I'm a fine seamstress, Samuel. And the money I make will be my contribution."

"I don't want your money, Abby," he said flatly.

"But—"

"No *buts.*" He threw a quick glance at Luke, then

turned back to Abby. "I said I got plenty to see us through."

His features unreadable, Abby continued to stare at him, trying to understand. Did he think so little of her then that her help wouldn't be appreciated? Didn't he see how important this was to her?

"I want to help," she said stubbornly.

"Help? By drivin' my horses up and down the mountain day after day? How the hell is *that* gonna help?"

"You didn't seem to mind before. . . ."

His fists clenched, and she could see his lips moving in some silent muttering. "That was *before*. You weren't talkin' about goin' down to Rock Creek regular. And while we're talkin' about this . . . how do you figure to do all your sewin' for folks in the dead of winter?"

She stood silent.

"Didn't think on that, did you?" He nodded victoriously. "Come wintertime, Abby, the cabin is mostly snowed in. That's why I get my supplies in before winter. 'Cause you can't count on gettin' down that road."

She gripped her fingers together. "All right, Samuel. Perhaps you're right."

"*Perhaps?*"

"But I could work until the judge comes, anyway." She lifted her chin slightly. "For all we know, I may not be here during the winter. The judge could very well give over the land to you, and then where would I be? I must have *something* to see me through the winter, one way or another."

His green eyes widened slightly at her statement. Then in a soft, hushed voice he said, "Whatever happens with the judge, Abby, you know you could stay here."

She could stay, he said. Abby swallowed heavily. He said nothing about love or marriage. Just that she could stay. Like Luke. She could earn her keep. Only she wouldn't be earning it by cleaning out the barn. Abby felt like crawling under the table and hiding. It was all her own fault. She'd given herself to him so eagerly, of course he would think poorly of her. But still, to make an offer like that. A stab of hurt and shame slashed through her. Somehow, she hadn't expected the ache to be so deep. If she'd had any doubts at all about becoming a seamstress, they were gone now.

Clearly, she'd been wrong. Samuel didn't love her. Yet.

"No, Samuel," she whispered, blinking back the tears in her eyes. "I couldn't stay where I don't belong rightfully."

His face paled, and Abby had to fight down the urge to go to him. But she stood in place, her hands tightly clasped, her chin lifted. Finally he lowered his gaze, shifted his feet, and turned to stand up.

When he did, his foot kicked the piece of leather from beneath the table leg, and his knee upset the delicate balance. The rickety table rocked, creaked, then tipped over. The skillet fell with a loud crash and stew spilled out onto the wooden floor. China plates brought all the way from Maryland shattered into delicately flowered ceramic shards, and hot coffee seeped through the cracks of the floorboards.

Harry whined softly and backed away from the mess. Maverick took a position next to Luke and seemed reassured by the boy's hand on his neck.

For a long moment no one said anything. Samuel's gaze locked on Abby's, and they stood grimly staring at each other. Finally he spoke.

"I told you once, Abby. I like things the way they are. If you hadn't tried to 'fix' that damned table . . . none of this would have happened." He spread his arms wide and shook his head. "Why'd you have to change everything?"

She knew he wasn't talking about the table. "I only tried to make things right, Samuel." Abby's voice was choked.

Luke watched as slowly Samuel's arms dropped. Then the big man turned and walked outside. The boy looked at Abby and saw the tears she was fighting so hard to hide. Quietly Luke motioned for the dogs to follow him and left the cabin so Abby could let go and have her cry.

Once outside, Luke ignored the sounds of Samuel's hammer and walked instead to the deserted barn. He went back to the corner stall and fell onto the stacked hay. Something was very wrong.

His small hand moved over Maverick's big head as he went over the scene in the cabin again. He didn't understand exactly what had happened, but Luke was pretty sure that Abby and Samuel hadn't been that angry over a few broken plates.

They'd been talkin' about something else altogether, he decided. And whatever it was, he was afraid that his peaceful time in the cabin was near over.

"Where'll I go now, Maverick?" His small voice was swallowed by the silence of the immense barn. The dog turned and licked Luke's face as though sensing the child's distress and hoping to ease it. "Why is it I can't find me a place? A place to stay?" Luke's fingers curled in Maverick's fur and tightened when he added softly, "I tried really hard this time, boy. I surely did.

And I thought, maybe . . ."

Leaning down toward the big dog, Luke buried his face in Maverick's neck and cried. Softly at first, as though he didn't remember how, Luke let the tears come until they shook his small body with the full force of the blow that had smashed his newfound safety.

Samuel lay in the dark, staring up at the ceiling. The bundling board was back in place, and he could hear Abby breathing quietly. It irritated him that she could sleep so easily.

He turned his head when Luke started muttering in his sleep. The boy was tossing and turning in his blankets, wrapping himself up tightly in the tangled mess. Samuel sighed and threw his forearm over his eyes. It was the first time in days that Luke had spent a restless night. And Samuel knew that what had happened over supper was somehow responsible.

A log in the fireplace snapped and broke apart. The wind outside made a steady droning sound that was the perfect lonely accompaniment to Samuel's bleak thoughts.

What had made her do it? What had happened to convince Abby to suddenly find a way of making money? He'd thought she was happy. And after the night spent in each other's arms, Samuel'd allowed himself to believe that perhaps she would want to stay. Instead, she started talkin' about the judge and maybe havin' to leave.

Samuel shifted position and tugged at the quilt. The judge. How the hell had he forgotten about the judge and the damned hearing? When Abby first arrived at the cabin, all he'd been able to think about was getting this whole mess straightened out and having the cabin to himself again. Now, after only a few weeks, just the thought of Abby leavin' turned him to butter.

Luke moaned softly, and Samuel winced. Who would have thought that he'd come to care so much for a scrawny, independent little cuss like that? But he did. And Samuel knew without a doubt that if Abby left, so would Luke.

Dammit, he *knew* she loved the mountain. The cabin. And she even seemed to have some feeling for him. Maybe, he thought suddenly, he could ask her to marry him. Then they could both stay on the mountain. Luke would stay. They could all be a family. A real family.

His lips twisted sardonically, and he flopped over onto his side. Marry *him*? *Abby*? No. A pretty little thing like her wouldn't want to marry up with a big, ugly, ignorant fool who lives on mountaintops to avoid people. But, his brain taunted, she went to bed with you. She *must* care something about you. . . .

He punched his pillow and closed his eyes determinedly. Beddin' and weddin' are two almighty different things, he told himself sternly, and there ain't no use in pretendin' otherwise.

Why was she so hell-bent on ruining everything? Why couldn't she just be happy with the way things were? Like him.

"Samuel—" Abby caught his arm just as he was walking out the door.

He stopped but didn't look at her. "What is it, Abby?"

"Would you like to go to town with me today? You and Luke, I mean?"

His green eyes focused on her. She noticed the red streaks and knew he'd gotten as little sleep as she had. She'd lain awake for hours, thinking over every little thing he'd said at dinner. And though she was willing to admit that perhaps Samuel didn't love her . . . she was quite sure of her own feelings. She loved Samuel. That wouldn't change. And she refused to feel shame for what they'd done together. Somewhere deep inside him, Abby knew that Samuel cared for her. If not love, then at least a fondness. And that was a start.

"Why?" he asked.

Abby took a deep breath. He wasn't going to give an inch. If they were to make up at all, she knew it would have to be her doing. And since she wasn't at all sure exactly why he was acting so strangely, it wouldn't be easy. The only thing she could try was being completely honest.

"Samuel," she began, her fingers smoothing over the back of his hand, "why are you so upset? Does it really matter so much if I want to help buy supplies?"

His free hand clamped down over hers, stilling her movements. He couldn't think when she touched him. Samuel's brain raced, looking for the right thing to say. How could he tell her that he was terrified of her earning her own money? She would never understand that to him it meant one thing. Having money of her own would make it too easy for her to leave him.

He couldn't. Instead, he lied. "That ain't it, Abby. It's just that I don't like the idea of you goin' up and down the mountain all alone regular like." She smiled, the shadows lifted from her eyes, and he went on. "There's wild animals—some folks just as wild—and anything could happen to the horses or wagon, leavin' you flat-out stuck. And alone."

"Oh, I'd be very careful, Samuel," she said, "and maybe you could go to town with me. . . ."

"I got plenty to do right here, Abby. Gettin' ready for winter and such—"

"Oh," she cut in quickly, "I didn't mean *all* the time. But *sometimes?*"

His thumb moved slowly across the back of her hand, and as he stared down into her eyes, Samuel knew he was lost. All through their quiet, uncomfortable breakfast together, Samuel had *wanted* to say something. But he'd had no idea what. He remembered the cautious uneasiness in Luke's eyes. The forced, polite remarks Abby'd made in hopes of easing the tension. And he remembered wishing that he could put an end to everyone's discomfort. Here was his chance.

"Sometimes," he agreed softly.

"Starting today?"

Samuel shook his head resignedly. He ought to have known by now that once you agreed to something, Abby didn't much care for waiting around. "All right, Abby. Starting today."

She stood on her toes to kiss him quickly, then grinned and started through the door. "I'll get Luke. We'll be ready in just a shake!"

Standing in the doorway, Samuel stared after her. She moved with an easy grace that never failed to captivate him. He leaned against the doorjamb and studied the sway of her hips, the determination in her stride. Suddenly he chuckled and noted that today she was wearing some kind of pink dress with a bright blue ribbon wrapped around her waist and tied in a huge bow at the small of her back.

A *dressmaker?*

Poor Minerva.

*   *   *

By the time they reached Rock Creek, Samuel was glad he'd given in to Abby. Luke was smiling again, despite the fact that wariness still shone in his eyes. Abby, as quick to forget as she was to forgive, had chattered happily all the way to town. Clearly, she was willing to put their little disagreement behind them. Samuel only wished he could.

Not that he was angry, he told himself. It was just the thought of Abby havin' some ready cash that worried him.

Samuel left Luke and Abby at Mullins's Mercantile and went on down the street to the Lucky Lady Saloon with Alonzo Mullins. Samuel still found it hard to accept that the people of Rock Creek were not only unafraid of him, but actually seemed to *like* him.

"Sure am glad you showed up when you did, Sam," Alonzo was saying. "Minerva's a fine woman, don't get me wrong now, but she liked to run my legs clean off this morning. Do this, do that. It's a wonder the woman's lips don't drop off into the dirt, the way she's forever flappin' 'em!"

Samuel chuckled softly and climbed the three short steps to the saloon. Alonzo pushed ahead of him into the darkened building and heaved a sigh of satisfaction as he marched to the bar.

"Gimme a beer, Dave, will ya?" he said to the bartender, then turned to his companion. "Beer all right with you, Sam?"

Samuel nodded.

"Make it two."

Drinks in hand, Samuel followed Alonzo to a table in the far corner. As they sat down, Alonzo took a long gulp of his beer and sighed happily.

"One thing I'll say for Sarah Dumont. Her beer's always cold."

Samuel's fingers toyed with the long, thick stem of the heavy glass goblet and let his gaze drift lazily over the Lucky Lady. One of the fanciest saloons he'd ever seen, Samuel had never really felt comfortable stopping by for a drink before. He'd always expected someone to start a fight. Usually, it was some young sprout eager to prove himself against a much bigger man.

With a start, Samuel realized that he hadn't done much worrying about things like that since Abby's arrival. He'd been much too busy worrying over his reaction to *her*.

"Like I said before, Sam," Alonzo said, breaking into his thoughts, "I'm glad you came to town today."

Samuel leaned into the curved back of his chair and laid his forearms on the worn, maple armrests. He studied the other man thoughtfully for a long moment. For the first time Samuel noticed that Alonzo was decidedly nervous.

The thin man's lips were twitching, his pale fingers drummed on the scarred tabletop, and he was having trouble meeting Samuel's direct gaze.

"Somethin' wrong?" Samuel asked quietly.

"Hmmm?" Alonzo jumped. "Oh, no. No, nothin' wrong. Not really. It's just that—"

The batwing doors behind them swung open, sending a shaft of sunlight into the dim saloon. Buck Whitehall signaled to the bartender, then walked to the table and sat down opposite Samuel.

"Did ya tell him yet?" he asked Alonzo.

"Not yet," the man grumbled. "Been workin' up to it."

Samuel's eyes narrowed slightly as he looked from one man to the other. The bartender set a beer in front of Buck and walked away.

Buck lifted the drink to his lips, drank, and commented, "Hell, I'll say it if you won't."

"*I* was elected," Alonzo retorted. "*I'll* do it."

Samuel shifted uneasily. He didn't much like any of this.

"Sam," Alonzo started, "the folks of Rock Creek done elected me to talk to you."

"He *knows* that," Buck grumbled.

"*And*," Alonzo said a little louder, with a pointed look at Buck, "if *some* folks would hush, I'd do just that." He turned his gaze on Samuel and lowered his voice slightly. "The thing is, Sam, folks was mighty impressed with how you handled yourself during that little set-to at the barn raisin'."

Samuel nodded and fought down the urge to get up and leave.

"Well, thing of it is," Alonzo went on "our sheriff, Pete James? Well, he ain't never been much of a lawman—" He broke off and waited for Samuel's reaction. There wasn't one. "And ever since that little fracas down to the Coleses' place, well, folks've been talkin' your name up some to be the new sheriff." Now that he was finished, Alonzo's breath rushed out, and he grabbed up his beer and drank it down.

Samuel's jaw dropped open, and he quickly snapped it shut. He sat silently, watching the other two men. Whatever he'd been expecting, it hadn't been *this*. Deliberately he kept his expression blank. He needed time to think.

Both men were watching him with anticipation. He had to say something. Anything.

"Uh," he began, surprised to find that his voice worked, "I don't know about this. I'd have to think on it some."

"Hell, 'course you do." Alonzo smiled and pushed himself to his feet. "We wasn't expectin' you to just jump at the job." He tugged at Buck's jacket, urging him to stand. "In fact, I already told most of the folks that I reckon you're not gonna want to give up your mountain to move down into town."

Buck stood and added, "But *I* said that any man'd rather have a job with ready money instead of livin' hand to mouth trappin' and such."

Samuel didn't say a word. After another long moment of silence, Buck and Alonzo started backing away from the table, hesitant smiles on their faces.

"Well, now," Alonzo said, "you just take your time, Sam. The sheriff ain't much, but he ain't doin' any harm, neither. So there's no rush, y'understand."

"We'll leave you be now, Sam," Buck intoned and slapped at Alonzo's shoulder to get the man moving a little faster.

"Uh, right." Alonzo moved for the door. "Minerva'll be gettin' a little fractious by now. If she don't get to order me about some every now and then, she gets ornery."

The creaking saloon doors swung wildly with the men's departure, letting sunlight flash and dim like the sun was winking.

Sheriff. Samuel lifted his beer and took a long drink. Sheriff? Who would've thought it? Of course, he told himself silently, he wouldn't take the job . . . and yet . . . He smiled and rubbed his hand across his freshly shaven jaw. A small seed of pleasure rested deep within him.

For the first time in his life Samuel knew what it felt like to be wanted. No, he corrected. Not just wanted. Needed. He knew all about Sheriff James. A good enough man, he supposed, but not one on close terms with hard work. Why, now that he thought on it, Samuel couldn't remember a time when he'd seen the sheriff *outside* his office.

He chuckled softly as he thought that the man's boots must last forever. They almost never hit the ground. As far as Samuel knew, they never got farther than bein' propped up on the big desk at the jailhouse.

Imagine that, he told himself. Folks want Samuel Hart to be *sheriff*. Samuel smiled behind his hand and looked quickly around the nearly empty saloon. Didn't want anyone to see him sittin' by himself grinnin' at nothin'.

With the fingers of his right hand, Samuel absently drew patterns in the water rings left by the beer mugs. Just two months ago, if someone had told him that he'd be offered such a job, he'd have thought the person completely mad. His brows quirked as he realized that two months ago, no one would have told him anything, 'cause nobody talked to him.

Not until Abby.

He sighed and leaned back. Closing his eyes, he willed her image up before him. Samuel could hardly credit the changes that one little woman had made in his life. Not only did he have a real home . . . even down to a *child* . . . but for the first time ever, he had *friends*. People who were actually glad to see him. Folks wantin' to chew the fat with him. A whole town wantin' to trust their safety to *him*.

Samuel opened his eyes and stared down at the

scratched tabletop. If not for Abby, he'd be what he'd always been. A man alone. No, he amended silently. A lonely man. There was a difference.

He couldn't let her leave.

Chapter Sixteen

"Samuel Hart?"

He glanced up at the owner of the husky, whisper-soft voice, then hurriedly clambered to his feet.

Sarah Dumont smiled at his obvious discomfort. Clearly, she told herself, he was a man not used to being around women much. As he straightened up and righted the glass of beer he'd spilled in his hurry, Sarah took pity on him and gave him a friendly grin.

"Slow down, Mr. Hart. I'm not known for bein' a deadly foe. *Dangerous* maybe. But not deadly."

Samuel shifted from foot to foot uneasily. "Sorry about that mess, ma'am. Don't know when I been that clumsy."

She waved his apology aside. "It's not the first beer spilled in here, and it for sure won't be the last." Sarah turned and called to her bartender, "Dave, bring us a couple of beers and a towel for the table."

That done, she looked up at Samuel again. "Mind if I sit down for a while?"

His gaze shot to hers, then quickly turned away. Pulling a chair out from the table, he said gruffly, "Pleasure, ma'am. A pleasure."

She sat down, smoothed her skirts, then leaned her elbows on the table, neatly avoiding the spilled beer. Samuel still stood uncertainly. Glancing up at him, she shook her head slightly. "You gonna stand all day, or are you goin' to join me?"

"Sorry, ma'am." He sat down before the only dry spot, in the chair right beside Sarah. Stiff as a board, Samuel curled his fingers over the ends of the armrests.

Sarah noticed and rolled her eyes. She must be gettin' old, she told herself. Time was when men fought each other to sit by her side. And she *never* remembered a time when a man was *this* jumpy just sittin'.

Dave brought a fresh round of drinks and wiped the table clean without a word spoken. As soon as he was gone, Sarah lifted her glass and admired the bright golden yellow liquid for a moment before taking a sip. She noticed Samuel watching her and explained, "I don't like to be rushed, Mr. Hart. I *do* enjoy takin' the time to fully enjoy *all* life's little pleasures."

Samuel looked down, and if she hadn't known better, Sarah would have sworn he was blushing. But she knew that was impossible. Grown men didn't blush. She waited for him to swallow his gulp of beer, then she said what she'd come to say.

"I saw how you handled yourself at the barn raisin'."

He looked up.

"Made the rest of the men around here look like boys in a schoolyard brawl."

"Well, uh . . ."

Sarah lifted one hand to shush him. "But that ain't what I wanted to talk to you about." She smiled at his obvious surprise. "Oh, I know about how the town's wantin' you to be sheriff . . . prob'ly a good idea. But that's their business."

Puzzled, Samuel stared at her.

"I stick to runnin' my own business." Then she chuckled softly. "Guess that ain't all the time true, or I wouldn't be sittin' here with you." Sarah shot him a quick look. "I don't mean nothin' by that, you understand . . . but I don't go up and talk to just anybody anymore. Don't have to. I own this place."

"Yes, ma'am."

Her lips quirked. "You think you could call me Sarah instead of ma'am? I'm commencin' to feel like a homely schoolmarm at a box social!"

Samuel smiled and nodded.

Sarah's breath caught, and for just a moment she found herself wishing that she *was* a schoolmarm and that his lady friend didn't exist. The big ol' mountain man had cleaned up into something special. But, she reminded herself firmly, the time for changin' her ways was long past, and not many men were willin' to overlook a little thing like bein' a madam.

"Anyhow," she went on, "like I was sayin'. Most times I mind my own business. Better that way. For everybody." Sarah looked up and met his gaze. "But this time . . . well hell, I *may* be wrong about this, too."

"What?"

She had his complete attention now. "You recall those two cowboys who started the ruckus at the barn raisin'?"

Samuel nodded.

"Well, they were in here later that night. The two of 'em so drunk it wasn't safe to strike a match." She reached up and smoothed the sides of her hair back.

"They were doin' a lot of talkin', too. Mostly about you. And your lady friend."

His brows drew together over suddenly narrowed eyes. "What'd they say?"

"Only that they were real mad with you. And that they were still set on havin' a dance with your woman."

He relaxed a little. "That don't sound too bad. Could be it was just the whiskey talkin'."

"Could be." Sarah pushed away from the table and stood up. She ran her hands over her hips, smoothing the fall of her bright green, knee-length satin skirt. "Either way, I figured you ought to know."

He nodded and stood up. " 'Preciate it."

Sarah followed him to the door and stepped out onto the porch with him. "You know, them two ain't really so bad as they think they are."

"Yeah." Samuel adjusted the brim of his hat and squinted out into the sunlit street. "I know." Most of the men he'd had trouble with in his life weren't really *bad* men. And these two cowhands were probably no more than young and stupid. But that didn't make them any less dangerous.

He looked down when Sarah's hand touched his arm. She was staring thoughtfully up at him.

"This ain't any of my business, either," she said softly, "but if that lady friend of yours ever ups and leaves . . . you come see me, Samuel Hart." A slow smile curved her lips as her hand slid up the length of his arm to the back of his neck. "I do believe you and me'd get along just fine."

Samuel backed away and went down the steps to the street. Once at a safe distance, he said, "Yes, ma'am. Thank you."

Sarah leaned against the porch post and watched the big man walk away. Her eyes skimmed over his muscled body and long-legged, light-footed stride. She gave a long sigh of regret, then turned around and went back where she belonged. Her saloon.

Minerva stood beside Abby, giving her last-minute instructions on the dress she would be making.

"Now, remember, Abby," she said with just a touch of panic in her voice, "no fancy froo-froos. Just a good old-fashioned Sunday church dress."

"I understand, Minerva." Abby ran her hand over the plain navy blue wool fabric. "But I still think a few yellow rosettes would look stunning. We could line them along the edges of the bodice and—"

"Abby—"

She frowned. "All right. No rosettes."

Minerva breathed a sigh of relief. Although she wouldn't be able to rest completely until she had the finished gown in her possession and was sure that it would be fit to wear. Heaven knew it had taken every ounce of her stubbornness to talk Abby out of using *orange satin* for a church dress!

Shielding her eyes from the sun, Minerva saw Samuel hurrying down the street toward them. Looking just past him, she spied Sarah Dumont standing on the porch of her place. As Samuel came closer, Minerva shook her head. Yep. Just as she'd thought. Samuel Hart had the same look every other man carried on his face after he'd spent a little time with Sarah. Like he'd been poleaxed. Minerva nudged Abby and pointed toward Samuel.

"Looka there. Don't know what it is that woman's got," Minerva said with reluctant admiration, "but durned if she don't turn every man she talks to into a red-faced, blithering idiot."

Abby followed her friend's gaze. She noted Samuel's agitated appearance, then looked on down the road and saw Sarah turn and go back into the saloon. What in heaven was going on? Samuel looked worried.

For two days Samuel had hardly stirred from the cabin. He kept thinking about Sarah Dumont's warning. It was prob'ly nothing, he knew. But still, he didn't want to take any chances with Abby's safety. Course, he didn't want to tell her any of this. He knew what her reaction would be. She would brush aside any concerns he had and insist that the two cowhands were perfectly harmless.

Besides, he told himself, he kind of enjoyed having her so curious about his visit with Sarah Dumont. Samuel chuckled, jabbed the pitchfork into the pile of hay, and tossed a forkful down to the barn floor below. He could see it in her eyes every time she talked to him. It was *killin'* Abby not to ask what he and Sarah had talked about. And the suspicion that Abby was just a little bit jealous was just too good a feeling to let go of so soon . . . so Samuel hadn't said a word.

And Lord knew that there was plenty for him to do around the cabin to keep him busy. He'd spent most of the last two days finishing up Abby's room. Tonight would be her first night in there, and Samuel sincerely hoped she'd be wanting him to join her.

It seemed like a hundred years since he'd touched her last.

He paused in his work, bent down, and looked out the second-story barn window toward the cabin. The fresh coat of white paint really made a difference in how the place looked. The cabin appeared almost proud of itself, settin' there all nice and shiny, surrounded by dark green pines and autumn gold aspens. Samuel sighed and told himself that it would have looked even better if he hadn't let Abby talk him into painting the trim such a bright pink! But, he thought with a smile, better on the outside of the place than the inside!

His gaze shifted slightly to the cabin yard. Abby had set up a chair and table in the bright sunshine and was working on that dress for Minerva. From what he could tell, she hadn't been exaggerating her abilities with a needle and thread. And she was almighty fast, too. The dress was near completed.

Samuel watched as Abby set the dress in her lap and raised her arms high over her head to stretch her muscles. Slowly, languidly, she moved her arms and rolled her head from side to side. Samuel gripped the handle of the pitchfork tightly and tried to breathe evenly as the fabric of her simple gown pulled across her breasts. Her eyes were closed, and she seemed to be soaking in the sunlight. Her deep chestnut hair shone with flashes of red and fell almost to the ground as she leaned back in her chair, a soft smile on her face.

"Samuel?"

He jumped, grabbed at the windowsill, and looked over his shoulder at the loft ladder. Luke's head appeared as the boy climbed up.

"Samuel?" he said again, louder this time. "I finished collectin' the eggs. You gonna let me help with the animals now like you said?"

"Uh . . . yeah." Samuel took a deep, shuddering breath and turned his back on the window. He crossed the loft, and when Luke started down the ladder, Samuel followed.

*   *   *

"He sure is a fine-lookin' wolf," Luke said softly.

Samuel's hand moved carefully over the animal's bandage. He kept a wary eye open, ready just in case the wolf changed his mind about accepting help. When he was finished, he slowly backed out of the cage and closed the door behind him. Not until he was safely outside again did he answer the boy.

"Yeah, he is, Luke." Samuel sat in the dirt, looking up at him. "But he's still a wild animal . . . and even more dangerous when he's hurt."

"He don't seem to mind you none."

"True." The man glanced at the cage behind him. "But you just never know when or if he'll turn on you."

Luke mumbled something Samuel didn't quite hear. "What was that?"

The boy shrugged and said offhandedly, "Nothin'. Just that he's no different from some folks that way. I mean about . . . turnin' on ya."

This was the first time Luke had volunteered anything at all about his past, and Samuel wanted to hear more. There had to be a reason that a child like him was all alone.

"You know some folks like that, do you?" he asked.

The fawn belonging to the caged, injured doe wandered over toward the boy. Its long spindly legs shook with each step, and its sharp nose twitched delicately as it sniffed at Luke's bent head.

Thoughtfully the boy ran his hand over the curve of the fawn's neck and down its back. The little animal moved closer to the affection, nuzzling Luke's arm. Quietly the boy said, "Used to. While back."

Samuel held his breath. He didn't want to make any mistakes now. Finally he decided to wait and let Luke decide if he wanted to go on.

After a small eternity passed, Luke spoke again.

"My real folks, they died on a wagon train." He looked up at Samuel. "We was headed for California. My pa, he wanted to get a farm. Heard most anything'd grow out there." Luke let himself slump down onto the ground, where he sat with his shoulders slumped, hands in his lap. "But Ma—well, she took awful sick. Don't rightly know what it was, but she was real poorly for quite a time, then—she died. Pa buried her on the trail. He found a nice little tree to put her under so's she'd always have a shady spot to rest." He took a deep breath. "Pa didn't seem to care much about anything after she went . . . and one night while he was ridin' guard on the wagon train's animals, somethin' spooked his horse, and he fell off and broke his neck."

Samuel watched the boy. It pained him to see the remembered hurt on the child's face. Even more so to watch him try to hide it.

Luke sniffed, rubbed one hand over his eyes, and added "Anyhow, the captain of the train took me in. I'd knowed him since Independence, always seemed a nice fella." His fingers continued to pet the tiny deer. "But the thing was, he turned out to be kinda like that wolf there. Real nice most of the time, but every once in a while he'd turn on a body for no reason." Luke raised his gaze to Samuel. "I stayed with him almost three years. But the last time he hit me, I lit out. That was pretty near a year ago now. Been on my own since."

Samuel kept his face from showing any of the fury that was raging inside him. Luke was ten years old.

So that meant that the bastard wagon train captain had started in hitting on a six-year-old boy! At that moment Samuel wanted nothing more in his life than to have that man in front of him for just five minutes! Five minutes would be all he needed to make sure the man never harmed another child.

Luke sat across from him, still as death. His eyes fixed on the deer, his hands slack.

Samuel remembered his first look at the boy. Half-starved, shoeless, cold, and more lonely than anyone should have to be. And still, after all he'd been through, Luke had a shining heart. Ready to love. Wanting to trust.

It made a man ashamed of complaining about his own little problems.

He looked at Luke. The boy seemed to be waiting for something. Perhaps Samuel's approval? "You done a fine job on your own, Luke. I know some grown men couldn't have done no better."

The boy smiled, obviously relieved. "Yeah, I did all right, I reckon." He looked at Samuel and added softly, "But it surely is nice havin' a place to stay . . . and *folks*."

"I know just what you mean, boy." Samuel glanced from the smiling boy to Abby, still sewing in the sun. "It surely is nice." He turned back to the child. Samuel said slowly, "I want you to know somethin', Luke."

The boy's wide blue eyes stared at him.

"What I said the other day . . . about you earnin' your keep? Well, I meant that . . . and . . ." Samuel rubbed his hand over his jaw nervously. "Hell, I just want to tell you that you got a home. Right here. As long as you want it, boy."

Luke grinned briefly, then glanced over at Abby.

"No matter what happens between me and Abby . . . or who ends up ownin' this place . . . it's *your* home." That was a safe promise to make. Samuel well knew that once Abby heard the child's sad tale, there would be no stopping her from cuddling and coddling him to death. No matter what . . . Samuel wanted Luke to feel—safe.

The boy's lips twisted, and the muscles in his throat quivered. Samuel knew Luke was doing everything he could to keep from crying. In fact, he felt an unfamiliar dampness in his own eyes. To spare them both, he quickly changed the subject and said a little gruffly, "How about you and me go on over to the creek and catch us some fish for dinner?"

"You mean it?" The boy's eyes lit up in anticipation.

"Hell, yes, I mean it. We done enough work for one day!" Besides, Samuel told himself. The creek is only a short holler away. If Abby needed him . . . if anything should happen . . . he could be back to her in seconds. Right now he just wanted to make the boy in front of him happy. "Well," he said, "git! Go fetch the poles. I'll put the fawn back in with his mama and get some bread dough from the cabin for bait."

Luke grinned, leapt up, and raced for the barn.

Abby tied a knot in the thread and neatly snipped it off with her scissors. Minerva's dress was finished. As she tucked the needle back into its case, Abby thought regretfully that the yellow rosettes would have given the simple gown such an elegant touch. But then, she sighed and told herself, it was more important to prove to customers that she was able to do the work well and quickly than it was to give them fashion advice.

She rolled her head on her neck slowly, to ease out the kinks in her tired muscles, and listened absently to Samuel and Luke as they squabbled over their checker game. Abby glanced covertly at the pair across the room from her.

Man and boy were seated opposite each other at the no-longer-rickety table. Abby smiled. Samuel had fixed the table only the day before, and she'd been wise enough not to say a word about it. As they bent over their game, arguing affably over which move would be the better one, Abby took the time to study Luke.

Relaxed and happy, the boy seemed perfectly content with his world. Samuel was probably right, she knew. It was best if they simply treated Luke as they always had. No doubt it would only dredge up dreadful memories for the child if they spoke of his past again. Abby's fingers clenched in her lap. Still, every time she thought of the tale Samuel had repeated to her, Abby wanted to scream. That anyone should treat a child so shamelessly . . . She shook her head. It was over. Luke was safe now. And would always be. She completely agreed with Samuel's promise to the boy and knew that she would do everything in her power to see that he was never hurt again.

Carefully she folded Minerva's dress and let her gaze drift over the cabin. Everything neat and tidy, and the little house glowed with warmth. From the crackling fire to the soft lamplight, to Luke's and Samuel's voices, the cabin filled her with a comforting peace. Maverick and Harry snored gently by the hearth, and the wind outside batted at the windowpanes. She was home.

With her lips curved in a smile, Abby pushed herself to her feet and said quietly, "I'm off to bed."

Luke and Samuel looked up from their game of checkers.

"Good night, you two." She smiled and gathered up her sewing kit. "We'll have to be up early if we expect to make it to church in time for the services."

Samuel grimaced, and Luke whined, "Aw, Abby, why ever did you tell that preacher we'd go to service?"

"We've been through this already." She tried to look stern and failed. "Reverend Knight made a special effort to invite us." Actually, she told herself, it was *Mrs.* Knight who'd hustled down to Mullins's Mercantile with the special invitation . . . but they didn't need to know that. "Besides," Abby went on when Samuel started to speak, "as Samuel's always saying, soon it will be winter, and there'll be too much snow to make it down the mountain."

Luke's face brightened.

"Don't see no need to go," Samuel said softly, not meeting Abby's gaze.

"We're a part of this town, Samuel. It's only right to worship with our friends and neighbors."

He began to mumble again, but she ignored him. "Oh, and Luke, thank you again for dinner." Abby smiled. "Best fish I ever ate!"

"Samuel cooked 'em," Luke said.

"But *you* caught them," Abby retorted. "Without you, he'd have had nothing to cook."

Samuel feigned outrage. "Told you, they weren't bitin'."

Abby winked at Luke. "Well, they weren't biting *your* hook, anyway, Samuel."

Luke muffled his giggle with a hand over his mouth.

"All right, have your laugh. Both of you." Samuel shook his finger at Luke. "But I'm winnin' this here game, ain't I?"

"Ain't over yet," Luke crowed and brushed his too-long hair out of his eyes.

Abby shook her head and walked to her room. At the door she turned and looked back. Samuel's gaze was waiting. Her heart thudded painfully, and her insides twisted as she read the desire etched on his features. And though she'd already called herself a fool many times over for risking a pregnancy, Abby knew she wanted him just as badly. Whatever the consequences, she would accept them readily to have more time with Samuel.

If she ended up having to leave this place, she wanted at least to carry the memories of him with her. And if she carried a child away, too . . . well, she could always move west and tell folks her husband had died.

Heat rushed up her cheeks. Abby could hardly credit that she had come to this. That she was willing to risk everything she'd always held dear . . . her reputation, her pride . . . for the love of Samuel Hart.

She shook herself from her wayward thoughts and saw Samuel's eyes reaching for her. Abby knew that he would come to her as soon as he could.

Slowly, pretending a calm she didn't feel, Abby went into her new room and closed the door behind her. Quietly she undressed and slipped under the blankets.

Her new room was small, but large enough for her. The smell of the forest still clung to the unpainted boards, and she inhaled it gratefully, hoping to calm herself.

The last two days had stretched her nerves to the breaking point. She and Samuel hadn't had a moment to themselves, even though the only time he'd left the cabin had been to go fishing with Luke.

In fact, it was almost as if he felt he *couldn't* leave the cabin. After knowing the man as well as she'd come to the last few weeks, Abby was quite certain that staying so close to the place was driving him crazy! Why, he hadn't even taken the dogs for one of his long walks in the woods. All in all, he'd been acting very peculiar.

She sighed tiredly and told herself she was being foolish. Reading something into his actions that wasn't there. For heaven's sake, *most* men didn't go traipsing off into the woods! Abby frowned. But Samuel *did.* And the more she thought about it, the more she realized that his strange behavior had all started with his visit from Sarah Dumont. Maybe she should just come right out and ask him what was going on. Yes. Yes, that's just what she would do. At her very first opportunity.

She reached behind her head and pulled her mass of hair over one shoulder. Idly her fingers twisted it into one long braid. Abby then settled back against her pillows, drew the blankets up under her arms, and waited.

Chapter Seventeen

Samuel was awake long before the first rooster crow shattered the stillness. In fact, he'd *been* awake most of the night. Tossing and turning in his makeshift bed on the floor, his mind had conjured up images of Abby, waiting for him in the darkness.

He glanced across the room at Luke. The boy was stirring slightly and would soon be full awake. Groaning softly, Samuel turned away and stared blindly up at the ceiling. Years of trying to protect himself from an adult's rages had no doubt made Luke a very light sleeper. It was the only explanation.

Closing his eyes, Samuel remembered the night before. Not long after Abby retired, he and Luke had finished their game and gone to their beds. Samuel had waited what seemed an eternity for the sound of Luke's soft, regular breathing to tell him the boy was asleep.

Finally Samuel crept out of his blankets, stood, and moved carefully across the room. His tread was so quiet, not even the sleeping dogs noticed his passage. Bathed in the light of the dying fire, Samuel reached for the knob on Abby's door.

"Wha'cha doin', Samuel?"

He froze.

Samuel spun around and squinted into the half light. He was just able to make out Luke, sitting straight up in his bed.

Harry jumped up and trotted to the boy's cot. Maverick raised his head, gave a halfhearted whine, and went back to sleep.

"What?" Samuel whispered, stalling for time.

The boy rubbed at his eyes and moved over for the little dog that had joined him. "I said wha'cha doin'?"

"Oh." Samuel straightened up and turned away from the child's interested gaze. Giving Abby's closed door a frustrated glance, he bent down and picked up a log from the stack of firewood. Whispering over his shoulder he said, "The, uh . . . fire's dyin'. Just feedin' it some."

Maverick opened one eye and stared at him. Samuel frowned.

"Oh."

Samuel laid the log on the fire and stared as the flames licked hungrily at the fresh wood. "Go on back to sleep, Luke. Everything's all right."

"G'night, Samuel," Luke muttered and lay back down, drawing the little dog close.

"Yeah. G'night." Samuel leaned his forearm on the mantel and breathed deeply. He glared down at the big dog still staring at him accusingly from one wide eye. "You go to sleep, too, you no-good hound. . . ."

Maverick snorted and closed his eye again.

Samuel glanced at the closed door to his right. Though his whole body ached for her, he knew that Abby would be sleeping alone. Grimly, then, he'd gone back to his own pallet by the fire and said the ABCs over and over, trying for some peace in forgetfulness. It didn't come.

The rooster crowed again, and Samuel opened his eyes, pushing thoughts of the foiled night aside. He only hoped Abby would let him explain.

Luke was outside collecting the eggs when she stepped out of her room. Samuel immediately went to her side.

"Abby . . . about last night . . ." he started.

She held up one hand. "Please, Samuel, you don't owe me an explanation."

"But—"

"Please. I'd rather not talk about it right now." She walked to her trunk, bent down, and lifted the lid. "Where is Luke?"

"Gettin' the eggs. Look, Abby . . ."

She stood up and turned to face him. "You two have to get ready for church."

"Abby—"

"This is for you." She held out a package wrapped in plain brown paper. In her other hand she held a smaller version of the same gift. "This is for Luke," she said softly. "I made them this week as a . . . surprise." Her voice caught on the last word.

"Abby, dammit all . . ."

She stiffened. "I've told you before, Samuel. There is no need to swear at me."

"There is if you won't listen!" He pushed one hand through his hair. "There ain't much time. Luke'll be back soon." He tossed the package onto the table and grabbed her shoulders. "Abby, I was goin' to come to you last night."

She looked away.

"Dammit, I was. But Luke woke up and saw me and I . . . well, hell. I didn't want him to watch me goin' into your room and all. Wouldn't be right."

Her gaze flicked back to him. With slow deliberation she studied his features while he held his breath. Finally a hesitant smile curved her lips, and her body relaxed into his.

Samuel's arms closed around her, drawing her tight against him. He sighed heavily, relieved beyond measure that everything was now right between them. He'd seen her red, puffy eyes, and he knew that she must have spent most of the long night before crying.

He bent lower and planted a kiss on top of her head. "Guess the only thing to do is build Luke a room, too."

Abby giggled and nestled closer.

Samuel groaned, squeezed her tightly, and added, "I'll start today."

She leaned her head back and looked up at him. "*After* church."

They stared at each other in a silent contest of wills. Finally Samuel grinned. "Yes, ma'am."

The front door flew open, and Luke came in behind the dogs. "'Mornin', Abby!"

She tried to move away, but Samuel held her fast. "Good morning, Luke," she said. One last kiss to the top of her head and Samuel released her. Abby walked over to the boy and said softly, "I have a present for you."

"For me?" His eyes widened as he looked from the package to Abby's smiling face. Quickly Luke set the basket of eggs on the table. He took the gift from Abby, his small fingers moving gingerly over the plain wrapping.

"Yes, open them," Abby urged. "Both of you."

Samuel and Luke glanced at each other, then tore at the paper. Abby stood back and watched them proudly. She waited for their reaction, her face lit with anticipation.

"Oh, my," Samuel breathed quietly.

"Lordy," Luke said in a hush.

"Well?" Hands on her hips, Abby smiled at each of them delightedly. What a wonderful surprise! She could see by their faces that she'd succeeded. They were absolutely stunned! All those stolen hours late at night and early in the morning had been worth it.

"I can hardly wait to see you two in them," she said happily. "Oh, I can tell you, it was quite a chore finishing them up in time for church today. . . ." She laughed softly. "And trying to work on them without you two catching me was a trial indeed!" She clapped her hands together. "Well . . . are you surprised?"

Samuel and Luke looked away from her to each other. New shirts in hand, they stared speechless at the gifts Abby had so painstakingly made for them. And in that long moment of silent communication, a decision was made. Turning back to the beaming woman, Samuel spoke first.

"You sure did surprise me, Abby." His fingers tightened on the fabric as he glanced down at it again. The red-and-yellow-striped material seemed to scream at him. He suppressed a shudder. "It's a fine shirt."

"Yes'm," Luke threw in. A smaller, matching shirt hung from his hands. He looked up at Samuel for encouragement, then glanced back at Abby. "I ain't never had a shirt like *this* one."

She grinned and moved toward them. She smoothed Luke's cheek gently with one hand and clasped Samuel's hand with the other. "Oh, I'm so happy you like them. I so wanted you both to look your handsome best for our first time in church together!" She took a deep breath and released it in a rush. "Now, you two get ready while I fix breakfast." Turning for the front door, she said, "First, I'll get the kindling!"

As soon as she was safely outside, man and boy looked at each other, then disgustedly studied their new clothes.

"Samuel," Luke said desperately, "what're we gonna do?"

He shot a look at the boy. "We're gonna get ready for church."

"But—"

"Luke, I ain't gonna hurt that woman."

The boy nodded grimly. His lip curled up as he lifted the shirt and looked at it from every possible angle.

"'Sides," Samuel added, "I don't know about you, but I ain't never had a body work for a week on somethin' special just for me."

Luke sighed heavily. "All right. But I'm tellin' you, Samuel, this here is a *fightin'* shirt."

"Hmmm?"

"Some fool in town is bound to say somethin' about this dang thing, and I'm gonna have to fight him."

Samuel lifted his shirt higher up, holding it by two fingers. His nose wrinkling, he said thoughtfully, "Well, now, as cold as it's gettin', Luke . . . we just may have to wear our coats all morning."

Luke's gaze flew up hopefully to the man's face. "Even in church?"

Samuel frowned. *"Especially* in church!"

The tiny church in Rock Creek had one of the best heating stoves Samuel'd ever seen. Even this close to winter, everyone inside was fannin' themselves with hymnals and casting curious looks at the only two people to keep their heavy coats on.

Sweat rolled down his back underneath his shirt and Samuel knew his face was beet-red. All he had to do was look down at the boy beside him. Luke looked about ready to faint, but his jacket was buttoned up to the neck.

Reverend Knight seemed willing to talk forever, since he was so toasty warm, and Samuel was positive that the man had decided to read about the prodigal son just for his benefit. The reverend looked right at him every time the man could tear his eyes off of Abby's hat. Samuel could hardly blame the man for that, though. He'd stared at it for quite a spell that morning himself. Somehow, that one-eyed dove was losin' its feathers. If Samuel didn't know better, he'd swear the damn thing was molting. It wasn't bad enough that it had only one eye . . . now it was damn near bald!

The preacher smiled and nodded at Samuel again, and the big man tried not to groan. He shifted uneasily as dozens of eyes turned toward him. Why'd that reverend have to fix it so everybody in town kept watchin' him? Even Sheriff James was present, and the man didn't look too pleased to see Samuel.

He fidgeted nervously for the hundredth time, and Abby nudged him with her elbow. When she leaned toward him, he bent his head close, trying to avoid the dancing pink feather.

"For heaven's sake, Samuel," she hissed, "you and Luke both are in a fever sweat! Why don't you take those coats off?"

"We got a chill comin' on, Abby." He glanced at the preacher and hoped he wouldn't get into any trouble for lyin' in a church. "Best if we stay covered up." Then he straightened and gave the Reverend Knight his undivided attention. He ignored Abby's mumbled comment.

As soon as services were over, Samuel and Luke were the first out the double doors. They raced down the flight of steps and stood in the cold morning air, breathing deeply. The citizens of Rock Creek filed out of church more slowly, and Luke and Samuel were there, nodding greetings absently.

"You two feelin' all right?" Alonzo Mullins stopped opposite them, pulled out a huge red bandanna from his breast pocket, and mopped his high forehead. "You look as hot as I feel!" Shaking his head, he added, "I think Reverend Knight keeps that place so hot to remind us all of Hell—and danged if it don't work. Why, I feel saved every time I leave!"

"'Lonzo!" Minerva said on a gasp as she came up behind him. "On the very steps of the church!"

"Where better to talk about Hell, woman?" He winked at Samuel. "Preacher Knight jaws about it every week!"

She clucked her tongue disapprovingly. "Abby and me are goin' down to the store. You all bring the children along directly. We'll have cake."

The two women started off down the street, leaving their menfolk surrounded by rambunctious children who'd been too long confined.

"You children run on ahead now. You're about to split my head wide open with your hollerin'," Alonzo said, urging his brood toward the house.

Luke glanced uneasily back at Samuel. The big man shrugged as if to say there was no way to avoid the shirt problem forever.

Alonzo and Samuel started walking, keeping a comfortable distance between themselves and the screeching, running kids.

"Now," Alonzo said, "you gonna tell me why you kept your coat on all through the reverend's long-winded talk?"

Samuel stopped. He glanced uneasily around them before speaking. "Abby made me and Luke a surprise gift."

Alonzo's brows rose. "So?"

Sighing, Samuel undid the buttons of his coat. When he was finished, he pulled the edges of his jacket apart.

Alonzo blinked. A long, low-pitched whistle slid out of his pursed lips. "Well, what *do* you know? I thought nobody'd *ever* buy that material."

Samuel rolled his eyes.

The other man rubbed his jawline. "Funny thing. Looks a lot brighter when a body's wearin' it. . . ."

"I know." Samuel pulled his jacket closed again. "Luke's got one just like it."

Alonzo chuckled, then stopped quickly when he caught Samuel's eye. Trying to keep a straight face, he said, "Well, it's a good thing you kept them coats on after all. As hot as it gets in that church . . . folks see somethin' as bright as you two, they'd be about convinced they'd come to the gates of Hell!"

Samuel grinned sheepishly as his friend slapped him on the back.

"Let's go get us some of that cake before my bunch of terrors eat it all up," Alonzo said on another laugh.

"Thunderation!" Obadiah whistled and continued his slow walk around Luke. Shaking his head much like his father had, Obadiah rubbed his eyes and stopped in front of his friend. "I ain't *never* seen a shirt that godawful ugly before!"

Luke's hands balled into fists, and he ground his teeth together. He'd known there would be trouble, but he'd been hoping it wouldn't be with his only friend. "Take it back," he said, his gaze locked with Obadiah's.

"Why?" The other boy laughed. "You gotta know it's true!"

"I said take it back!" Luke advanced on his friend. The alley beside the mercantile was dark and shadowed, even in the afternoon. Obadiah took two more steps back and stopped when he came up against the side of the building.

"Awright! I take it back." He frowned at Luke. "What's the matter with you anyhow? You really *like* that shirt?"

"Hell, no." Luke smoothed his hand down the front of the hated shirt gently. "But . . . well, Abby made it for me and . . ."

"Oh. Yeah, *I* know what you mean." Obadiah patted his friend's shoulder. "One time my ma made me a silly-lookin' suit." He shook his head slowly. "I looked like a danged fool, but Ma sure was pleased." Obadiah grinned. "Like to took me near six months to grow out of that durned thing!"

Relieved, Luke laughed, and the two of them started out of the alley together.

"Well, looky here . . ."

The boys stopped dead and looked up at the two men blocking the alleyway.

The cowhands walked toward the boys, laughing and weaving on their feet.

"Chris, you ever seen anything like that before?" Jason pointed at Luke's shirt.

"No, I never." The shorter man's voice rose. "Don't he look pretty, though?"

Luke shrugged Jason's hand off his shoulder. "Leave me be."

"Say, Chris," the tall blond said as his hand clamped down on Luke, "ain't this the kid what was with the pretty lady?"

"I do believe you're right, Jas."

While the two men were talking, Obadiah shot out the alley and ran around to the back of the store. Trouble was comin'. He just knew it. He hit the door at a dead run, throwing the door into the wall. His mother and Abby jumped when he rushed in, gasping for air.

"Durn it, boy . . ." Minerva started, then noticed the fear on her son's face. "What is it?"

"Luke . . . alley . . . cowboys . . ." he managed finally.

Minerva ran for the front room and the men at the same time that Abby raced out the back door.

Abby had no idea what she would do when she got there. She only knew that she had to get to Luke. Coming around the corner of the store, she heard the drunken voices.

"She your ma, boy?"

"Watsa matter with you, boy?"

Then she heard Luke call out, "Let go o' me, you no-good son of a sorry mule!"

Feet flying, Abby turned into the alley and kept right on going. It didn't matter what she might face—she wasn't about to let Luke be hurt again. Not if she could stop it. She crashed into the tall blond cowboy, sending him sprawling into the dirt. As she turned for the other one, she saw Luke had already started.

Kicking, punching, and biting, Luke had the man backing up, howling in outrage. Without another thought Abby joined him. She lifted her hem and kicked out at the drunk while at the same time snatching his hat off and slapping him with it.

Dirt flew in the narrow alley. Abby scratched her forearm on the rough wooden siding of the Mercantile but paid no attention to the splinters.

"What kind of man are you, picking on a defenseless woman and child?" she shouted. "Did your mama know what kind of man she raised?"

The hapless cowhand held his hands up in front of his face, trying to deflect the blows.

"You're a man to be proud of, aren't you?" she yelled.

"You tell 'im, Abby!" Luke shouted gleefully and kicked the trapped cowboy in the shins.

"Hey, lady, leave off!" Chris yelled, and whiskey-soaked air fanned her cheek.

"I'll teach you to—" An arm wrapped around her waist from behind and swung her off her feet. She pulled at Jason's arm, trying to free herself. "Let me go, you worthless drunk, or so help me, Hannah—"

"Shit, lady, shut up, will ya?" Jason's voice came low in her ear. "We didn't want no trouble. We was only funnin' the kid some. If you don't shut the hell up, we're gonna have the law down on us. . . ."

Abby gasped. "Don't you swear at me, you . . ."

A shadow fell across the alley. Jason looked up, saw Samuel, and muttered, "Holy God Almighty . . ." just before he dropped Abby to the ground.

"Chris! Chris! Let's go. C'mon!" Jason yelled frantically.

Abby was back up in an instant, slapping, scratching, and kicking. Her hair hung about her face, partially blocking her sight, and still she went at him. Behind her, she could hear Luke cussing a blue streak while the other cowhand tried to peel the boy off.

Samuel didn't say a word. He was beyond speaking. From the moment he saw Minerva's face, he'd somehow known that these two men were behind the trouble. For days he'd worried and thought about the danger Abby was in. He'd been afraid for her safety. And now . . . it was all so ridiculous. These two were no serious threat.

In just moments Samuel had seen that if they'd wanted to, the two drunks could have freed themselves from Abby and Luke. All it would have taken was a couple of punches. But they hadn't done it. In fact, from what Samuel could see, they were doing everything possible to keep from hurting the woman and child even while taking their abuse.

He fought down a smile. It wouldn't do to laugh at Abby and Luke while they was busy fighting! And though he was almost enjoying the scene, he knew he should stop it before someone really *did* get hurt. Deliberately he stepped farther into the alley and shouted, "That's enough!"

His voice boomed out, breaking into Abby's and Luke's concentration. They both stopped their attack for a moment, and that was all the chance the two drunk cowhands had been waiting for. As one, they turned and ran down the length of the alley, made a sharp right turn, and kept on running.

Abby looked from Samuel to her escaping prey and immediately started after them, shouting, "They're getting away!" It only took a few steps for Samuel to catch her and lift her off her feet.

"Let me go, Samuel!" she shouted, pushing her hair out of her eyes. "We've got to catch them!" She swung her legs uselessly in an effort to get down.

"Let 'em go, Abby."

He spoke so softly, she thought for a moment she hadn't heard him. Blowing at her fallen hair, she glared at him. "What did you say?"

"I said, let 'em go. You done punished 'em enough."

Samuel grinned. She had dirt on her nose, her bright green dress was ripped at the shoulder, and her hair had come completely down. To him, she'd never looked lovelier.

To think, he'd spent all his life worryin' over losin' his temper with folks . . . he'd probably said more ABCs than all the children in Colorado put together. And Abby . . . why, she was about the most even-tempered female he'd ever come across. He'd yet to see her cross or mean. And then this!

Just like a mother bear defending her cub, she'd torn into those two like a screamin' tornado. And it had been quite a sight. His heart seemed about to burst, he was so proud. To be loved by a woman like that would be a real responsibility.

Samuel spared a glance for the boy standing beside him. Covered in dirt, his new shirt ripped up the side, Luke was staring at Abby like she was the Angel Gabriel.

"You all right, boy?" Samuel asked, never loosening his grip on Abby.

"Shoot, yeah. I'm fine." He looked down at his shirt, then up to Abby. "Sure am sorry, Abby. Them yahoos ruint my new shirt."

He sounded so disappointed, Samuel narrowed his gaze to study him. If he didn't know better, Samuel would swear that the child was really upset.

"Samuel," Abby said softly, "put me down, please."

When her feet touched the ground, Abby went to Luke and enfolded him in a warm hug. As she patted his back gently, she told him, "Don't you worry about that shirt, Luke. It's only torn at the seam. I'll fix it up like new first thing tomorrow. I promise."

Over Abby's shoulder, Luke's gaze sought out Samuel. The big man had a hard time smothering his laughter at the sight of the boy's disgusted face.

But Samuel's amused grin became tender as he watched the little boy turn his face into Abby's shoulder and wrap his arms around her. Somehow, Samuel didn't think Luke would much mind wearing his new shirt anymore.

He knew he wouldn't be hiding his ugly new shirt under a coat anymore, either.

Chapter Eighteen

Abby pushed at the partially opened door again, but it still didn't catch and close.

"Oh, Abby," Minerva said, "don't bother with that durned door. It never *did* shut proper. 'Sides, it's only open a crack. The men know we're back here."

"But I wanted you to try the dress on," Abby said.

"Well, I'm gonna." Minerva reached around behind her and began to undo the buttons on her severe black gown. "Any of them come to the back of the house, they'll knock before they come in." When she was down to her chemise, Minerva took a deep breath and forced herself to say, "All right, Abby. I'm ready. Let me see it."

Abby walked to the nearest chair, picked up the navy blue dress she'd made, and shook it out. Then she held it up for Minerva's inspection.

Slowly a pleased smile crossed Minerva's face. She crossed the room to Abby and took the dress from her.

Carefully she checked the seams and hems, making admiring coos over the tiny, even stitches. Her fingers moved over the tucks Abby'd taken in the wide skirt just below the waistline and the full-cut sleeves.

Minerva shook her head slowly. She could hardly believe it. It was as fine a job as anything she'd ever seen. And to think . . . *Abby Sutton* did it. Well, she told herself, that should teach you something. Never judge a horse by the bridle it's wearing! 'Cause to look at the outlandish getups Abby was forever wearin', no one would have guessed that she was such a fine hand with a needle.

"Do you like it?"

"Like it?" Minerva looked up at Abby and grinned. "Why, it makes the dress I bought from that woman in Wolf River look like a horse blanket!"

A broad smile lit Abby's face as she hurried to Minerva's side to help her try the dress on. "Now, let's just make sure it fits properly. . . ."

After the last button was fastened, Minerva stood before the full-length mirror in the corner of her bedroom. She met Abby's reflected gaze and said softly, "Abby, I ain't never owned a dress that suited me so well."

"Oh, I *am* pleased." Abby walked to the nearest chair and plopped down. "Do you think the other ladies in town might be interested?"

"Huh!" Minerva tugged at the sleeves on her new dress, then turned sideways to check the hang of the gown. "You just wait till folks see me in *this* rig. Especially Charity Whitehall! That woman can't sew a button on a shirt without it falls off . . . and her with them three girls . . . Shoot. You could work just for *Charity* and do real well."

"That's wonderful, Minerva."

"Just you remember," Minerva said, turning to look at Abby. "I found you first, I get first call."

"Agreed!" Abby grinned happily and leaned back in her chair. While she watched Minerva primp and preen in front of the mirror, Abby let her mind wander. She still couldn't quite understand Samuel's reaction to that fight she and Luke had had in the alley.

Idly she toyed with the fresh white bandage on her forearm. Not even removing several splinters from her arm had upset him. He'd still had the same, pleased look on his face. Alone in Minerva's kitchen, while the other woman took care of cleaning Luke up, Abby had given herself into Samuel's care.

She closed her eyes and saw him again, bent over her, gently removing the small wood slivers. His touch tender, his eyes warm, his smile had only faltered when she winced with the pain.

"I'm sorry, Abby, but they've got to come out," Samuel said softly.

"I know." Abby twisted her arm to look at the row of splinters. "But it still hurts."

"Next time you should have your fight out in the wide open." His voice was stern, but amusement shone in his eyes. "Away from wood walls."

"Next time?" Her offended gaze flew to his. "I don't believe there'll be a next time. I don't often get into fights, you know, Samuel. And I wouldn't have this time, but those two bullies were tormenting Luke, and I couldn't let that go on, now, could I?"

He smiled again and tugged at a long splinter. "Course not. Now, hold still."

"Ow!" She pulled her arm away, but Samuel snatched it right back.

"Might as well behave. I'm gonna get 'em all, y'know."

Reluctantly she gritted her teeth and held her arm steady.

"I'll try to be careful," Samuel said.

"I know." She watched him silently for a moment and tried to ignore the painful tugs at her flesh. Then Abby suddenly touched the sleeve of his shirt with her free hand. "Do you really like your new shirt, Samuel?" He looked up at her, and she went on. "I mean, I heard Alonzo teasing you about the bright colors . . . and I know that you once told me you didn't like it, but"—she lowered her gaze—"when I saw those beautiful red and yellow stripes, I just thought it would look so handsome on you that I bought it anyway and—"

He kissed her. Just a brief touch of his lips.

"I think this here is the best-lookin' shirt I ever saw, Abby." His breath touched her face, and his green eyes moved over her features lovingly. Abby's heart skipped, then thudded. "Don't you pay no attention to the likes of Alonzo. He's only jealous that he don't have such a fine shirt."

Abby smiled and hesitantly touched his cheek.

"And," Samuel continued with a smirk, "if Luke don't wake up again like he did last night, I'll come to your room and show you just how thankful I am . . . for the shirt—for everything."

She grinned mischievously. "And how are you going to make sure he doesn't wake up?"

"I ain't figured that one out yet." Samuel smiled wryly. "But I'll think of somethin'."

He leaned toward her and covered her mouth with his. After a long moment he pulled away just a bit.

"Oh, yes, ma'am. Believe me. I'll think of somethin'." He winked and added, "I didn't about kill myself gettin' that room done in a hurry to be stopped by a wakeful child!"

"Abby! Abby girl, wake up!" Minerva gave the woman's uninjured arm a good shake. "For corn's sake, Abby!"

"Huh?" Abby's eyes blinked, then flew wide open. Good Lord, she'd gone right off into her thoughts without even noticing.

Minerva stood in front of her, hands on her hips, and a grin on her face. "By the looks of you . . . I imagine you wasn't thinkin' much on dressmakin'?"

A hot blush rushed to Abby's cheeks. "No. No . . . I'm uh, sorry, Minerva. I was, uh . . ."

"Uh-huh." The other woman nodded. "Reckon I know just what you was thinkin' about. I mean, *who*."

Abby smiled softly.

"So," Minerva said, "you love him, do ya?"

Abby's golden brown eyes lifted to her friend's. "Oh, yes, Minerva. I do." It felt so good to say it out loud. "For the longest time, now."

"Can't say as I blame you." Minerva cocked her head to one side. "Gonna marry him?"

"He hasn't asked me." Abby sighed and frowned thoughtfully. "He hasn't even said that he loves me."

"So?"

"*So?*" Abby stood up and crossed the room nervously. At the opposite wall she stopped, held back the white lace curtains, and stared out the window. "So, if he doesn't love me, how can I marry him?"

"Horse patties!" Minerva snorted.

"What?" Abby choked out a laugh.

"I said, horse patties!" Minerva crossed the room to stand beside the other woman. "Hell, of *course* he loves ya. Anyone can see *that!*"

"I don't know." Abby sighed and looked back out the window. "If he does, why doesn't he say so?"

"Abby . . ." Minerva plopped down on the edge of the bed. "*All* men are slow on the draw when it comes to love." She shook her head slowly. "Oh, they'll buy a pig in a poke or decide to ride hundreds of miles for no more reason than because they're tired of the same old thing . . . but *love?* Shoot." She patted the mattress beside her and waited for Abby to sit down before continuing.

"Why, my man Alonzo?" Minerva smiled at some secret memory. "Hell, he didn't even *know* he loved me until I *told* him! You never seen a more surprised man in all your life! But by thunder, he knew the right of it once I said it."

Abby grinned and shook her head.

"You think I'm foolin', don't you?" Minerva reared her head back and looked at her friend. "Well, I'm tellin' you the honest to God truth . . . sure as I'm settin' here."

"Well, then," Abby asked softly, "how did you do it?"

"Easiest way is straight out." Minerva nodded and smoothed down the front of her new dress. "That way the poor man don't miss nothin'. I walked right up to Alonzo one day in the middle of town—not Rock Creek . . . a little place back home in Arkansas—and I says, 'Alonzo Mullins, you love me and I love you. Think it's time we done somethin' about that!'"

Abby's jaw dropped. It was hard to imagine. "What did he say?"

"What do you think he said? Just what he always says. 'Yes, Minerva.'" she gave Abby one firm nod. "Yessir, we was married the very next Sunday and set out for Colorado a week later."

"But—"

"Oh," Minerva went on, "I don't want you to think the man's got no mind of his own. He does, and we've had some rip-roarin' fights over the years . . . but all in all, it's been a real good life." She leaned over and patted Abby's knee. "And with five kids runnin' around . . . I guess that proves right enough that he's a mite fond of me, don't it?"

"I guess you're right." Abby bit her lip and began to think.

Luke and Obadiah raced through the parlor, headed for the front door, but Alonzo's voice stopped them.

"What the hell you tearin' through this house for, boys?"

"Sorry, Pa." Obadiah glanced over his shoulder toward the connecting door to the Mercantile, then back to his father.

"Well?" Alonzo waited.

The connecting door flew open, and the four other Mullins boys ran into the parlor. As one, they skidded to a stop in front of their father.

"Obadiah and Luke're goin' down to the livery to watch 'em break horses," Nimrod complained, "and they won't let us go along!"

Alonzo and Samuel looked at the two oldest boys, who managed to look everywhere in the room but at the adults.

"Obadiah, I reckon you can take the little ones, too."

"Pa . . ."

"Hush." Alonzo waved one hand at his oldest son. "Go on, now. But first you can go through the store and each of you can have *two* licorice whips."

All six boys grinned.

"Mind you, I said *two*."

"Yessir, Pa." Obadiah turned back for the store, his brothers hot on his heels.

Luke paused for a moment. "Thank you, Mr. Mullins," he said, then ran to join his friends.

Once the door was closed and quiet was restored, Alonzo turned to Samuel.

"That's a fine boy there."

Samuel smiled. "Yeah. Yeah, he is."

"He gonna be stayin' with you permanent?"

"I think so. I already told him he was welcome." Samuel stretched his long legs out and crossed them at the ankles. "Abby feels the same. No matter what happens about the cabin . . . Luke can stay."

"That's good. That's good." Alonzo carefully packed tobacco into his pipe, then reached for the matches on the table beside him. "Speakin' of the cabin and all . . ." He paused, held the flame to the pipe bowl, and sucked at the stem until the tobacco caught.

"What?" Samuel turned in his seat to watch the other man.

"Well, telegram came last night," Alonzo said slowly. "Judge is gonna be here early." He puffed at his pipe. "Appears he ain't got as much to do on the circuit as he figured he might."

"When? When's he gonna be here?"

"Next week some time. Prob'ly not till Thursday or so."

Samuel ran one hand over his face and tried to think. Next week? That soon? But he wasn't ready. He still had to arrange to get a copy of his deed sent up from the county seat. He snorted. What the hell was he thinkin'? Worryin' over land deeds when the most important thing was . . . what would happen between him and Abby? He knew good and well that her claim would never stand up in court. *He* owned the land and the cabin. And he was pretty sure that *she* knew it, too.

But once the judge said so official-like . . . then what? Would she just up and leave? Oh, he knew that the cabin was the only reason she'd come to Colorado in the first place, but was it the only reason she'd *stayed?*

No. He shook his head slowly. No, he couldn't believe that. She cared for him. She *did*. She'd as much as said so lots of times. But, his brain reminded him, she'd never actually said so *out loud*, had she?

Shit. What should he do?

"Sam?" Alonzo's voice brought him back from his mental wanderings.

"Huh?"

"I *said*, you give any thought to the town's proposition?"

"What proposition?"

Alonzo rolled his eyes and sighed. "For godsake man! You get so many job offers, you can't remember 'em all?"

Job offers? Samuel thought for a moment. "Oh. The sheriffin' job."

"Yeah. You thought on it any?"

"No, 'lonzo. I ain't had the time to think on it." Samuel frowned and told himself since Abby's arrival he hadn't had much time for anything . . . except her.

"Then you best start thinkin'." Alonzo took his pipe from his mouth and studied it. "Townfolks is serious about this. They want you. They're even willin' to help build you a place here in town." He smiled wickedly. "Never needed no sheriff house before. Ol' Pete, he just nods off in one of his cells with the other no-goods . . . like the ol' sayin'—Birds of a feather . . ."

Samuel smiled absently and stood up. "All right, 'lonzo. I'll think on it."

"You do that." Alonzo waved his pipe stem at the big man. "Best remember somethin' else, too."

"What's that?"

"If you're plannin' on keepin' that youngster with you, you'll be wantin' him to get some schoolin', won't you?"

"Yeah, I guess."

"Well, it ain't likely he'd be able to go up and down that durned mountain in the wintertime to get to school, is it?"

"No, reckon not." Samuel hadn't considered schoolin' for the boy. And of course, there was Abby. If she *did* stay, he couldn't see her snowed in for months at a time. What if she needed a doctor or somethin'? What if somethin' happened to *him*? Hell, she'd never survive in the winter. *Alone.* Just her and Luke.

Samuel began to silently recite the ABCs. He needed something familiar to do. Suddenly there was so many different things to consider. A mental image of Abby, struggling through waist-deep snow just to get to the barn sprung up in front of him. And Luke. Hell, boys was always breakin' somethin' or other. What if he broke a leg or an arm? Would he, Samuel, know the right things to do so's the boy wouldn't be further harmed?

His heart pounded, and his brain raced with visions of all kinds of disasters. The ABCs weren't working.

With a snort, Samuel acknowledged that they rarely *did* work when the problem was Abby.

"Sam?" Alonzo asked. "Sam? You all right?"

Samuel started, looked down at the other man and forced a smile. "Yeah. Fine." No point in tellin' any of this to Alonzo, he thought. "It's just time we was headed back for the mountain, is all. Don't care to be gone too long."

Alonzo started to push himself to his feet. "I'll fetch Abby for you."

But Samuel was already moving. "Don't worry. I'll go get her. If Luke and Obadiah come in, hold on to Luke for me, will ya?"

The other man nodded, but Samuel saw him lean his head back against his chair and knew that Alonzo was settling in for a nice Sunday nap. Couldn't blame him none, either. In fact, Samuel smirked, if his mind wasn't so busy hoppin' from one thought to the next, he'd like nothin' better than gettin' home and maybe convincin' Abby that they all needed a "nap."

He walked quietly through the Mullinses' living quarters at the back of the store. As he moved down the long hallway, he studied the flowered wallpaper and the framed portraits of Mullin family members. There were even a couple of daguerreotypes taken of the children not long ago.

It was a real nice place. He smiled as he realized that for the first time he could remember, he wasn't jealous of someone else's home. Because finally he, too, had a home. A woman. A family. Samuel pulled a deep breath into his lungs. At least, for now.

Maybe it was about time he did something permanent about his new family. Maybe, he told himself, he should take the chance that Abby *did* love him as fiercely as she loved Luke. Every time she looked at him, he could swear he saw love in her eyes. It was there in her touch. In the things she did for him. Maybe it was finally *his* turn to love and be loved. But what if . . . his mind started.

No. He shut down on that thought firmly. He couldn't think about that now. If he started in thinkin' on all the reasons Abby had to refuse him, he'd never work up the nerve to ask her anything. And one thing he knew for certain, the reward of having Abby's love was worth the risk of pain.

Samuel stopped short. He would do it. Tonight. He would ask her to marry him.

Then he heard the voices. Soft, teasing, with a little laughter. Minerva and Abby. He moved closer to the partially opened door, raised his hand to knock, and paused. He heard Minerva say, "Course I'm right, girl. Now, do you want to marry him and stay at the cabin or not?"

He held his breath.

"Certainly I'm going to marry him, Minerva! I don't want to leave that cabin ever!" Abby laughed quietly. "Now all I have to do is convince Samuel!"

Samuel's heart stopped. His mouth dry, his insides twisting, he turned away from the door. She didn't want to leave the cabin. She had to "convince" him. "Certainly" she was going to marry him—and he hadn't asked her. The cabin. It all came back to the cabin.

Had she really done all of this to get the cabin? Was a home *that* important to her? So important that she was willing to *bed* a man to keep it?

Hurriedly he walked back down the hallway. He had to get outside where he could breathe. What a fool! What a stupid, blind fool! What was he thinking?

How could he have imagined even for a moment that a woman like Abby would actually *love* him!

Of course she bedded him for the cabin! Why the hell else would a woman as beautiful as her bother with a big, ugly, ignorant man? She could have anyone. Anyone at all. Why would she pick *him?*

Samuel slipped through the kitchen, out the back door, and across the road to the livery stable. Luke and Obadiah were sitting on the top fence rail feeding carrots to the horses. The other boys were nowhere in sight.

"Hey, Samuel," Luke called. "Want to see—"

"Ain't got time," Samuel managed to say. "Go fetch Abby. We got to get back to the mountain."

"But Obadiah and me, we were gonna—"

"Do it *now*, Luke."

Even seeing the boy's face dissolve into worried lines and creases wasn't enough to stop Samuel. If he could, he'd go back to the mountain alone. But he couldn't just ride off, no matter how he felt. Somehow, he would have to face Abby and not let her see that he was dead inside.

He had to get back to the mountain. Back to the woods. Where he could think. Where he belonged.

Deliberately Samuel reached into the back of his wagon and picked up his coat. Then he pulled it on over the red-and-yellow shirt and buttoned it up to the neck.

Abby watched Samuel walk out the front door without a backward glance.

Even during supper, he'd hardly said a word. Oh, he'd been polite. Giving one-word answers to any question she posed him. Listening to Luke tell him about the day's adventures. But since they'd left Rock Creek, something had been terribly wrong.

Abby dropped the dishtowel to the tabletop, wiped her hands on her apron, then untied it and tossed it on the nearest chair. She glanced at Luke, still seated at the table.

"I'll be back in a moment, Luke. I want to talk to Samuel about something."

The boy looked up and nodded. Abby could see the worry in his eyes and knew for certain that she wasn't imagining things. Samuel's polite distance was affecting the boy, too.

To think, she told herself as she walked to the front door, only this afternoon everything had seemed so simple. Outside, her gaze moved over the cabin yard until she spotted the big man out by the animal cages. Determinedly she started walking.

She came up behind him silently. He was just closing the door on the empty wolf cage.

"Samuel?"

He barely glanced at her. "What?"

"Samuel, why did you let the wolf go? Is he ready?"

Samuel straightened up. He stood, back to her, legs spread wide, his head tilted back as he stared at the sky. "Ready enough."

She went closer and touched his arm. He pulled away. Swallowing heavily, Abby asked, "What do you mean, ready enough? Wasn't he well?"

Samuel took a step aside. "Well enough to get by, I reckon."

"But—"

"Abby," he ground out, "the animals are my look-out. *I* say when it's time for 'em to be set free. *Not* you."

"I know that, Samuel, but—"

"No *buts*." He stared off into the distance as though he could see right through the surrounding pines and aspens. As though he were watching the wolf make its own way back to its home. Its world. "He's better off out there. Much longer in that damned cage and he would'a died." His voice softened, and Abby had to strain to hear him. "Some animals got to be free to wander. Don't belong in no cages."

Abby reached out to touch him, then let her hand fall to her side when he took another step away. "Samuel," she said, her throat convulsing slightly, "can't you tell me what's wrong? What's happened?"

Samuel finally turned to face her, and she wished he hadn't. His familiar features blank, unreadable, he simply stared down at her as if waiting for something. Abby wanted to touch him, reassure him somehow, but she was stopped by the look in his eyes. His pale green eyes were shadowed. Sad and haunted. In fact, Samuel looked much as he had when she first came to the mountain. Only this time he wouldn't talk to her.

In the face of his silence, Abby turned and walked to the cabin, her feet dragging at every step.

When the last light was blown out and Abby was in her bedroom, the door closed firmly behind her, Luke lay awake in the darkness. He heard Samuel shoo one of the dogs away and wasn't surprised when Harry jumped up onto his bed.

Luke swallowed back his nervousness and whispered a question into the dark. "Samuel, why was Abby cryin' a while ago?"

"Don't know. Reckon you'd have to ask her that."

"But, Samuel—"

"Luke"—he drew in a deep breath and tried to keep his voice level—"this don't have nothin' to do with you. I already told you. No matter what else happens, you're welcome here. I want you to stay."

"What about Abby?"

Samuel cringed a little at the boy's wistful tone, but there wasn't anything else to be said. Nothin' was gonna make the child feel better, Samuel told himself. Hell, there wasn't anything that'd make *him* feel better, either. It was best the boy understood that right off.

"I don't got nothin' to say about Abby, boy. Reckon what she does now is up to her."

Luke didn't answer, and after a few minutes Samuel was almost positive he heard the child sniffling. His jaw clenched tightly, Samuel tried to ignore the sound. Just as he tried to ignore the solitary tear that rolled down his own cheek.

Chapter Nineteen

Her eyes ached and burned. Oh, not from crying. She'd long ago run out of tears. But staying awake all night, staring into the darkness, hoping for an answer to the riddle of Samuel's behavior, had made her eyes as irritable as she felt. Absently Abby rubbed at them with her fingertips and tried to think.

What could have happened in town to create such a turnaround in a man? She'd thought yesterday that perhaps if he had a little time, he'd talk to her. But only an hour ago, over breakfast, Abby had realized that he was going to do no such thing.

In fact, he'd seemed even colder this morning than the night before. His jawline was covered in red-gold stubble, his eyes looked more cherry-colored than green, and Abby knew that Samuel was still cut off from her. And judging by the rigid line of his mouth, she told herself, he had no intention of telling her why.

Abby stood in the cabin's open doorway staring out at the barn. He was in there. Immediately after eating, he'd stalked off without a word to either her or Luke. She could still see Luke's face, mirroring his disappointment and dread at what was happening. Poor little thing had run off into the woods right after Samuel went to the barn, and she hadn't seen him since.

The longer she stared at the big, silent building across the yard, the angrier she got. No matter what Samuel was sulking over . . . he had no right to treat Luke so badly. And by heaven, she thought firmly, it's high time she told him so!

Determinedly Abby marched across the quiet yard to the barn. Huge black clouds rushed and stretched across the sky, masking the sunlight and bathing the ground in a vague half light. The barn's wide double doors hung open as if in a challenge.

Abby stopped just outside, straightened her shoulders, lifted her chin, and mumbled a short prayer for strength. Strength to face Samuel down and risk losing everything she thought she'd gained.

Before she could lose her nerve, Abby walked into the cavernous building. Quickly she looked around and spotted Samuel in the far stall, saddling one of the horses.

He was leaving?

Her heart thudding in her chest, Abby hurried down the aisle.

"Samuel?"

He glanced at her over his shoulder, then turned back to cinching up the saddle. "What?"

"Are you going somewhere?"

He snorted. "Yeah."

Abby moved closer until she stood on the other side of the stall door. She crossed her arms atop the wood rail and waited for him to look at her. After what seemed forever, he did.

"What do you want, Abby?"

She stared up at him. There was no softness in his face. No warmth in his eyes or his voice. He looked at her as he would a stranger. An *unwelcome* stranger.

"Samuel, what's *wrong?*"

"Nothin'." He opened one of his saddlebags, looked inside, then closed the flap and tied it down.

Abby walked around to his side and laid her hand on his arm. He stared down at it until she pulled back. "If nothing is wrong," she demanded, "why are you leaving?"

"Goin' to the county seat. Get a copy of my land deed."

"But, why? The judge isn't due for a couple of weeks yet."

He shook his head. "Nope. He'll be here the end of the week." Samuel reached around behind Abby and pulled his slicker down from the stall post. "You best get yourself ready, too, Abby. Figure out just what you're gonna tell the man to make him give you my place."

"What?"

"You heard me." He pushed his arms through the sleeves of his slicker, then glared at her as he buttoned it. "That's what all this"—he flung his arms wide— "has been about, ain't it?"

"All of what?" Abby said, her tone dropping to a dangerous level.

"All of what you been doin'." He took one step closer to her, forcing her to step back and tilt her head to see him. "Cookin', cleanin', sewin'." His eyes narrowed. "Hell, you was even willin' to take *me* to bed! Just to get my place! So don't go standin' there all sweet as sugar and pretend any different! I *know!*"

"You know what?" Abby stood her ground and forced herself not to look away from his accusing stare. She could hardly believe what he was saying to her. But she knew *he* believed it.

"I know exactly what you was after all the time. I heard you tell Minerva. . . ."

Tell Minerva? Abby's brain raced trying to recall everything she and her friend had talked about the day before. She blushed a little when she remembered admitting flat out that she loved the mountain of stupidity standing before her. But surely, if he'd heard *that*, it wouldn't have made him this angry!

"Yeah," he snorted, "you *should* be blushin' for the shame of it! I ain't never heard of the like. A 'good' woman givin' up her honor for a piece of land!" He took a deep breath, and Abby watched his chest swell with his power and rage and hurt. "And then you tell Minerva 'Of course I'm gonna marry Samuel,'" he mimicked. "'I don't never want to leave that cabin. I'll *convince* him!'"

Abby's jaw dropped. *That* was all he'd heard? And from that little bit of conversation he'd decided that she was no good? He'd taken everything they'd shared, all of their feelings, and thrown them away for *nothing*?

"So," he said, nodding victoriously. "Now you know, don't you? You know I heard you makin' your plans, and you're busy right now tryin' to find a way to change my mind. You gonna *convince* me, Abby?"

For a long moment Abby was stunned speechless.

She stared up into the face of the man she loved and knew that no amount of "convincing" would do the slightest bit of good. He'd already made up his mind about her.

No, she told herself as she silently fumed. She wouldn't try to change his mind. Right now she had a strong hunch she wouldn't be able to *find* his mind! How any man could be that empty-headed was beyond her. She thought back to that first night at the cabin. When she'd been so sure he was simple-minded. Strange that it had taken so long to find out that she'd been right!

His familiar features were set in grim, harsh lines. She'd never seen him this way, and she didn't like it. But he'd done it to himself! And because of his own doubts, he was trying to destroy her and Luke, too. Well, before he left, he was going to listen to a few things from her!

Deliberately Abby kept her gaze locked with his and took a step closer. The big man backed up a pace, and she saw a flicker of surprise flash in his eyes. Get set for more, she warned him silently.

Pointing her index finger, Abby jabbed him in the chest. "All right, *Mr.* Hart. I stood still and listened to all of your nonsense—"

"Nonsense?"

"Nonsense!" She kept walking, and he kept backing up until his back was flat against the barn wall. Then, poking him in the chest for emphasis, Abby gave him both barrels.

"You dare to look me in the eye and tell me that I 'gave away my honor' for a piece of land? Who do you think you are, Samuel Hart, to say a thing like that to *me*?"

He shifted position a bit, but her hard gaze refused to let go of his.

"After knowing me all these weeks . . . living in the same house with me . . . you can say that?"

"You know you—"

"Hush!" she shouted. "You had your turn. What about you, Samuel? Hmmm? Look at you! Look at the size of you! Did little ol' me *force* you into bed? I sure hope I didn't hurt you any! And, you said yourself, you durn near killed yourself finishing up my room. . . . You couldn't *wait* to get back in my bed! So don't start pretending now that you were taken advantage of! For heaven's sake!" She leaned in closer, glaring at him. "You sound as though you were some prim old maid that a wandering gypsy had seduced!"

"*Gypsy?*"

"I told you hush." Abruptly she turned her back on him and began to pace furiously back and forth the length of the stall. The horse stirred uneasily, and she immediately patted its neck. Samuel had relaxed somewhat, but when she spun back around, he flattened up against the wall.

"And as for the rest of it—the cooking, sewing, cleaning—*I* thought we were both working together . . . making the cabin a home. I had no idea that what I was really doing was trying to steal it! And Luke!" She crossed the few feet separating them quickly and jammed her finger back in his chest. "What about Luke? Do you know what you're doing to that poor little boy? How you're hurting him by this foolish sulking of yours?"

"*Sulking?*" he roared. "I ain't sulking, woman! I'm spittin' mad!"

"At Luke?" she shouted back.

"Course not at Luke! At you!"

"Fine. Then *be* mad at me!" Fists on hips, she stared him down. "But don't you hurt that boy any longer! He's been through enough without having to deal with an idiot who's too blind to see what's right in front of him!"

"*Idiot? Me?*" He pushed away from the wall and came within inches of her before stopping. "You call me stupid 'cause I don't want to hear any more of your lies?"

"Lies? What lies?"

"Well . . ."

"Can't think of any, can you, Samuel?"

"Don't matter. I know what I heard yesterday."

"Do you really?" Abby's voice dropped. She cocked her head to one side and took a deep breath. Funny, but when she'd considered taking Minerva's advice and telling Samuel that he loved her, she hadn't expected the scene to be anything like this! Slowly she shook her head and let her gaze travel up and down the length of him until he began to stir uncomfortably.

"If you had eavesdropped a little earlier," she started, and smiled when he looked away, embarrassed, "you would have heard far more interesting things."

"I imagine."

"No, Samuel," she said softly, "I don't think you do. I don't think you can imagine for a moment what we were talking about yesterday. You know why?"

He didn't answer.

"I'll tell you why. Because you don't know how to love, that's why."

He turned and looked at her, surprise shining in his eyes.

"That's right, Samuel. You see, if you'd been listening earlier, you would have heard me tell Minerva that I loved you."

His lips twisted in a disbelieving smirk.

"And you would have heard me agree to her advice." Abby didn't even care anymore if he believed her or not. Her first wave of anger had died down now to a smoldering tower of hurt. She just wanted to tell him everything and then leave. "You see, she advised me to do what she did to Alonzo."

His brow furrowed in confusion, he stared at her.

"Yes, Samuel. If you hadn't acted the ass yesterday, I would have proposed to you."

She felt his surprise.

"You . . ."

"Yes, you heard me. Propose." She smiled and shook her head. "I *was* going to tell you how much you loved me, since you didn't seem to realize it yourself."

"I—"

She held her hand up for silence. "Oh, don't worry. It won't happen now. You see, I don't want to marry a man who thinks as little of me as you do, Samuel. So"—she turned away and left the stall, talking all the while—"when you get back from the county seat with your precious piece of paper, Luke and I won't be here."

"What?" He followed her down the long wide center aisle. "What the hell do you mean, you and *Luke?*"

"Just what I say. We will go into town and stay with Minerva until the judge arrives. After the hearing, we'll decide together what to do." She smiled. "Either move in here when you clear out, or move on."

"Luke ain't goin' nowhere."

"Yes, he is. He's going with me."

Samuel grabbed her arm, but she yanked herself free.

"I promised that boy that he had a home here no matter what," Samuel said.

"Yes, Samuel. But if you asked him today if he'd like that, I don't think you'd care for his answer."

His teeth ground together, and he began to mutter furiously.

Abby tilted her head to one side and said, "I've often meant to ask you something, Samuel. And since this will most probably be my last chance, what exactly are you always mumbling to yourself?"

He glared at her for a long moment, then took a deep breath. "It's somethin' my ma taught me to do. Say the ABCs so's I don't lose my temper with folks."

She smiled sadly. "Hmmph! Doesn't seem to work, does it?" Then she turned and left the barn as quickly as she could manage it.

Samuel stood in the shadows, alone in the quiet building. He watched her cross the yard and enter the cabin, closing the door behind her. His brain raced with everything she'd said, and his chest heaved with the effort of breathing.

Mentally he started the ABCs again. This time he only got as far as the letter *G* before he turned and slammed his fist into the nearest wall.

"I swear, that man must be the most loggerhead-ed, rattlepated, chuckleheaded man I ever heard tell of!" Minerva shook a blanket out over the narrow cot with such a flick of her wrist that the wool covering snapped. "Don't know why I never said so before . . ."

Abby stretched across the second cot that had been set up in the Mercantile's storeroom. Slowly and deliberately she tucked the sheet into what would be Luke's bed for the night.

Ever since she'd left the cabin, Abby had gone over and over the things she and Samuel had said to each other. And every time she had to fight down tears of anger and frustration. Thankfully, Minerva had been more than willing to take them in for as long as they wanted to stay.

Poor Luke, though. He was wandering around the store with the hangdog look of a puppy that had been deserted in the middle of the road. Abby sighed. Of course, she'd been right. The boy hadn't wanted to stay at the cabin. It was probably due more to Samuel's manner in the last two days than anything else. But whatever the reason for Luke's presence, she was glad to have him. It was hard enough leaving Samuel.

She slapped the pillow near her hand. Why did the man have to be so mule-headed?

"That's the spirit, girl," Minerva said. "Only thing is, you should'a done that to him!"

Abby smiled and sank down onto the cot. "Oh, Minerva. How did all this happen? Everything was going so well." She looked up. "Now he thinks that all I want is that damn—dang cabin!"

"If you mean damn—say damn," Minerva advised.

"I don't know what I mean anymore," Abby groaned. "But if that's what he really thinks, maybe that's just what I should do!"

"Huh? What?"

"Maybe I'll just fight for that . . . *damned* cabin—and win!"

Minerva shook her head slowly. "Now, Abby, you know as well as me that Samuel's claim to the land is the stronger one. You ain't got a chance in hell of winning." She watched Abby's shoulders slump lower. "Besides, if you *did* win somehow, that'd prob'ly mean losing Samuel. You ready for that?"

"I've already lost him, Minerva. He won't even talk to me."

"Hmmph!" Minerva came over and sat down beside the younger woman. "You can't never be sure about anything as long's there's a man involved. They have the most contrary minds of anything God put on this earth." She patted Abby's shoulder sympathetically. "Appears to me that you picked the Good Lord's favorite knothead, too." Abby leaned against her friend and smiled when Minerva added, "But you know, Abby, I wouldn't be a 'tall surprised if that man o' yours didn't straighten himself out before too long."

Abby sniffled. "I don't suppose there's much chance of that. Besides, I don't know if I want him back."

Minerva laughed out loud. "Hell, sure you do. You just want to make him *earn* his way back! As well you should. Don't give in too easy, girl. I always say . . . a little crawlin' never put permanent dents in any man's knees."

Three days, Samuel told himself. He looked in stunned surprise at the cabin. Abby'd been gone three days, and the whole damn place was fallin' down around him.

He glanced over at the table and winced at the pile of foodstuffs and pots and pans. Hell, he'd had to go through every nook and cranny in the cabin just to find a pan to cook him a meal that first night. Don't know why she had to hide everything, he thought disgustedly. Yes, he did. She liked everything to look neat and tidy. Lord knows, she'd told him that often enough.

He snorted and let his gaze wander over the rest of the place. With her gone, the little cabin seemed a helluva lot emptier than it had before. There was no smell of bread bakin'. No soft voice singing. No laughter. No nonstop chatter.

Her bedroom door stood open, and Samuel found himself staring at the big wide bed they used to share. It was just as she left it. Quilt neatly pulled up, pillows plumped, he'd even left the bowl of flowers on the bedside table even though the blossoms in it were withered and dead. For some reason, Samuel hadn't been able to bring himself to change a thing in that room. He'd even been sleeping on the floor in the main room. He was sure he'd never be able to sleep in that bed again.

For the thousandth time Samuel's tired brain recalled everything Abby'd said to him the day she left. In his mind's eye he saw her again, standing toe to toe with him. Her golden eyes flashing, that long, chestnut braid of hers swinging wildly with her every move.

She never flinched when his voice boomed out around her, his anger rushing over her with the force of a flash flood. She shouted back at him, demanding to be heard. To be believed. And then when he wouldn't, she turned from him. But not, he thought, in anger. It was more . . . disappointment.

She was disappointed in him.

He rubbed his jaw anxiously. Could she really have meant all those things? Was it possible that she really did love him? That she wanted to marry him not for his land but for himself? How could she expect him to believe that? Didn't she realize that nobody, save for his mother, had ever cared for him? Hell, until Abby came along, he'd never even had a friend to call his own, let alone a woman!

Could it really be that easy? Samuel stared at her bed through hungry eyes as if he could make her appear just by wishing it were so. Jesus! Had he really held every one of his dreams in his hands and then thrown them away?

Or was he right? Was it just the cabin? Was she saying and doing all this just to claim the home she said she'd always wanted?

Lord, his head hurt.

Maverick limped across the cabin and plopped down beside his master. The dog lay his big head on Samuel's knee and stared up at the man with sad, sympathetic eyes.

"You wonderin' where Abby and Luke are, boy?" Samuel reached down and rubbed the dog's head, scratching the animal behind his ears. "Yeah, it *is* awful damn quiet around here, ain't it?"

Maverick whined and thumped his tail against the floor.

"*You* think I'm crazy, dog?" Maverick's tail thumped even louder. Samuel smirked slightly. I *must* be crazy, he thought—sittin' alone in my house talkin' to a dog and expectin' an answer!

This was all Abby's fault, he told himself. Before she came, he was happy. He didn't have anybody in his life, and he didn't *want* anybody. Samuel stopped suddenly and frowned. That wasn't true, he admitted silently. Sure, he'd always wanted somebody. Somebody to love and to love him back. But he'd never felt the loneliness of his solitude this deeply until Abby had been here and then left.

Somehow, the quiet was louder now. The mountain

was colder. The night was darker.

Samuel's head fell slack against the chair back. If he kept this up, he was gonna go right out of his mind. How had all this happened?

Squeezing his eyes shut, he tried to remember how it was before he loved Abby Sutton.

The next day Samuel was in the barn, trying to keep busy, when a voice hailed him from the yard.

"Samuel! Samuel! You here?"

Samuel walked outside and grinned. He'd never been so glad to see anybody in his life. "'Lonzo! Good to see ya! Come on in and set for a while!"

Alonzo's eyes widened as he studied the big man. "Lord, man! What in hell's happened to you?"

Samuel glanced down at his dirty wrinkled shirt and brushed at it self-consciously.

"I ain't talkin' about your clothes!" Alonzo went on. "You look like you ain't slept in a week, and that beard you got rid of is about back!"

Rubbing at his jaw, Samuel tried to think of something to say. He could hardly admit to the man that he hadn't done much of anything since Abby left. Just like he couldn't admit that since she'd gone, nothin' was *worth* doin'.

Finally Samuel decided to ignore the man's statements. "'Lonzo, what are you doin' up here?"

Alonzo stayed in the saddle and shrugged. None of this was his business anyway. "Come to tell you. Judge is in town. Says he'll hold the hearin' tomorrow."

Samuel's face tightened. Bowing his head, he asked, "Abby know?"

"Hell, yes, she knows." Alonzo screwed his face up. Hadn't he been listening to Abby and Minerva talk about nothing else since the night before? He looked at Samuel again. The man looked almost as bad as Abby did. Didn't seem to make much sense, he told himself. If they was *that* miserable apart from each other, why didn't they just get back together? In fact, it seemed so simple to Alonzo, he risked Samuel's annoyance by saying, "Why don't you come back to town with me and talk to that woman? Get this mess all straightened out?"

"No." Samuel shoved his hands in his pockets. Even after all the thinking he'd done the night before, Samuel couldn't face her. If he was right, he never wanted to see her again anyway. And if she was telling the truth, how could he face her? "No, best just leave it be till tomorrow."

"As you say." Alonzo sighed heavily and rested his hands on the pommel of the saddle. He'd done all he could. No man appreciated another man buttin' in. "But I surely will be glad to have this dang hearing over."

"Why're you so interested?"

"Oh, hell, I don't give a hoot *which* of you ends up with this cabin"—Alonzo leaned down and chuckled tiredly—"but I'll tell you somethin', the Good Lord didn't mean for a man to live in a house with *two* women!" Straightening up again, Alonzo added, "Don't get me wrong none. They're both fine women . . . but just a *mite* headstrong, if you know what I mean."

Samuel grinned in spite of himself. Then he realized just how long it had been since he'd smiled. Since that last trip to town with Abby. Shaking his head to clear it of her image, Samuel said eagerly, "Why don't you climb on down and come have a cup of coffee?"

"No, but thank you just the same." Alonzo shifted

position in his saddle uncomfortably. "The sooner I get back to town and off this durn horse, the better I'll like it." He pulled at the reins and turned the animal for town. "We'll be seein' you tomorrow, Sam." Alonzo raised his right arm in a wave and started off.

Samuel watched the other man until he'd disappeared in a bend of the road. Alone again, Samuel looked over his shoulder at the cabin and knew he didn't want to go in there and listen to himself talk to the dogs again. Instead, he walked back to the barn, hoping to find something to do. He just had to get through one more day.

One way or another, it would all be settled tomorrow.

Chapter Twenty

"Lady," Judge Hackett proclaimed solemnly, "court ain't in session till I say so." His gaze swept up Abby's small form until he reached her hat. His eyes widened slightly, and he stared at her bonnet when he continued. "And I sure as hell ain't sayin' so until after I get me a cup of coffee."

Abby nodded forcefully, sending the one-eyed dove into a thrashing dive. It hung, suspended by one leg, over the brim of her bonnet until she reached up and patted it back into place. Smiling, she said blithely, "Oh, I completely understand, Your Honor, and ordinarily, I would never think to bother you—particularly this early."

"Yes, yes..." His eyes narrowed in his attempt to tear his gaze from the incredible bird. Finally he succeeded. Shaking his head, he asked, "Well, now that you're here, young woman... what is it that's so durned important?"

Abby took the older man's arm and swiftly guided him to a corner table, far from the interested ear of the Lucky Lady's bartender. When they were settled and the judge had taken a few sips of his strong, black coffee, Abby took a deep breath and said, "It's about the hearing."

"No, no, no. I'll not listen. T'wouldn't be fair to the other party . . ." The judge smoothed his gray mustache down and took another gulp of his coffee. It was much too early in the day to be dealing with all of this, he told himself. This was supposed to have been a simple case.

"But that's just it, Your Honor." Abby leaned on the table, gave a quick look around, and whispered, "If you'll just listen to me, a hearing may not be necessary."

His bushy silver brows shot straight up. Abby watched him and waited. His weathered, lined face was deeply tanned from the sun, making his sharp blue eyes seem even more piercing than they actually were.

"All right, Miss . . . uh . . ."

"Sutton." She held out her hand and smiled. "Abby Sutton."

The judge signaled for another cup of coffee, then said, "Say what you want to say, Miss Sutton."

"Simply this." She delved into her string bag and pulled out a piece of paper. Sliding it across the table to the judge, she said, "Last night I wrote this out and signed it. Minerva Mullins also signed it as a witness."

The man lifted the paper and squinted at it. Moving it first close to his nose, then as far away as his arm would stretch, he finally set it down and sighed.

"Don't have my spectacles with me. What is it?"

"Simply a note saying that I give up any claim to the land that Samuel Hart's cabin stands on."

He cocked his head. "Why?"

Abby shrugged and laced her fingers together. "Well, Your Honor, there was never really a chance of my claiming that land. I had hoped that . . ." She sighed and looked away briefly. "But you don't want to hear any of this."

"On the contrary, young lady, I'm very interested." The older man picked up his coffee cup and leaned back in his chair. "Why would a person back out of a land dispute at the very last minute? Has this Hart fellow paid you a sum for your interest?"

"No . . ." Abby took a deep breath. She'd thought about this decision for most of the night. It hadn't been an easy one to come to. But she knew it was the only thing to do. Minerva was right. She'd never really had a claim on that land. She'd known that since the first night, when she'd found out about Samuel.

And then, after falling in love with the man, Abby had hoped that she'd never have to leave. That she'd finally found the man and the home she'd always dreamed of.

But since that wasn't going to be, she'd just as soon leave. Quickly. Before she had to see Samuel. She'd already waited for three days, hoping he'd come to his senses. He hadn't. Abby frowned. Samuel obviously believed that she was a no-good, conniving, scheming hussy! Seeing him again wouldn't change his mind.

Besides, if nothing else was gained, at least if she left town, the big knothead would realize that she'd been telling him the truth. That she hadn't wanted his cabin—if he didn't come along with it.

Abby glanced up at Judge Hackett. His vivid blue eyes seemed softer now, more sympathetic. And suddenly she decided to tell the man the whole story.

"You sure this is what you want to do?" Luke slouched against the wall of the storeroom and stared at Abby.

"Yes . . . well, no . . . All right," Abby conceded. "I'm not sure." She looked at the boy and forced herself to look excited by their coming adventure. "But, Luke, I can't stay here. Not now."

"'Cause of Samuel," he whispered.

"That's right." Abby straightened up. How could she find the words to explain herself to the child when she really didn't understand any of this.

"Don't like him no more?"

"No, that's not it." She walked over to him and knelt down. Hands on his shoulders, Abby waited for the boy to look at her. "I like him fine, Luke." She touched his cheek. "In fact, I love him. Expect I always will."

Luke squeezed his eyes shut and groaned. "Then why're we doin' this, Abby? Why don't we just go home? Back to the cabin?"

Abby pulled him close and wrapped her arms around him. When he laid his head on her shoulder, she stroked his hair gently and said, "Because he doesn't love me. *I* can't go back to the cabin, Luke. Samuel doesn't want me. You'll just have to trust me to know what's best." She pulled away slightly and tipped his chin up with her fingertips. "But *you* can go back, honey. You know that Samuel would love to have you at the cabin again . . . it's all right with me. I would understand."

The boy wiped his tears away with the back of his hand and shook his head. "No'm. It just wouldn't be the same with you gone. I figure to stay with you . . . if you want me."

Abby gave him a teary smile. "Of *course* I want you! Now, why don't you go see Minerva and get those blankets she promised us?"

"All right." With his hands in his pockets, his head bent, Luke shambled slowly out of the storeroom, headed for the stairs.

Abby sat back on her heels and drew a shuddering breath. What if she was doing the wrong thing? Was she being fair to Luke?

And could they really make it, *walking* over the mountain? She shook her head stubbornly. Certainly they would make it. Luke insisted that he knew the way. He'd done it himself. Alone. And if a ten-year-old boy could do it, Abby resolved, so could she.

The Mercantile clock struck nine, and Abby leapt up. Samuel would be coming to town soon for that hearing. She wanted to be well away from Rock Creek before he arrived. Quickly she walked back to her cot and began once more to pack their bags.

At ten-thirty Samuel rode down the center of Main Street. The wind shrieked down the narrow road. Pine trees quivered and golden aspen leaves were tossed and twirled through the air. Samuel turned the collar of his coat up and glanced at the sky. Menacing black clouds hovered over Rock Creek, and he knew without a doubt there would be snow before evening. Maybe a lot of it.

He cast one quick look at the Mercantile, then forced himself to turn away. He didn't want to run into Abby. At least, not until they were standing in front of the judge. After three days of living without her . . . he had no idea what he'd do when he first saw her. Kiss her into submission—or strangle her for shattering his peaceful life!

He nodded briefly at the townspeople he passed and couldn't help but wonder why no one seemed very friendly. Even Preacher Knight, standing on the boardwalk in front of the livery, gave him a hard and disapproving stare.

Samuel shrugged and tried to ignore it. But now that he'd become accustomed to a warm welcome, hostile glances were harder to shrug off.

As he stepped down from his horse and tied it to the hitching rail outside the Lucky Lady Saloon, Samuel felt dozens of pairs of eyes boring into his back. His shoulders twitched uneasily, but he straightened up and marched into the dark saloon.

Only a few of the tables were occupied. Like most small towns, when there was a legal matter to attend to, the nearest saloon became a courthouse, and sales of liquor stopped until after court was closed.

Samuel looked toward the bar and spied an older man with a long mustache and a hard gleam in his blue eyes. Since the man was also dressed in a somber black coat and was standing behind the bar, Samuel guessed him to be the judge.

Then the man spoke. "You Samuel Hart?"

"That's right." He took a step closer and pulled off his hat.

"I'm Judge Zebulon Hackett." The man waved imperiously at Samuel. "Step up here, boy, and we'll get this business settled."

A few muttered comments floated about the room, but they were too low-pitched for Samuel to understand them. He walked up to the bar and stopped directly opposite Judge Hackett. He stood still while the older man looked him up and down, then frowned disgustedly.

"So you're Samuel Hart."

"Yeah . . ." Samuel said warily. He didn't much care for the look on the judge's face, and the mutterings behind him were getting louder now. He distinctly heard *someone* say, "Imagine doin' that to a poor little thing like her. . . ."

Her? The only *her* they could be talking about was Abby. Samuel's brow wrinkled. Where the hell *was* Abby? Shouldn't she be there?

"Before I pass judgment on this matter," Judge Hackett said slowly, "I want to know do you have anything you want to say?"

"About what?"

Hackett groaned and slapped his hand down on the bar. "About what we're doin' here, man! About why I was sent for! About your damn cabin and the poor woman you dispossessed."

"Dispossessed?"

Judge Hackett's lips twisted and his mustache twitched. "Dispossessed. Cast out. Got rid of. Chased away."

"Now, wait a minute . . ." Samuel's chest swelled with indignation. He pointed a finger at the judge, who stared at him accusingly.

"Out of order!" Judge Hackett shouted and slapped the bar again.

"You tell 'im, Judge!" someone shouted.

Samuel spun around, looking for the owner of the voice, then quickly turned back when Hackett started speaking again.

"You sayin' it ain't true about chasin' Abby Sutton off your land?"

"I didn't chase her off—"

"Did ya ask her to stay?"

"Well, no . . ."

"Did ya even bother to talk to her about all this?"

"No . . ." Samuel glared at the man defensively. "I figured that was *your* job!"

Judge Hackett shook his head. "Nope. Pushin' the blame off on the law won't do you no good." The older man looked up at Samuel through hard eyes. "Now, you listen to me. I got a letter here, written by Abby Sutton."

Samuel's eyebrows rose.

"That's right," Hackett said. "In the letter she says she don't want your damn land, nor your cabin. Says she gives up all rights to it. Wants you to have it."

Samuel stared blankly, as if he'd been hit in the head with an ax handle.

"You *should* be surprised!" Judge Hackett shook one finger at Samuel and leaned forward. "She told me everything, and mister, if I had my way, you'd be horsewhipped for treatin' a fine little thing like you done! But I can't do that. Instead, I have to give you full title to your land."

Stunned, Samuel's jaw dropped.

"But that don't mean I have to look at you!" He turned away and grabbed a bottle of whiskey off the nearest shelf. "You get out of here." Then louder, he said, "Bar's open!"

As thirsty men pushed past him, Samuel walked slowly toward the double front doors. He couldn't believe it. Abby gave up the cabin? The land? But she'd wanted it so badly. It just didn't make sense.

Unless, he told himself in amazement, unless she really *did* want *him*. Not the land.

He stepped through the batwing doors and stopped on the boardwalk. Behind him he heard men laughing and talking with the judge and realized that he hadn't argued with a single thing the man had said to him. Suddenly he knew it was because he'd deserved it. That and more. Why, he wouldn't blame Abby if she never spoke to him again. He glanced down the street at the Mercantile and started moving toward it. He had to try. He had to talk to Abby. He had to try to convince her to forgive him.

He couldn't lose her.

"You're too late," Minerva said flatly. "She's gone." At his blank look she continued. "You figure she was just gonna sit around Rock Creek waitin' on you? That there is a fine woman. Too good for the likes of you! She needs to find her a man who'll know how lucky he is to have her!" She glared at him, then turned and walked to the counter. "Like I told you . . . she's gone."

"Gone?" Samuel followed the woman across the store. "What do you mean, gone?"

She frowned at him over her shoulder. "How many things you figure I could mean?"

"Now, Minerva," Alonzo said softly, "maybe you should tell him—"

"Lonzo, you hush!" She glared at her husband, then at Samuel. "The only thing I'm gonna tell this big ol' . . . *man* is that he durn near broke Abby's heart!"

Samuel sighed and stared at the ceiling. "I *know* that, Minerva, that's why I want to find her now."

"Want to finish the job?"

"*No!*"

Minerva didn't turn a hair when Samuel's voice thundered out. "Don't you take that tone with *me*, Samuel Hart. I'll not be talked to in such a manner!" She took two quick steps toward him and heatedly poked him in the chest. "And I'm not the kind to go runnin' for cover when a jackass brays too loud!"

Alonzo shook his head and smiled.

Samuel took a deep breath to steady himself. "I'm sorry, Minerva."

She blinked.

"You're right. I *am* a jackass!"

She blinked again, then narrowed her gaze to study him.

"And that's why I want to find Abby," he continued. "To tell *her* I'm a jackass."

"Hell," Minerva said quickly, "she *knows* that!"

Samuel rubbed his jaw viciously. "Well, does she know that I want her to marry me?"

A slow smile spread over Minerva's face. "No, she don't. You know, there may be some hope for you yet, Samuel."

"Pleased to hear you think so," he said softly. "Now, will you tell me where she is?"

Minerva glanced uneasily at Alonzo. He shrugged and nodded. "All right. Her and Luke took off a couple hours ago."

"Took off? For where?"

"Anywhere." Minerva looked at him worriedly. "Truth is, I'm a mite concerned, 'specially now that the weather's turnin'."

"Where are they?" Samuel's face was tight. His voice strained. If Minerva was worried, there was no telling what had happened.

"Walkin' over the mountain."

"*What?*"

"I know, I know." Minerva gripped her hands together. "I tried to tell her. Tried to get her to take horses and head for Wolf River first. But she wouldn't. A harder head I never met."

"Why didn't you stop her?"

"You ever tried to stop Abby when she's got her mind set on somethin'?"

Samuel sighed. He had. And he knew how useless it was.

"Where the hell are they goin'?" Samuel asked.

"All they said was 'west.'"

"Son of a bitch!" Samuel cursed softly. He looked down at Minerva and saw the worry on the woman's face. Immediately he said, "Will you get me some supplies, Minerva? I'll get the horses."

"You're goin' after her, then?" Minerva smiled, more relieved than she cared to admit.

"Hell, yes." He stomped over to the front door and yanked it open. Looking up at the sky again, he muttered, "Fool woman can't even tell there's a storm blowin' in!"

Samuel raced out the door, and Minerva turned to her husband. She blinked back sudden tears and said, "You was right, 'lonzo. He *does* love her."

"I know." Her husband smiled gently. "Let's get that gear together for him."

Something soft and wet touched Abby's cheek, and she shivered. She hadn't counted on it being so cold. For weeks they'd had nothing but the nicest weather. And now, the day when she needed it most, they got . . . a white flake swept past her nose. Snow.

She looked up anxiously. The clouds seemed close enough to touch. In fact, the higher she and Luke climbed, the more it seemed as if they were walking straight into the clouds. The heavy gray mist was settling around them, covering them in a bone-chilling cold. Abby looked ahead at Luke. The boy's head was bent as he tried to huddle into the collar of his coat. She knew he had to be tired and hungry, but he hadn't made a word of complaint.

Suddenly the enormity of what she'd done struck Abby. She was risking not only her own life, but Luke's as well. In her stubborn foolishness she'd attempted something that neither of them was prepared for. Perhaps the wisest thing to do, she told herself, was to hole up somewhere, wait out the storm, and then go back to Rock Creek. After she'd earned enough money, they could leave town again. Only the next time they would take a stage or hire some horses.

"Luke!" Her voice barely carried over the wind.

He turned and came back.

"Do you know where we are?" she asked.

"Sure." He squinted and looked around at the surrounding pines and aspen. "At least, I'm pretty sure."

Abby stifled the sudden fear that gripped her. Lost? In a snowstorm? Fear wouldn't help them now. Thinking fast, she said, "Look for a likely place, Luke. We'll settle in and wait out the storm."

He chewed at his lip nervously, then nodded. Together, they started walking again, this time searching for a safe place to hide.

Samuel cursed and used the pressure of his knees to urge his tired horse forward. The animal dipped its huge head and plodded on, leading the packhorse following close behind. The wind had picked up. Snow was flying, and Samuel watched the trees around him bend with the wind. He'd been riding for two hours and hadn't seen a trace of them. And with the snow covering tracks as soon as they were made, Samuel knew that he would need more luck than skill in finding them.

He reached up with one gloved hand and pushed his hat down more firmly. This was all his fault. It was his own stupidity that made Abby strike out on her own. If he hadn't been so damn stubborn, he'd have gone into town after her days ago. How could he have convinced himself that she was using him? It just wasn't in her nature to be anything but loving and honest.

The packhorse suddenly stopped, and Samuel jerked at the reins to get him moving again. Hell, he didn't even know if he was in the right place to start looking for them. For all he knew, they'd gone down the other side of the mountain. But he was counting on Luke taking Abby on the easiest route. And the other mountain face was mostly sheer drops with mighty few handholds.

He ducked as he rode under an ancient pine. Snow, dislodged from an overhanging branch, dropped down the collar of his jacket. Samuel turned slightly in the saddle, reached back, and brushed away what he could. Then he stopped. Squinting, he stared at a rocky ledge about fifteen feet off on his right.

There it was again. A brief flash of light. Like a fire. He turned the horses and made for it, hoping he was right.

Abby and Luke huddled around the small fire. Gently she fed the struggling flames one piece of wood at a time. She *had* to keep the fire going. Without it they would surely freeze.

Thank heaven, she told herself, that Luke had found this ledge. An overhang of rock with heavy brush on two sides, it at least offered *some* protection from the wind. Even though enough blustery air came through the barrier to threaten their small fire.

Abby looked up. Staring out into woods, she listened carefully. She heard it again. Someone or *something* was out there. Getting closer. Quietly she picked up a fair-sized branch and moved next to Luke.

"What is it?" the boy whispered.

"I don't know. But . . ."

A huge figure loomed up just outside of the firelight. In the stormy darkness Abby could only make out a big, burly shape. But Luke's eyes were sharper. He jumped up and ran toward it, yelling, "Samuel!"

Abby released her breath and dropped the heavy branch with relief. When she looked up, she saw Samuel walking toward her, one hand on Luke's shoulder, the other holding the reins of two horses he was leading into their campsite.

Once the horses were tied securely under the far end of the overhang, Samuel brought his full saddlebags and dropped them beside her. She looked up, expecting to see fury on his face. And truth to tell, she wouldn't have blamed him. It had been a foolhardy thing to do, coming out into the woods with little knowledge and a small boy to look after.

Instead, though, she saw a relieved smile curving his lips.

"Samuel, we sure are glad to see you," Luke said.

"Are ya?" His eyes never left Abby.

"Yes," she said softly. And though she *was* happy

to see him, Abby couldn't help but wonder why he'd bothered to come after them. And how he'd *found* them.

But he ignored her unspoken questions.

"Luke," he ordered, "get me the biggest branch you can find." While the boy started poking through their meager pile of wood, Samuel told Abby, "You got your fire placed all wrong. Should have it backin' up against the rock. Then the heat'll ricochet off the ledge and throw more warmth at ya."

Abby nodded and watched as Samuel used the branch to push their small fire up closer to the rocks. Once that was done, he banked the flames and stoked it up with more wood. Then he spread a blanket over the fire's previous spot and told Luke to lay down on the warmed ground and cover up. Abby sat perfectly still before the now blazing fire while Samuel took some of the supplies he'd brought and made a pot of coffee. Neither of them said anything until the coffee was ready and he'd poured them both a cup. He glanced over at Luke and noted that the boy was sound asleep.

"Tired out, huh?"

She nodded. "It's been a hard morning."

Samuel looked down into the black liquid for a long moment before he said softly, "I'm, uh—"

"Samuel, I know what you're going to say," Abby cut in.

"You do?"

"Yes, and you're right." She took a sip of coffee and went on. "It was a foolish thing to do. Coming out here, I mean. I should have waited and taken the stage. I had no right to risk Luke's life like this and—"

"Dammit, Abby." Samuel set his cup down and

moved to her side. "You talk more'n anybody I ever saw."

She stared at him and tried to edge away. His hand on her waist stopped her. "Please, Samuel, don't . . ."

"Abby . . ." His eyes moved over her face. Then slowly, tenderly, he leaned down and kissed her forehead.

She took a deep, shuddering breath. "Why are you here? I left so I wouldn't have to see you again."

"I know." He raised one hand and gently smoothed her hair back. Then his fingertips traced the line of her jaw. "I'm sorry, Abby."

Her gaze flew to his. In his pale green eyes Abby saw the tenderness, the love, that had been missing the last time they were together. "Sorry?" she breathed.

"For everything." His hand snaked farther around her waist and pulled her close. "Abby, I never did know much about women." He kissed her cheek with a feather-light touch. "And I ain't the brightest man God ever made . . ."

Abby kept quiet.

"But I know enough to admit when I'm wrong."

"You saw the judge, then? You know about the letter I left?" Abby pulled harder and managed to scoot away from him.

"Yeah."

"And *that's* why you believe me now?" She watched him and was pleased to see the shamefaced expression cross his face.

"Shit, Abby." Samuel threw a piece of kindling into the flames and stared as it was swallowed up. "I knew . . . even before the judge. I knew that you wasn't . . . all those things I said . . ." He stared helplessly down at his hands. "It's just that . . . I think maybe I was afraid to believe ya."

"Afraid?"

He snorted and let his head fall back on his neck. "Hell, Abby, *look* at me!" Samuel straightened and turned his gaze on her. "I'm just a big, homely man. Got no education. Don't hardly know what to say to a woman. Hell, I didn't even have a *friend* till I met up with you!" He dropped his gaze to the fire and muttered, "I just couldn't let myself believe that a fine lady like you would want the likes of me."

"But, Samuel—"

He shook his head. He filled his chest with air, then released it in a rush. Still staring at the fire, he said softly, "Don't ya see? If I let myself believe that and it wasn't true . . ." His voice broke when he finished, "It woulda killed me, Abby. Damn near did anyway."

"Samuel . . ." Abby inched a little closer. Tears filled her eyes, but she blinked them back. She still had to hear him say the one thing she'd waited for.

"While I'm doin' all this talkin'," he added, "might as well tell ya. I signed over the cabin to ya. It's yours. Just like your uncle Silas wanted."

"Bother Uncle Silas."

"Huh?" He swung his head around and stared at her.

"I *said* bother Uncle Silas." She shook her head gently. "And bother the cabin."

"You don't want it after all?"

"No, Samuel."

"But—"

"Samuel, why did you come after me?"

"Well, I had to tell ya about . . . everything."

"Is that the only reason?"

He looked away and rubbed his chin nervously.

"Samuel? Is that the only reason?"

"No," he muttered.

"Why else?"

He flicked a glance at her. "You ain't gonna let go o' this, are ya?".

"No."

As his lips twisted, Samuel sighed heavily, shot a look at the still-sleeping boy, then turned back to the waiting woman. Slowly Samuel moved beside her. Cupping her shoulders with his big hands, he met her steady gaze with his own. Taking a deep breath, he finally managed to say, "I, uh, love you, Abby. I want ya to marry me."

Abby Sutton looked into Samuel Hart's eyes and saw everything she'd ever wanted. She finally understood what it had cost him to say all this to her. How much he'd risked. How much he loved her. Raising one hand to his face, Abby stroked his jaw and smiled. "I love you very much. Yes, Samuel, I'll marry you."

The breath he'd been holding rushed out of him, and a wide grin spread across his face. Tenderly Samuel pulled her into the circle of his arms and lay his cheek against the top of her head. For the first time in days Samuel felt alive.

As his hands stroked her back, he whispered, "I'll get better at this, Abby. All I need is some practice."

She tilted her head up at him and smiled. Then suddenly she pulled away and reached for his drawn-up knee. Carefully Abby ran her fingers over his jean-covered kneecap until Samuel asked, "What the hell are you doin' now?"

Abby moved back into his arms and placed a kiss at the base of his throat. "Just checking," she said lightly. "Minerva was right. No permanent dents."

"What?"

"Never mind," she told him and pulled his head down for a kiss.

In his blankets Luke smiled, squeezed his eyes tightly closed, and turned over.

Epilogue

"Sam," Alonzo said heatedly, "you got to do somethin' about them cowboys. . . ."

Samuel sighed, nodded, and stood up. He walked around the edge of his desk and moved to the window. Staring out onto Main Street, he could see that Alonzo had a point. The boys that worked for the Triple K Ranch were in town again and causing another uproar. Looked like he'd have to take a ride out to the ranch and have another talk with their boss.

"Samuel"—Preacher Knight pushed Alonzo out of the way and stepped up close to the sheriff—"about the church picnic. Do you think you can manage to maintain order? What with the ranch hands coming in and all, I'd hate to see anything untoward occur."

Samuel nodded again, crossed to the door, and yanked it open. He stepped out onto the wide board-walk and looked up the street at the road leading to his cabin.

Two years. Two years he'd been sheriff of Rock Creek.

After he and Abby got married, it'd only made sense. What with Luke needin' school and Abby needin' folks around, it was really the only choice to be made. But sometimes, Samuel had a need to get back up on the mountain. To listen to the silence again.

He smiled and tipped his hat as one of the townswomen passed by. It was still something of a surprise to him how much everyone seemed to like him. But little by little, he was coming to believe that his mother had been wrong all those years ago. Oh, he told himself, she'd meant well. Wantin' to protect him and all. But still, maybe if she hadn't been *so* worried, maybe things would have been different. Maybe it wouldn't have taken him half his life to make friends.

But, he thought with a grin when he saw Abby headed his way, maybe he'd never have met Abby, either. Her hair piled on top of her head, his wife was wearing her new lavender and green gown, which wouldn't have been so bad all by itself. But, Samuel thought with a sigh, her latest hat really topped it off. Where she'd found those huge, artificial sunflowers, he'd never understand. Smiling, he sent a silent prayer of thanks to his own mother before reaching out to take his son from *his* mother's arms.

"Oh, thank you." Abby smiled. "I swear, that boy is getting bigger every minute!"

Little Sutton Hart reached out with one small fist and grabbed at his father's hat. Samuel caught the boy's hand in his own and kissed it. His son showed every sign of one day being as big as his father.

Samuel would never forget the fear he'd gone through waiting for Sutton's birth. Terrified that Abby would be much too small to deliver any child of his safely, Samuel had near lost his mind before Minerva came down to report that Abby had "slipped that child out as easy as shuckin' corn."

"Pa!" Samuel let the memory go and turned to face Luke. He wasn't quite sure just when the child had started calling him Pa, but Samuel surely did like it.

"Pa, Obadiah and me are goin' fishin', all right?"

The tall, lanky twelve-year-old in the pale green shirt waited impatiently.

"If it's all right with your mother." Samuel looked at Abby.

"Be home in time for supper?" she asked.

"Yes, ma'am," Luke replied, grinning. "Wouldn't miss your stew for nothin'."

"All right, then."

"Thanks, Ma!" he called and raced off toward the Mercantile.

"It's a wonder I can keep that child in clothes, the way he's growing." Abby shook her head gently, then turned and smiled at Samuel. "That reminds me. Samuel, I've finished that new jacket for you. You can wear it to church tomorrow."

Samuel groaned inwardly as he thought of the blue-and-red-checked material Abby'd been working on for a month. Then he sighed and smiled. Some things, he told himself, would never change.

As Abby reached for Sutton, Samuel looked once more toward his old cabin. Ever since moving to town, Samuel had managed to escape to the mountain every once in a while. For him, that place would always be special.

His wife followed his gaze and moved up beside him. Cradling her son in one arm, she wrapped the other about her husband's waist. "Samuel?"

"Hmmm?" he said, absently stroking her arm.

"I know Minerva would watch the boys." She waited for his gaze to meet hers. "Why don't you and I go up to the cabin for a couple of days?"

A slow smile curved his lips. "How'd you know what I was thinkin'?"

"Could be," she answered gently, "that I was thinking the same thing."

Samuel bent down and pressed a quick kiss on her lips. "Let's go talk to Minerva, huh?"